The Art of Deception

The Art of Deception

Peter Martin

Part One

Chapter 1

Christmas is a time for celebration, for giving and receiving presents, for being with your loved ones. For the children it's about excitement and wonder, Santa Claus, the elves and lots of gifts. And happiness. But for adults, it's often a succession of nights out partying, overeating, being sick and getting drunk.

For John Greaves, that Friday a week before Christmas Day was the night of the annual Sachs Gordon ball at the Scott Arms. He looked forward to relaxing and chatting with his colleagues and their partners, and dancing the night away with his wife, Angie, until they were ready to drop.

At seven that evening, he stood in their bedroom wearing his best grey suit and a red tie. His tall lean figure was complemented by the cut of the suit, and the bright tie contrasted well with his short black hair and oak-brown eyes. He smiled to himself, thinking of the night to come. He turned around to admire Angie in her blue chiffon gown.

As she walked past him towards the bathroom, he noticed an anxious expression on her face.

'You all right?' he asked.

'Yes, a bit of a tummy ache – that's all.'

'Oh dear, are you sure you're all right to go?'

'Of course, wouldn't miss your Christmas do for the world. I'll take a couple of tablets just in case, but I'm sure it'll pass.'

'I hope so. It wouldn't be the same without you.'

She went to him, moving her slender figure close. He stroked her long ash-blonde hair and looked into those deep blue eyes that still sent shivers down his spine.

'That's nice to know,' she said.

The doorbell rang.

'Must be the taxi,' John said. 'Are you ready?'

'Yes, I'll just get my coat. Can you answer the door?'

Outside, the weather was cold, helped by a brisk wind. John and Angie got into the back of the taxi, shivering.

It took twenty minutes to get to the Scott Arms. John paid the driver, tipping him generously and asking him to collect them at midnight.

John and Angie hurried into the building to get out of the cold.

'How's your tummy ache now?' John whispered.

'Gone off.'

'That's good. Just be careful what you're eating and drinking, eh?'

'I will.'

There were already several of John's colleagues in the foyer, among them Sarah Benson, a fellow accountant, with her husband, Jack. Sarah was tall with short blonde hair, in her late twenties. Jack had black hair and a well-groomed beard, and was even taller. They both looked immaculate.

John waved and saw her face light up with a smile. Sarah and Jack walked over to them.

'Hiya Angie, hi John. Great to see you made it in this weather,' Sarah said.

'How you doing, Jack?' John said, shaking his hand. 'How's the football these days?'

'Yeah, not bad. Doing well after a bad start. We're in third, and the way we're playing I reckon we could soon be challenging for—'

'Hey, I hope you two aren't going to be talking football all night,' Angie said, giving John a knowing look.

'Don't worry, my sweet. I might talk shop with Sarah instead.' John winked at his colleague.

Angie shook her head and Sarah laughed.

'Angie, trust me, that's the last thing I'm going to be talking about tonight,' Sarah said.

The doors opened, allowing the crowd into the room the firm had booked for the night. John said hallo to a few of his colleagues, before everyone went to their allotted tables. John and Angie had been placed opposite Sarah and Jack.

The food, a set Christmas meal, came to them within fifteen minutes. John was pleased to see that it looked very appetising.

'So, what are you doing over Christmas, guys?' Sarah asked.

'Just the usual family gatherings. John's mum and dad are coming to us Christmas Day and then we'll visit my dad on Boxing Day. Yourselves?'

'Much the same, although we're travelling down south on Boxing Day – Jack's off to a football match, surprise surprise. And I'll scout around the shops for a few bargains in the sales.'

'Nice one, Jack. Fancy your chances, then?' John said.

'Yeah, don't see why not – after all, our opponents are only midtable. We beat them 3-0 at our place in August, so there's no reason why we can't do the double over them.'

Angie rolled her eyes at Sarah and mimed a yawn. 'Hey, cut the footie talk down, you two.'

'Come on Angie, we've got to talk about something,' John said.

'This wine isn't bad,' Angie said.

'No – it's better than that horrible stuff they gave us last year!' Sarah said. 'And the food is good, too.'

'Going away in the new year?' Jack asked, draining his first pint of beer.

'Yeah, probably. We might go to Greece around Easter time, then Italy in the summer,' John said.

'Wow. I wouldn't mind going there,' Sarah said.

Jack tutted. 'What's wrong with this country? Wales has great scenery – and Scotland, too. That fortnight we had in Torquay last year was great, weather fantastic and at half the price of going abroad.'

'But we could still go abroad too. If you'd cut down on the football a little, we could afford it.'

'I'm not cutting down on the football, no way, so you can forget it,' Jack said.

'See what I mean – I've got no chance,' Sarah said. 'Don't know what he'd say if I ever got pregnant!'

John and Angie laughed, but Jack raised his eyebrows. 'Come on, you can't tell me you want to be tied down with a screaming sprog?'

'Don't be too sure,' Sarah said a little angrily. 'How about you, Angie? How come you've never taken the plunge?'

'Don't know, think we're too busy enjoying ourselves. Love the holidays, and the freedom to do what we want. Once you have a baby, all that changes. You're tied down, aren't you, and the baby has to become the centre of your life. I'm not sure I'm ready for that yet. And there's my career, too.'

'I'm sure it will happen at some stage,' John said. 'But to be honest we haven't really discussed it that much. Although I think deep down, we would both like kids. Maybe in a few years' time, when we're thirty or so, eh Angie?'

'Maybe. We'll have to see.'

The puddings were delicious, too. Angie seemed to be enjoying the wine as much as Jack enjoyed his beer. John, who had never been much of a drinker, only drank shandy; he hoped she didn't get sozzled.

After the meal, the disco started and Angie, bold as brass, dragged John up onto the dancefloor. Soon they were joined by Sarah and Jack. The four of them danced together for a time, with Angie seeming to have forgotten all about her earlier ailment. She giggled and made eyes at John, who laughed it off. It was Christmas, after all.

'We're going to sit down,' Sarah shouted in John's ear.

He nodded and told Angie. 'You want to sit down as well?' he asked.

She shook her head. 'Unless you haven't got the stamina.'

'No, no. I'm fine for the time being.'

So they carried on. Later, out of the corner of his eye, he caught sight of Jack and Sarah, gesticulating towards each other. They looked to be having a few words.

'Think Jack and Sarah are having a row.'

Angie giggled. 'That's funny – I wonder what that's all about?'

'Don't know, maybe it's about them having a baby.'

''Cos she wants one and he doesn't?'

John nodded. 'Something like that.'

'Oh dear. That's a shame. He ought to let her have one, can't he see she's desperate for a child?'

'Best leave them alone for a bit, eh?'

'Sure.'

Angie was starting to look tired. 'Going to have to sit down, John, I'm whacked. I'm so unfit it's untrue.'

John could feel sweat trickling down his back and wasn't about to argue.

As they moved back towards their table, Sarah and Jack stood up.

'Hi, John, Angie, we're going now. I feel a bit off, so I'll see you Monday, John. Been great talking to you both again.'

'Good luck for Boxing Day.'

Jack laughed. 'Cheers mate, we're going to smash them.'

They left, leaving John and Angie on their own.

'Looks like you were right,' Angie said.

'Yeah, I thought so. Feel sorry for Sarah, though. But they'll have to sort it out themselves. Hope that never happens to us, when the time comes.'

Angie smiled. 'It won't.'

John looked at his watch: eleven-thirty. He wiped his brow with the back of his hand, and sighed. 'We'll have to be going soon.'

'Time for another drink?'

'Angie, you sure you should? You've already had nearly a whole bottle of that wine, and you've had the giggles all night.'

'It feels good to let your hair down once in a while, don't you think? Lose your inhibitions.'

'Well, if you lose any more, you won't have any left.'

She laughed then whispered in his ear, 'If I have another drink, there's no telling what I might do to you when we get home.'

He laughed too. 'And what might that be?'

'You'll have to wait and see.'

'Oh, you spoilsport. So how about a liqueur coffee?'

'Yeah, that would be nice. I need warming up before we go out in the freezing cold.'

They'd only just started their drinks when he got a message to say the taxi he'd ordered was waiting outside.

'The taxi's arrived.'

'That's early,' she said.

'It's ten to twelve now. You want to let him wait?'

'No, no, don't want to be left stranded. But I'm not sure I can finish this drink, John.'

'Don't worry, leave it then.'

'Gone tired all of a sudden,' she said with a giggle.

'I told you not to have that last drink.'

'I know you did, darling. And I'm sorry if I've gone a bit overboard tonight.'

'Doesn't matter – it's only once a year. Come on then, I'll just say goodbye to everyone and then I'll get our coats.'

When he came back, she was in her seat, dozing.

He gave her a little nudge. 'Hey, Angie, you all right?'

'Oh, sorry. Yes, just a little woozy. Phew, what was in that coffee?'

'I couldn't tell you, except it probably contained whisky.'

He helped her up and with putting on her coat, then guided her out through the doors he'd pushed open. The taxi was right outside.

The driver got out and opened the door for them, and John followed Angie into the back seat, closing the door behind him.

She leaned against him, gently snoring away. He smiled; he had a feeling he might have to carry her out and upstairs, and so much for all the enticing promises she'd made earlier.

When they arrived at the house, he paid the driver and opened the car door. Effortlessly he picked her up and carried her to the house. Then with difficulty he opened the door, brought her in and laid her on the hall carpet.

He blamed himself for having suggested the liqueur coffee. But never mind – it was Christmas. She was entitled to one lapse.

After carrying her upstairs, he pulled off her coat and shoes and settled her on the bed. He worried about undressing her and getting her into bed. The dress came off easily, but the rest would be more difficult.

'What are you doing?' she mumbled as he tried to get her bra off.

'Trying to undress you,' he said.

She sniggered. 'Hey, I hope you're not trying to take advantage of me.'

'Would I ever?'

'Maybe, if you could get away with it.'

'No way – I'm not interested in self-gratification.'

She laughed. 'Self what?'

'Can you sit up?'

'I'll try,' she said.

He gave her a hand. Eventually together they got her nightie on, and she got back into bed unaided.

'Thank you, John. I don't know what I'd do without you.'

John smiled.

'So, what were you going to do to me tonight?'

She grinned again. 'You'll have to hurry back to find out, my darling.'

He rushed to the bathroom, undressed and washed, put on some deodorant and brushed his teeth. His heart beat faster as he got to the bedroom, but he found Angie spark out on the bed. He smiled to himself; he should have realised what would happen. Never mind – his time would come.

As he lay beside her, he thought about their earlier conversation. He felt so sorry for Sarah. He was determined never to be like Jack, if it ever came to it.

<><><>

On Sunday morning, John woke to find Angie gone. Perhaps she was in the bathroom. Then he heard a noise, as if someone was retching. He got up like a shot and walked to the door to see Angie bent over the sink, holding her stomach.

'What's wrong?'

She shook her head. She looked very pale, and he wondered if this had something to do with Friday night when she'd drunk and eaten too much. She'd been pretty out of sorts yesterday, come to think of it.

'This is the trouble at Christmas – everybody goes mad. Drinking and eating too much. And at some stage you have to pay for it.'

'I feel sick, and my stomach keeps heaving, but I haven't actually thrown up.'

'That might come later. It might have been something you ate that didn't agree with you.'

'No, John. It's not that. I know what it is. I shouldn't have been drinking at all on Friday, and God knows what damage I might have done.'

'Angie, you're talking in riddles. What are you on about?'

She suddenly pushed him out of the way and vomited violently into the toilet bowl. When she'd recovered, she wiped her eyes, took a deep breath and said, 'This was meant to be a surprise. I'm sorry, John – but I'm going to have a baby. I can't make it any plainer than that.'

John's eyes widened and for a moment he was lost for words. But he suddenly squeezed her tightly and yelped with joy.

'This is unbelievable! We were only talking about this other night with Sarah and Jack! Amazing! When did you find out?'

'Yesterday morning. So I was already pregnant on Friday when I drank all that wine, and that's why I'm so worried. And why I've waited until now to tell you.'

9

'Darling, don't be silly. OK, so you had too much to drink, but you weren't paralytic. I reckon there's only a very tiny chance of there being anything being wrong with the baby. But if you're worried, go and see the doctor.'

'I hope you're right.'

'I am. So what made you suspicious in the first place?'

'You know how irregular I am, but I'm almost three weeks late this time, so I thought I'd do a test to be on the safe side. I felt sick yesterday too, but today's the first time I've been sick.'

'Anyway, this is great news – the best Christmas present ever. At last our family will be complete!'

'I hope it will, although I'm not looking forward to the next few months, especially since it looks like I'll suffer with morning sickness.'

'You want this to be common knowledge yet?'

'No, not yet. Let's keep it to ourselves until we're sure everything's OK.'

'But we have to tell everyone! Our mums and dads first, of course, then friends and colleagues.'

'I'll hate that. Everybody congratulating me and asking me questions. Just the thought of it makes me cringe.'

'Well, that's only natural. You'll get used it, especially when the baby starts to show.'

'Tell me about it.'

'Still feel sick?'

'Yes, not so bad as earlier on, but my appetite's gone. Don't feel hungry at all.'

'I'm sure it will pass. They say the first three months are the worst.'

She pulled a face. 'The thought of the birth fills me with dread, too. In fact, the whole idea of being pregnant frightens me.'

He squeezed her hand. 'Listen, I'll be with you as much as I can. And any time you need to go to the clinic or the doctor's, I'll come with you. And remember at the end of it, we'll have our own beautiful baby.'

'Yeah, there's that I suppose.'

'You do want the baby, don't you?'

'Yes. Of course. This is just me being silly. It's just … Well, my mum was bad after she had me – she had postnatal depression. She suffered with it for a long time.'

'That's not to say you'll be the same. My mum had a bad case of morning sickness when she had me too. She felt sick through the whole pregnancy. You never can tell. And anyway, when it's all over you'll forget about it. There are other worries, like looking after our baby.'

'I know. That terrifies me, too. I've never even changed a nappy. How on earth am I going to look after a baby?'

'We'll manage, Angie. Other people do.'

Later that night, as John snored alongside her, Angie remained wide awake, pondering over this wondrous thing that had happened to her. While she'd wanted kids, she had no idea what to do, or how she'd feel. She should have been happy, but all she felt was terror around everything to do with having a baby. But she had family and friends who would rally round her when needed. Surely she'd get through this with their help? And John would be her rock, she knew, there to give her encouragement. Sometimes she wondered what she'd do without him.

Chapter 2

She woke early the next morning, feeling sick. She tossed and turned in bed, trying to get rid of the churning in her stomach. John, although half-asleep, seemed aware of her restlessness.

'All right, darling?' he mumbled.

'Just sick.'

'Can I get you anything?'

'No, no, I'm fine. Go back to sleep. It's only four o'clock – you can sleep for another two hours yet if you want.'

Within seconds he was asleep again.

But Angie had to get up. Downstairs in the kitchen she made herself a drink: black tea, as she suddenly couldn't face the thought of drinking milk. She took it into the living room and switched on the TV, but her mind wandered. Her heart beat fast and she was short of breath. Panic wasn't something she'd suffered from before, but now she found herself shaking. God, this should be the happiest time of her life and she felt like this. She couldn't worry John with it, though, when he was so thrilled about the baby.

He came down a little later in his dressing gown, yawning as he saw her sitting in front of the TV.

'You're up early, Mummy,' he said, bending down to kiss her on the lips.

'Couldn't sleep,' she admitted.

'Why's that?'

'I don't know. Perhaps because we had an early night.'

'Can I get you anything? A drink, or I'll cook you some breakfast if you haven't already eaten?'

'Thanks, but I'm not sure what to have to eat. Can't say I'm very hungry.'

'Feeling sick again?'

'Yeah, as sick as a dog. But I haven't been sick – yet.'

'That's something, anyway.' He looked worried, and she didn't know how to put his mind at rest when her own was still in such turmoil.

'How about some dry toast? That's supposed to be light on your stomach.'

She shook her head. 'Later. Think I'll have a shower and get dressed.'

'All right. Give me a shout if you need your back scrubbing.'

'OK,' she said, trying not to smile.

As the shards of hot water hit her, she felt a little better. When she came out, though, she felt giddy and had to hold on to the side of the bath. As she dried herself, her stomach acquired a life of its own, causing her to suddenly retch over in the sink … and then again and again. As before, nothing much came up, but it was unpleasant and she ached. She had to sit on the toilet for a while before those sudden urges to throw up passed.

'Shit! Shit! Shit!' If this was what she had to put up with for the next eight months, she thought she might die.

She got dressed, wiped her face with a tissue and ventured downstairs, taking a deep breath and wondering how on earth to hide her feelings from John. And also, she had work today. She was an estate agent and had at least five appointments to show people around properties. What if she threw up while showing clients around? How embarrassing would that be?

She dressed smartly in a beige suit and applied her make-up with a shaky hand. As she came downstairs, she smelt bacon and eggs; John was making himself a fry-up. The smell made her want to puke.

'Ah, there you are,' he grinned. 'Want some bacon and egg? Got plenty here.'

She shook her head. 'Can't face anything right now. And I've got to go to work in fifteen minutes.'

'Well, at least eat something. You're supposed to be eating for two, you know.'

'Very funny. John, I'm not in the mood for your silly jokes, please keep them to yourself.'

He opened his palms towards her. 'OK. Sorry.'

'I'll just have another cup of tea, and then I'll be off.'

'All right, sit yourself down and I'll make you one.'

Sitting at the table, she took in a deep breath, puffed out her cheeks and breathed out. She shouldn't go in today, but she had to. There was only one other person in the office, and nobody would be available to cover her appointments. They couldn't afford to lose out on potential buyers.

She felt John's eyes on her as she drank her tea, and waited for his inevitable comment.

'You ought to phone in sick; you look as white as a sheet. I could always ring up for you, say you're ill, if you like.'

'No, I can't take a sickie already. Too busy. And who knows what time I'll need to take off in the next few months? I'll just have to grin and bear it, and hope for the best.'

'OK, it's your call.'

She got up and grabbed her coat and briefcase. They kissed, and for a moment she had tears in her eyes. But then she smiled, pulled herself together and went out. She got in her Corsa and drove to the office, where she checked out her appointments and then set off again for a house just outside Dexford. Fingers crossed she'd be all right.

She didn't feel her usual confident self as she made her way to 18 Chevel Avenue, a pre-war semi in a quiet cul-de-sac. Mr and Mrs Osborne were standing on the footpath, waiting for her.

The house was empty, so she had the keys to get in. She shook hands with the Osbornes and went inside. Hopefully they'd like it.

Her morning went well, with two possible sales, and one of the owners she did a valuation for looked likely to use Elliott's estate agents to sell their property. The last appointment was at a flat on the fifth floor of an exclusive block that usually sold very well at inflated prices.

Once inside, the thought of climbing the stairs made her feel faint, so she took the lift, but the movement made her stomach lurch. Glad to be out of the lift, she pressed the doorbell and Mrs Reynolds showed her through to the living room.

'Cup of tea?' she asked.

'Oh, yes please, no milk and no sugar,' Angie said, noticing a baby of about twelve months fast asleep in a baby bouncer in the corner. She grimaced.

Within five minutes, Mrs Reynolds returned with the tea. Angie would have liked to drink the lot in one go, but that would be rude, so she just had a mouthful.

'How old is he?'

'Fourteen months. That's the reason we need to move. We want a detached or a semi with a big garden, somewhere for him to run around.'

Angie measured each room carefully and took photos, then discussed fees and gave a valuation. She felt sick again. Drinking her tea, she hoped it would pass, but it didn't.

'Sorry, Mrs Reynolds, is it all right if I use your bathroom? That tea has gone right through me.'

'Yes, of course.'

Angie rushed off, embarrassed, and just made it to the bathroom before she vomited in the sink. Luckily there wasn't much, as she hadn't eaten anything. She rinsed it away and wiped it with some tissues, hoping Mrs Reynolds wouldn't notice. But a few minutes later she came out, red-faced, to find the woman standing in the hallway.

'Are you all right?'

'Yes, I'm OK. I'm sorry, but I was sick in your sink. I've cleaned it all up.'

'Perhaps you ought to go home.'

'Yes, maybe I will. I'm pregnant, you see – I've only just found out – and it looks like I'm going to get morning sickness. My mum had it really badly.'

'Oh, I am sorry. I went through the same with him. It was nine months of hell – although he's made up for it since. Congratulations, anyway. I hope you have a better time than me!'

'Thanks, I hope so, too. If you want us to sell your flat for you, please give me a bell, and I'll set it in motion. You'll find our rates are very competitive, and as we're the biggest agent in the area, you should get lots of viewings.'

'Thank you. I'll be in touch. And good luck.'

Angie was extremely glad to get out of there. How humiliating. She guessed Mrs Reynolds was bound to go elsewhere after what had happened. When she got in her car, she broke down. Having wanted a baby at first, suddenly she wished she wasn't pregnant. Her emotions were all over the place.

Somehow, she got through the rest of the day, mainly because she spent the afternoon in the office, catching up with her paperwork. But she had never been so glad to get out of there.

As she parked on the drive of their four-bed detached house, she wasn't sure she could face John. She didn't want him to see her like this. It would be Christmas in a few days, and she was having a baby. She should be over the moon.

John usually put the dinner on if he got home first, which he had this evening as his car was on the drive. The oven would be on, but what if she couldn't eat it, or was sick? He'd be mortified.

She heard him in the kitchen, singing to himself without a care in the world. When she came in, he turned and gave her a warm smile, like he did when they first went out as teenagers, eight years ago. A smile that used to send her weak at the knees. She put her arms around him and held him close, kissed him tenderly, hoping she could get through this for his sake as well as her own. A baby should bring them closer together, make their happiness complete. But why did she suddenly feel so unsure?

Chapter 3

'So, how was your day?' John asked as they parted.

'Oh, just run-of-the-mill stuff, really. Might have made two or three sales – we'll see. I'll just get changed, back in five minutes.'

'OK, smart. The dinner's done. I'll dish it out, shall I?'

'Yes,' she said, hoping he hadn't noticed her flushed cheeks.

The plates were on the table when she came back.

'There you are,' he smiled. 'Are you hungry now, after this morning?'

'Not really. But I suppose I'll have to try to eat.'

'You do, now you're having a baby.'

'Thought you might get that in.'

'You must eat for you as well. Please try. I got out early, spent ages cooking this – and let me tell you, even if I do say so myself, it's delicious.'

'I'm sure it is.'

He ate his casserole quickly, trying not to look at how she was getting on. 'Want to go out anywhere afterwards?'

'I think I'll pass on that. My stomach still feels like it's working overtime.'

'OK, no probs. Shall we just drive over to my folks? We could give them the good news.'

'Can't we keep it to ourselves for a while? I don't want everyone fussing over me.'

John felt hurt. He wanted to shout it from the rooftops. 'Sure, if that's what you want. Will you do the same with your dad?'

'Yes – just until I get used to the idea.'

'OK, Angie. Whatever you say.'

John finished his meal while Angie picked at hers, eating tiny mouthfuls very slowly.

'Hey, if you can't eat any more, it's no big deal. It won't hurt my feelings. I can see you're not feeling great.'

'Sorry. Normally I'd have asked for more.'

'Yeah, I know. Have you made your doctor's appointment yet? You need to start the ball rolling with midwives and stuff, don't you? And they'll probably prescribe you something for the morning sickness, too. Why don't you make an appointment tomorrow?'

'Think maybe I'll have to.' She swallowed hard. 'John …'

'Yeah?'

'I was sick today, in a client's flat.'

'Oh God. Was it bad?'

'Could have been worse. Luckily, I managed to get to the bathroom in time, but I can't tell you how embarrassed I was. At least it was a woman. John, what am I going to do? If this keeps happening, I won't be able to do my job.'

'Hey, calm down, Angie, you're panicking. It's very early days. It will pass. Talk to the doctor, get some tablets, then everything will get better.'

'I hope so. Mind if I don't come with you to see your parents? I still feel queasy, and I'm tired. It's been a long day. I'm going to lie down for an hour.'

'They'll wonder why you haven't come too. What shall I tell them? Although, second thoughts, why don't I not go at all? I'd rather spend the evening with you.'

She smiled at him, but he had the feeling she would prefer to be alone.

'No, you go,' she said. 'Say I've got a headache. I'll feel guilty if you didn't, after all you only see them once a week, and they are getting older. Anything might happen to them.'

'Mid-sixties isn't old! And they're still pretty fit for their age. OK – I'll go, but only for an hour. Be home in no time.'

'And not a word about the baby – promise?'

'I promise.'

John put on his coat, kissed her, and drove off to his parents' house, five miles away in the village of Gladbury.

They lived in a detached bungalow, having moved when they both retired five years ago. His dad, George, had worked as a solicitor, while his mum, Susan, had been a legal secretary in the same firm. He often wondered how they'd got on so well, living in each other's pockets like that.

Arriving outside, he saw the lights strung up all around their house, something his dad took pride in every Christmas.

John rang the bell, and the slight grey-haired figure of his dad appeared.

'Hallo, son, great to see you. Come on in. No Angie?'

'No, she says sorry, but she has a migraine.'

'Oh dear, my mum used to get those and by God, when you get one, it certainly knocks you off your feet,' George said as they went through to the spacious living room.

Susan, a plump woman with dyed brown hair, smiled at her son and got to her feet to give him a kiss and a hug. 'How are you?'

'Yeah, not bad, thanks, Mum. Yourselves?'

'We're off to the Bahamas in the new year.'

'Oh, to be retired,' John said, wondering whether they really ought to be going on two holidays abroad this year with Angie being pregnant.

'Don't wish your life away, son. It'll come around soon enough,' George said.

'Drink?' Susan asked.

'A squash please, this is only a flying visit.'

She gave him a drink, which he sipped hurriedly.

'Didn't know Angie was prone to migraines,' George said.

'Yes … well, she doesn't get them often … but when she does, it's a stinker. And I can't understand why.' John hated lying to his parents.

'How long do they last?'

'Could be all day. So, are you still coming to us for Christmas dinner?'

'Of course, if you'll have us.'

'Great. See your Christmas lights are up already.'

'Yeah, it took me a while, but it's worth the trouble when I switch them on at night. There's only a few more final touches needed. You'll see them for yourself when you come over Boxing Day evening.'

'Looking forward to it.'

'Shame we haven't any children in the family. Kids love the lights,' Susan said.

'Yeah, Christmas isn't the same without children, is it, love?' George said.

She smiled at John fondly. 'I remember when you and Sheryl were young, we had such fun, especially with the elves. It would be so nice to have those times again …'

His heart beat faster, but a little voice told him to hold fire with his news; Angie was too emotional right now. It would have been a great Christmas present for them too – especially as Sheryl, his sister, couldn't have children – but he'd promised her.

He was glad to leave.

<><><>

Angie lay on the bed and closed her eyes, hoping this sickness would leave her. She wanted to take something but didn't know what. If it affected the baby, she'd never forgive herself.

She tried to relax.

In fact, she did sleep, then woke with a start, sat up, rubbed her eyes and looked at her watch: two-fifteen. She'd been asleep for forty-five minutes but was still sick and frightened. Not wanting to worry John meant she had no alternative but to confide in her dad. He lived alone, a widower since her mum's death fifteen years ago at the early age of forty. He had never remarried.

She took out her phone and tapped his number. It rang and rang and she was almost ready to hang up when he answered.

'Dad?'

'Hallo, Angie. How are you? Great to hear from you.'

'I'm OK.' There was a pause. 'Actually, that's not quite true. I've got something to tell you.'

'Oh yes? What's that?'

'I'm pregnant.'

Silence. Had he heard what she said?

'Dad? You still there?'

'Yes, of course.' She heard him sigh. 'Pregnant, you say. Are you sure that's a good idea?'

'That's exactly it – I'm not sure it is. It was an accident, Dad – I've no idea how it happened.'

'So what are you going to do? You know what happened to your mum … Does John know yet?'

'Yes. I had to tell him, Dad. I've been sick a lot and he'd have noticed soon enough. And now he's obviously thrilled to bits, but I can't stop thinking about Mum, her bipolar and everything – what if I'm the same? What if the baby inherits it? I know I should think about getting rid of it. But I'm not sure I can.'

'You'll be taking a big risk if you don't.'

'Yes, but if the baby is normal, and I'm fine, then I'll have aborted it for my own selfish reasons.'

'But if there's a problem with you, that will be much worse. Don't get me wrong, Angie – no one wants a grandchild more than me. And if your mum was here, she'd be over the moon. But you remember what she went through. What if the same thing happened to you? That'd be horrible.'

'Oh, Dad, I don't know what to do. I worry over the baby too, that there might be something wrong, but surely the doctors could do tests or something. They might spot something in the womb.'

'I don't think so, love. You're clutching at straws there. But I'm not the one you should be discussing this with. John's your husband, and he has the right to know.'

'I can't, Dad – he'd be devastated. He wants a child so much, it'd destroy him to know what having a kid might do to me. And there may be no need.'

'OK. I'm not going to interfere, love, but don't say I didn't warn you.'

Angie was silent for a moment. The front door opened and John shouted, 'I'm back.'

'Dad, I must go. John's come home.'

'All right. Remember I'm always here if you need to talk. Love you.'

'Love you too.'

She got out of bed and ran to greet John with a warm kiss.

'Hey, what's that for? I think I'll go out more often if this is the reception I get!'

'I missed you.'

'I've only been away an hour. How are you?'

'Been lying down. I think I slept a little.'

'Are you feeling any better?'

'A little. Want a drink?'

'Sure, if you're OK.'

They sat on the sofa.

John sipped his coffee. 'Come with me the next time I go; I hate telling them lies. Mum even me gave me some tablets for you to take for that "migraine" of yours. And they kept dropping hints about the patter of tiny feet. I felt so guilty.'

'I'm sorry. I'll tell them in my own time, though, not by them seeing me throw up. Don't worry – it won't be long and everyone will know, I promise.'

'How about when they come over for Christmas Day? Wouldn't that be the perfect time?'

'Please don't put pressure on me.'

'Or New Year's Eve?'

'John, give it a rest.'

She got up and walked upstairs, where she lay on her stomach, crying her eyes out.

John came up a few minutes later, sat on the bed and took her hand. 'Look, I'm sorry if I keep going on. I always wanted kids and now you've made me the happiest man in the world. That's all.'

Angie looked up with tear-stained eyes. 'I'm sorry. It must be my hormones playing havoc with my brain. Once I've seen the doctor, I'll be better.'

'Let's hope so. Listen, will you be all right for Christmas Day? With Mum and Dad coming over for dinner, I mean. I can take over if you supervise me.'

'No, they'll know something's up if we do that. I'll get through it, but if I'm sick, we'll have to cancel.'

'Yeah, I suppose.'

'Look, I can't help how I feel. There's always next year – the baby will be a few months old then. Sure they'll enjoy that much more.'

He squeezed her arm. 'It will be a big change for all of us – and hard work, too. But well worth it. Still can't believe I'm going to be a father. Wow, the guys at work will pull my leg something rotten.'

'Yes, they will.' She smiled, but she wished he'd shut up. It got on her nerves. Please change the record, she thought.

Chapter 4

Angie sat in the waiting room that Wednesday morning, her nerves frayed, and she wanted to cry. She needed to pull herself together, to be in control when she faced the doctor.

They were already running late and didn't call her until nine twenty-five. She worried about missing her first house viewing appointment at ten.

Dr Brodie was an overweight man with sparse black hair, in his early forties, she guessed; she'd seen him before, but only for minor ailments.

'Hallo, Angela,' he said, eyes twinkling through half-rimmed glasses. 'And what can I do for you?'

She told him about the sickness.

'Quite common, I'm afraid. But it usually passes after a few weeks. There are over-the-counter tablets that help, but if the symptoms worsen, I can prescribe another medication. I suggest you avoid spicy foods, eat dry toast or plain biscuits and drink plenty of fluids. And get lots of rest. Make sure that husband of yours looks after you, eh?'

'OK. Thank you, doctor.'

By the time she arrived at her first appointment – she only just made it – she was feeling incredibly stressed, but the young couple looking to sell their semi were friendly enough. The wife was expecting herself, but looked four or five months gone. Angie didn't mention her own pregnancy; the last thing she needed was an excited mums-to-be discussion about prams and car seats. She wanted to stay away from that stuff for as long as she could. And the fewer people who knew, the better.

After work, she drove home. John was back early and Angie, relieved, slid easily into his arms and kissed him.

'Glad you're here.'

'Me too. Got out on time, and the traffic was light. Fish and chips waiting in the oven. You all right?'

'Yeah, not bad. Still sick even after taking one of the tablets the chemist gave me. But I've eaten better – at least that's something.'

'I hope you're making sure you eat enough. You must eat properly for the baby's sake, Angie – and for yourself.'

'Yes, I'm aware of that, thank you. Don't go on, John. I'm under enough pressure. I'm worried about work, too; if I can't show clients around properties, what will they say? And what if I'm sick in front of someone? It was a near thing last week. I'll be so embarrassed. And then there's Christmas dinner with your parents ... ' She sniffed back tears.

John lifted her chin and looked her straight in the eye. 'Darling, let's just take this one step at a time. Get through work for the rest of the week, and then it's Christmas on Friday, and the weekend. We can just relax for a few days.'

She nodded. 'Sorry. I'm getting in such a state, I know, but I don't want to let anyone down.'

'You're not. Once everyone knows you're pregnant, people will be understanding, I promise.'

'You're probably right.'

'Now, let me get changed and we'll eat, OK?'

<><><>

John climbed up the stairs to the bathroom, concerned at Angie's anxiety. She'd always been confident in everything she did, at home and at work, and yet suddenly she was going to pieces. He needed to be strong for her, support her as much as he could.

He returned downstairs in more comfortable clothes and sat at the kitchen table. He tucked into his food but noticed that Angie was only picking at the edges.

Finally, she put down her knife and fork and sat back. 'Sorry, John. I can't face any more. This food makes me want to throw up.'

'That's fine. No need to apologise. I didn't cook it, did I? And even if I had, I wouldn't have taken offence. It'll get better, I promise. Do you want anything else instead?'

'Don't know – a banana, maybe.'

'Yeah, why not? Nothing better than a banana when you're sick,' he smiled.

'Or a tin of fruit. I can't face dairy products.'

'Sure, coming up. No pun intended.'

As he watched her eat the fruit, John smiled. 'Just think, Angie. Next year there'll be three of us. Funny thought, isn't it?'

She slammed her spoon into the bowl. 'John, stop going on. All right, I'm having a baby, but can we please change the subject?'

John jumped at this uncharacteristic outburst of temper. Must be hormones again, he told himself. Better hold his own temper or else they'd have a row.

'OK, let's talk about something else. What are we doing about your dad over Christmas? I know he doesn't like a fuss, but we'll have to see him at some stage.'

'I'll see him on Christmas Eve to give him his present, and invite him to ours on Boxing Day. But I don't think he'll come. You know what he's like – just wants to be by himself.'

'Well, we can't force him to come.'

'No. I wish he'd make more of an effort, though. It's like he's never got over mum's death. All those photos of her everywhere.'

'I know. It's almost as though he blames himself for the accident.'

Angie suddenly started to cry.

John put his arm around her, frowning. 'Hey Angie, what's wrong? Have I upset you?'

She shook her head. 'What if I can't cope with a baby? What if I can't eat right, and it affects the baby – it'll be my fault! I'll never be able to live with myself.'

'Angie, stop it. We should be celebrating this, instead of contemplating doom and gloom.'

She gave him a sad smile. 'Sorry, I know you're right. But these last few days I'm getting down over the most trivial things. Never experienced anything like it.'

'Me neither,' John replied.

'Very funny. I can imagine what you'd do if you were in my shoes.'

'Yes, well I'll never be in your shoes. I've done my bit; the rest is up to you.'

'John, you're treading on very thin ice. I expect you to do more than your bit.'

'I intend to, I promise,' he said and got up. 'Hey, time for an early night. You need to conserve your energy.'

Chapter 5

Angie didn't sleep well. The sickly feelings returned, and she rushed off to the bathroom while John was asleep. Although she retched over the toilet, nothing came out. She needed to take another tablet, but the urge to vomit remained. Around five o'clock she got up and watched TV until she had to get ready for work.

She was in the kitchen eating a piece of toast when John joined her.

'Hey, you're up early,' he said.

'Couldn't sleep. I felt sick. Oh God, this is going to be a nightmare.'

'Well, if the tablets aren't helping, go back to the doctor.'

'I will, but it's only been a couple of days. Maybe I should give it a bit longer.'

'Better have my breakfast and get off. The sooner I'm in, the sooner I'm out. What are you up to today?'

'I only have a few appointments, so I'll be in the office for part of the day. We're supposed to be going for our Christmas meal at lunchtime; what if I throw up? How embarrassing would that be?'

'Tell them the truth.'

'Not yet.'

'You can't keep it a secret forever.'

'No need to go on, John. I'll do it when I'm ready.'

On the way to work, Angie kept thinking about lunchtime. Normally she revelled in these social occasions, but now she was almost tempted to ring in sick.

Having parked the car, she walked the short distance to the office. The weather was cold and windy and she shivered as she pushed the door open. Bethany on reception gave her a warm smile. Young and pretty, she was wearing a sequinned Christmas jumper. Angie frowned; she wasn't feeling remotely festive.

'Anyone else in yet?' she asked.

'Peter and Duncan.'

'Let them know I'm here if they need me.'

'OK, Angie. Nice to see you in the office for a change.'

'Yes, it's good to be in the warm. It's bitterly cold out there. Pity I have to go out later this morning, but people still seem to want to sell their houses even at Christmas.'

Bethany smiled. 'Want a drink?'

'Tea, please. Black, no sugar.'

'That's not like you.' She grinned. 'Had too much to drink last night, did you?'

'No, nothing like that. Just trying to watch my weight a bit. You wouldn't believe how many calories there are in a latte!'

Angie went into her office and switched on the computer, still feeling sick. It had just booted up when Duncan Drysdale, her boss, shouted her. Tall and thin with thick, prematurely grey hair, he'd taken over the agency from his father five years ago.

'Angie, how you doing?' he asked.

'Yeah, good, thanks. Be glad when today's over. I need a rest.'

'Don't we all. It's been a hectic year with house prices going up and properties starting to sell again. But that's great for us … and I'm pleased to say, you'll be due a five percent bonus in your next pay packet. I wanted to thank you for the work you've done. Hopefully when you get back from your appointment, you'll join us at the Railway Tavern for a drink and a bite to eat.'

Angie blushed. What she'd feared was now impossible to avoid. She was lost for words.

'When are you going over?'

'Around twelve. If you're not back, we'll carry on – just come over when you can, we'll be there until two. In fact, I'm closing the office at lunchtime – all right?'

'Yes, great.'

'The firm is paying. It's a small thank you for all the work you've done over the past year.'

'OK, Duncan, thank you. It's nice to be appreciated. I'll be there as soon as I can, I promise.'

'Good. I'll see you later.'

Once she got outside, panic set in and she struggled to hold back the tears. But first things first: her appointment with an old couple, living in an enormous detached property and wanting to downsize to a bungalow. Very pleasant they were, too, telling Angie about the family, their five kids who had all flown the nest. But they carried on for over an hour. When she left, she drove straight back. As it was well after twelve, the office had closed, as the note on the door explained.

She got out of the car, tempted to make an excuse and go home. But they'd guess something was wrong, as they knew she was usually up for any social occasion.

So she sauntered across to the pub, spotting Bethany in the window as she passed, waving frantically. No chance of getting out of it now.

Angie pushed her way through to the table. Bethany, Duncan, Peter the younger estate agent, Danny the junior, and Elaine, who worked part-time at weekends, were all there.

'Angie!' Duncan exclaimed, getting to his feet. 'So glad you've made it. Come and take a seat, we've been waiting for you.'

'Sorry.'

'No problem. How were Mr and Mrs Caruthers?'

'Talkative. I couldn't get away, and now I know their whole life history. But I think they've decided to use us for the sale.'

'Good on you, Angie, looks like it's another one in the bag.'

'Hope so.'

'Angie,' Bethany said, 'I got you a drink in – rum and black. That's still your favourite, isn't it?'

Angie froze. 'Sorry, Bethany – remember the diet? My early new year's resolution, I'm afraid.'

Bethany looked at her strangely. 'Sorry, I should have realised after this morning.'

'No worries, I'll get myself a drink.'

'Hey,' Duncan said, 'everything is on me. What would you like instead?'

'Just a mineral water, please.'

'You sure? It is Christmas!'

'Yes, quite sure. Thanks.'

'How about a bite to eat? We've already ordered ours.'

'Oh, err … I'll have a chicken salad. Thanks.'

'OK, I'll order it for you,' Duncan said, and called over a waitress.

Angie breathed in deeply and closed her eyes.

'Are you all right, pet?' Elaine said. 'You look pale.'

Angie squashed in to sit beside her. 'Just a bit under the weather. Not been well. Must have eaten something that didn't agree with me.'

'That's a shame, with Christmas coming up.' She dug a playful elbow into Angie's ribs. 'You sure it couldn't be anything else?'

'Err … no.' She shook her head, but her face grew hot.

Elaine's eyes widened. 'Oh my God, I'm right! You're pregnant, aren't you?'

Angie couldn't look at her, but sensed them all staring.

'Are you, pet?'

Eventually she nodded.

'How wonderful,' Peter said. 'What a coincidence, with Polly already three months gone. We can swap sob stories!'

Angie laughed nervously. 'Maybe. Has she got any tips for morning sickness?'

'Oh dear – suffering, are you? Sorry to say Polly's blooming. No sickness at all. And she's eating like a pig, more than me right now.'

'You've kept that quiet, Angie,' Duncan said.

'Well, I only found out a few days ago. It's very early days still.'

'If you need any time off, don't worry – I'm sure we'll accommodate you. After all, you've been a diamond to us over the past five years.'

'Hopefully I won't need to take many days off. I want to get through these nine months and have a healthy baby.'

'I'm sure you will,' said Elaine.

'But what if I'm bad when I'm out visiting clients. How embarrassing if I was sick then.'

Duncan frowned. 'Yeah, you have a point. Maybe we should cut down your appointments a bit. Bethany's itching to get out there, aren't you, Bethany? Why don't you take her with you after the holidays, and when she's fully competent, you can spend a bit more time in the office.'

'OK. Thanks, Duncan. I appreciate it.'

<><><>

She came home early, and John wasn't there. So she lay on the bed and fell asleep; no wonder, after last night.

When she felt something on her lips, she jumped. Opening her eyes, she saw John's smiling face in front of her.

'You all right? Did I startle you?'

'No, no, no. I was having a weird dream. For a second, I thought you were someone else – a guy I went out with years ago. He didn't like it when I broke up with him. Kept sending me horrible texts, threats like *if I can't have you, no one else will.* My dad sorted him out in the end, but he frightened me. I dreamt he was going to kill me.'

'I wonder what made you dream about him now suddenly?'

'No idea. Stress?'

'Yeah, could be. So how was your last day?'

'All right. Duncan took us out for a meal – paid for the lot himself. And he told me I have a bonus coming for all the hard work I've put in during the year.'

'That was decent of him.'

'But they found out I'm pregnant. I didn't want anyone to know yet, but I couldn't lie when Elaine came right out and asked me.'

'That's good. So can we tell everyone now?

'No. I want a peaceful Christmas without all and sundry fussing over me.'

'Angie, you've told the guys at work – what's wrong with telling our families too?'

'Don't push me. Let's wait until the new year,' she snapped.

'Why? Not ashamed of being pregnant, are you?'

Angie stormed out. If he told anyone without her permission, there'd be hell to pay.

Chapter 6

John was the first to wake on Christmas Eve. He thought about going out to the shops without telling her, seeing as she hadn't got up yet, but decided against it. She'd kick up an almighty fuss. So he waited. At least she must have had a good night's sleep.

She came into the kitchen half an hour later in her dressing gown, looking irritated.

'John, why didn't you wake me? We're supposed to be going shopping. There'll be nothing left!'

'Sorry – but I thought it best not to wake you. Are you still suffering?'

'Yes, but I want to make sure Christmas goes off smoothly, with your parents coming round for dinner.'

'You'd better get a move on, then. The shops shut at lunchtime, don't they?'

'OK. Let me have a drink and get dressed, and I'll be ready.'

'What about having a bite to eat too? You've got to eat, Angie.'

'I'm not hungry, that's all. Don't start that again, John. I'll eat when I can – and not before.'

Within half an hour they were driving to Dexford town centre, and only just got a spot in the supermarket car park.

They went around the store, getting their last essentials for Christmas. John had expected her to take over as soon as they started, but she hardly spoke and allowed him to put in whatever he'd written down. She seemed in a trance. He frowned, but carried on until they came to the checkouts.

'All right, Angie? Listen, I've got everything I think we need. Is there anything I've missed?'

'No. Come on, John, let's get these things paid for. I want to go home. I feel sick again.'

'OK. I'm being as quick as I can,' he said, putting the last items on the conveyor.

He stuffed everything into the bags haphazardly while Angie stood by the trolley waiting to get out. He would have appreciated some help, but considering how she'd been the past few days, he kept quiet.

She pushed the trolley through the car park – almost getting hit by a car in the process – then left it to him to put the shopping in the boot. He drove off without saying a word, but out of the corner of his eye he saw her place a hand in front of her mouth.

Oh God, no – not in the car, he thought.

'You all right, darling?'

'No, not really. Can you drive a bit faster?'

'I'm trying. But it's better to be sick in here than have an accident.'

She shrugged her shoulders, while John drove as fast as he dared, and they made it without incident. But when she got out, she rushed to the front door, opened it and ran inside. John had to bring the shopping bags in himself while she was locked in the downstairs toilet.

He'd had time to make a cup of tea before she came in holding her stomach.

'Have you been sick?' John asked.

'No. But I kept heaving – good job I didn't have any breakfast. Those tablets aren't working.'

'Can you increase the dose? I don't want it to spoil our Christmas.'

'God, is that all you care about, your bloody Christmas? What a shame if your poor little wife is poorly and you can't enjoy yourself!'

'It's not like that. But if you can take the full dose, do it.'

'I'm not putting the baby's life at risk for the sake of a few tablets and Christmas.'

John needed to stop this turning into a full-blown argument.

'OK. It doesn't matter. I'm sorry.'

'Me too. Let's grab a bite to eat. I'll try a tin of soup with some bread, maybe I can keep that down.'

'Don't forget we're supposed to go your dad's this afternoon. We've wrapped his presents, haven't we?'

'Yes. I told him we'd be there at three.'

'Right then, let's eat and chill out before we go. Are you going to tell him about the baby?'

She nodded, but he thought she looked uncomfortable.

<><><>

After lunch, she dozed but didn't sleep. Instead she thought of the afternoon to come with her dad, hoping he'd remember that he wasn't supposed to know about the baby, and hoping he wouldn't mention her mother's illness. John still thought Marion had died in a car crash, and Angie wanted it to stay that way.

'You awake?' John said.

She opened her eyes, rubbed them and smiled. 'I wasn't asleep, just resting my eyes.'

'Come on, let's go. We don't want to be late for your dad.'

'I won't be long. I'll just get changed and freshen up.'

He was already wearing his overcoat when she came downstairs.

'Got the presents?'

He pointed. 'In that plastic bag on the settee.'

'Good, come on then.'

The house was a neat and tidy semi on the outskirts of Dexford, a shiny Fiesta parked on the cobble-paved drive. There were smart blinds in the windows and the red door was new.

'Like the door,' John said as they walked towards it.

'Yes, me too. Better than that battered old thing he had before.'

She rang the bell. Within seconds, the door opened and there stood her father, Alan, a stocky man with a weathered face, muddy brown eyes and thick, grey hair brushed back from his forehead.

'Angie, John – great to see you,' he said. He kissed Angie on both cheeks and shook John's hand. 'Come on in, out of the cold. Come through to the living room.'

The first things anyone entering the house noticed were the photos on the walls. Pictures of his wife Marion, and of Angie. Blonde and beautiful, they could have been sisters. Angie as an adult – the woman Marion never knew – was the image of her mother.

Angie and John sat by each other on the white leather settee while Alan sat in the armchair.

'Right then, you two – want a drink?'

'Just a lemonade,' Angie said.

'Fruit juice, please.'

'Well, you're a proper pair of killjoys, aren't you? Come on! It's Christmas!'

John shrugged. 'I'm driving.'

'And I'm pregnant,' Angie said.

Her dad acted his part perfectly. 'What? Did I hear you right? Pregnant?'

'I found out a few days ago.'

'Was it an accident?'

'Dad!'

John intervened. 'Does it matter? What matters is that she's pregnant, and that we're happy and so will you be, grandad.'

Alan smiled. 'Yes, I am. Can't believe it. A grandad, eh? Makes me feel old all of a sudden.'

They both laughed.

'This calls for a celebration. Shame neither of you can drink.'

He returned from the kitchen with a lemonade, an orange juice, and a glass of something fizzy.

'What you got there, Dad?'

'Asti what-do-you-call-it. I'd meant to open it tonight anyway, but it seems I'll have to drink it by myself.'

'We'd love to help you, Dad, but we both need to be careful.'

Angie's father gave them sandwiches and slices of Victoria sponge cake, which he'd made himself.

'This cake is delicious,' Angie said. 'You've become a good cook since Mum died.'

'Yes, I was determined to keep you well fed, although I must admit I learnt a lot from your mother. This is one of her recipes – do you remember it?'

'You made it just as good. Tastes as if mum had cooked it herself.'

'Glad you like it. I've kept them all, and I even cook a few for myself when I'm here on my own.'

Angie felt tears building up. 'Wish she could be here to see our baby.'

Alan put his hand across the table and squeezed hers. 'You've no idea how much it hurts me too. It's been a long fifteen years, but never a day goes by without me thinking of her. She would have been so happy … although I don't imagine she'd like being called nanny.' He had tears in his eyes too. 'You never really get over losing a loved one. I live with it, but I'll never forget her.'

'Never wanted to meet someone else?' John asked.

'No, never. I have my memories, and no one can take those away from me. I'm not lonely – I've kept myself busy in my garden, and I've got my allotment and the fishing. And I've got my workshop, of course. Doing up all that old furniture keeps me busy and provides me with a living. That takes my mind off Marion.'

'Dad, you can always come to us whenever you want. And when your first grandchild is born, we'll come even more often.'

'Thanks, love. I know you mean well, but I won't impose on you – I've told you that before. But if you want to visit me, you're more than welcome. Anyway, now you're here, why don't we swap presents?'

'Sure. John, give Dad the bag.'

'Here you go. Happy Christmas,' John said, picking up the bag.

'Thanks, both of you.' Alan got to his feet. 'Let me get yours, they're in the bedroom.'

'All right, darling?' John asked while he was gone.

'I'll have to be, won't I?'

'You didn't eat as much as normal, but more than you have recently. I'd say you might be on the mend.'

'Maybe, but I feel sick again already. No idea how I ate all that, but I didn't want to hurt Dad's feelings.'

'I understand. Good on you. I know how close you are to your dad.'

Alan returned, carrying his own bag.

'For you both,' he said with a smile.

'Thanks, Dad. Shall we open them now, or wait until tomorrow?'

'Open them tomorrow. I'll only get embarrassed if I've bought the wrong thing.'

'Are you sure?' Angie asked.

He nodded. 'Let's just have another drink … but if you need to shoot off, that's fine by me.'

'No, Dad, we'll stay. But I should let you know I've been feeling sick a lot. If I run off to the toilet, it's not your food, honestly!'

He smiled. 'That's OK. Thanks for letting me know. Must be awful to have that all the time.'

'It is but I just have to live with it, I'm afraid.'

They stayed another hour, watching TV. Angie seized her chance when John went to the bathroom.

'Dad, you were amazing – you ought to be on the stage. I don't like lying to John, but he doesn't know what we know, and I'd hate to worry him. It would upset him too much if he knew about Mum and that I might end up like she did.'

'I'll say it would. Have you thought any more about getting rid of it?'

'I can't, Dad. It's not the baby's fault that Mum killed herself. I know there's a chance I'll be affected with the same problems, but I won't have an abortion just in case – even though it worries me a lot and it's giving me sleepless nights on top of the morning sickness.'

'Remember what we went through, love. Your mum never had any problems until after you were born, either – and then suddenly she was like a different person. Mood swings, hallucinations, delusions. We kept a lot of it from you, of course, but it was terrible.'

'Let's not talk about it anymore. This is my problem and I'll deal with it.'

John came downstairs and she looked at him gratefully.

'We'd better make a move, Dad. I feel queasy again and I'm tired. It'll be a busy day tomorrow.'

'That's fine. I'll phone you in the morning. Pop over before the new year?'

'Yeah, sure.'

'Enjoy Christmas, both. Hope you like your presents, but if you don't, I can always change them. I've got the receipts.'

'That won't be necessary, Dad. We always treasure what you buy us. You have a good one, too.'

Angie sat in the car in silence. Tears were coming, and she couldn't stop them. John was bound to notice.

'Hey – you all right?'

'Yes, sorry. I keep thinking about Mum and how she'd have loved having a grandchild. It doesn't seem fair that I lost her so young. It's hard to express how I felt when she died – what Dad and me went through together. She was such a warm person, would do anything for you, the best mum ever.'

'I wish she was here, too. I wish I'd met her. You're the spitting image of her.'

'I may look like her, but there's some of my dad in me too. I'm like him in my ways – or at least, I was until I got pregnant. I barely recognise myself these days.'

'You'll be fine once the sickness has gone. Your old self again.'

'I wouldn't be too sure. It's emotional as well as physical. I want to cry all the time and I don't know why. I should be happy, but I'm not.'

'I've told you before – it's just your hormones. You'll settle down. In a year's time we'll look back and wonder what on earth we were so worried about.'

Angie smiled, but she prayed she'd made the right decision.

Chapter 7

John put the bag of presents down while Angie went into the kitchen to make a cup of tea. When she returned, she sat in the armchair rather than next to him on the sofa.

This worried him. 'Everything all right, Angie?'

'I don't know. No. I feel strange – like my emotions are all over the place, somehow. I'm frightened.'

'There's no need to be. You can talk to me about anything and you know I'll help if I can. And if you'll let me.'

'I keep thinking back to when Mum died and how hurt I was. The thought of never seeing her again scared me to death. We used to talk about growing up, and what she experienced when she was my age. It was like having a big sister. It's not quite the same with Dad; we're very close and I love him to bits, but he can't ever be my mum.'

'You'll never replace her, that's true. But if we have a daughter of our own, your relationship with her might be similar.'

'That's ages away. What do I do until then?'

'Talk to me, your dad, your friends, anyone you're comfortable with.'

Angie sighed.

He changed the subject. 'Hey, shall we open these presents?'

'Not on Christmas Eve. We have to do it in the morning.'

'Don't you think we're too old for that claptrap?'

'No, John,' she snapped. 'It's a family tradition and I won't break with that for anyone, not even you.'

'All right, don't get mad. It was only a suggestion. No need to bite my head off.'

'Look, I still feel bad. I miss my mum and I'm struggling to come to terms with having a baby, so I don't need your sarcasm.' She got up from her seat.

'Where are you going?'

'To bed. And you can forget about me cooking the dinner and having your parents here tomorrow, too. I can't face it. I'm sorry, but that's how it is.'

John shook his head. 'So what are we doing with the turkey?'

'Is that all you can think about – your bloody stomach? I don't give a shit about the turkey. Just do what you want. I don't care.'

He felt his face reddening with anger as she stormed off upstairs. To fly off the handle like that over nothing was ridiculous.

He needed a beer to calm himself down. He watched TV for half an hour and then went upstairs; she was in bed, with her back to him.

What if she meant it about his parents not coming? He'd have to speak to her in the morning. And as for the turkey, it seemed he'd have to sort that out himself.

He undressed and got in beside her, being careful not to touch her. He imagined she was asleep, so he put on his alarm clock for six and tried to drop off, without much success.

<><><>

Bang on six o'clock, the alarm beeped. John was already awake and turned it off at the third ring. He risked a glance at Angie, but she was still asleep.

Downstairs, he made for the kitchen to deal with the turkey, trying to remember what Angie had done last year. He checked it was thawed properly, washed it, placed it in a roasting tin, added knobs of butter under the skin, then smoothed foil over it and put it in the oven. He longed to ask Angie if he'd done everything right, but he couldn't.

At nine, he returned upstairs to see if she'd stirred. Quietly he opened the bedroom door; she lay in the same position, like a corpse. Pulling back the covers, he risked speaking to her.

'Angie, are you all right?'

She opened her eyes, looked at him and turned away.

'Come on, darling, what's wrong?'

She burst into tears and he put his arm around her.

'I've got everything under control. The turkey's in the oven. You've nothing to worry about.'

'I ... I can't face it, John – I mean it. Please tell them not to come. I'll be sick, I know I will. It will be so humiliating. Phone them. Please.'

'But what do I say?'

'Tell them I'm ill ... say I'm sorry for the inconvenience.'

'Why don't I just explain you're pregnant and having a bad time? They won't be angry – they'll be happy for you, honestly.'

'No, no, no. You mustn't, or I won't be able to look them in the eye.'

'Angie, why ever not? Isn't this a celebration, our first child? We should shout it from the rooftops. And your dad already knows, anyway.'

'What if there's a problem, and I need a termination?'

'That won't happen, I promise you. Trust me, please. Let me phone them, so they can make alternative arrangements.'

She hesitated, thinking it over. 'They'll be so angry; my name will be mud.'

'No, it won't. They'll be thrilled.'

'All right, do it,' she said, burying her face in the pillow.

He took out his mobile and pressed the number, moving out of the room so that Angie couldn't hear.

His mum answered the phone. When he told her the news, she wept with joy.

'Oh, John! How wonderful! Our first grandchild. Incredible! I'm sorry she's not well, but these things happen during pregnancy. It's a shame we can't see you, but you must put Angie and the baby first.'

'If she's any better later on the week, you can pop round then, or we'll come to yours.'

'Don't worry about that. It's most important for Angie to look after herself, and you must take care of her too.'

'I will. I feel awful about it, though. What'll you do about your Christmas dinner?'

'It won't be a problem. The pubs are open. I'll get your dad to ring around; there's bound to be a few that aren't fully booked. Why don't we come over at the weekend instead?'

'OK. And I'll ring you later, let you know how she is.'

'Thanks, son. You look after yourself, and Angie too. Merry Christmas to you both. Give her our love.'

He heaved with relief when she'd gone, thankful at how understanding she'd been. But he felt guilty that his parents now had to go out and pay a fortune for their Christmas meal when they should be coming to them. While Angie couldn't help being ill, her timing could have been better.

He walked back into the bedroom, where Angie was hunched over on the bed with her head in her hands, crying again. He sat beside her, taking hold of her hand.

'I've told them, darling. And they were fine – they're going out to a pub instead. They wished you all the best and said for you to look after yourself. I told them to pop around in a day or two, if you're well enough. You OK with that?'

She shrugged her shoulders and sniffed back her tears. They sat in silence for several minutes before she lifted her head and looked at him through blood-shot eyes.

'I'm sorry, John. I kept hoping I'd be all right, but it's no good. I wanted so much to give them Christmas dinner but it's impossible. Can you forgive me?'

'There's nothing to forgive. You can't help being ill, and it's just a shame Mum and Dad had to be the victims of your illness. I could have cooked everything, and I'm sure Mum would have helped. As it is, the turkey's in the oven. Just got to put the veg on, and we're good to go.'

'Always the optimist, eh? It'll all go to waste now.'

'It's only food. If the stress of being the hostess had caused you to miscarry, then it would be worth crying over, but a few quid's worth of food won't hurt us. We can always freeze the leftovers. Anyway, that's the least of our worries. I've got to say I'm concerned, Angie. The way you've been in yourself ever since you found out you're pregnant isn't normal. I think after the holidays you should see the doctor again, find out if there's anything he can give you, you know, to settle you down a bit.'

Angie's mouth dropped open. 'You haven't got much faith in me, have you? OK, so I'm having problems with morning sickness, but that's all. I don't need a shrink, for God's sake. Are you trying to get back at me because your parents aren't coming over?'

'That's not it at all. But it's not only the sickness, it's your mental state too. You're acting irrationally, overreacting to things you'd normally take in your stride—'

'I'm not listening to this. Piss off and leave me alone.'

'Please, Angie. At least think about it.'

'Why don't you get on with cooking your precious Christmas dinner that no one will eat except you?'

John knew he shouldn't have mentioned his fears, but they were out in the open now. There was no going back.

He strode downstairs. She would come round, and in the meantime, he'd continue with the meal. He wasn't an expert cook, but he'd watched her enough times to know what to do.

By twelve-thirty the dinner was done and everything was on the plates. It didn't look bad, in the circumstances. He went back upstairs.

She still sat on the bed, staring into space.

'Angie.' He spoke softly and she glanced in his direction. 'Listen, dinner's ready if you're hungry. I've done the best I can, hope it's at least edible.' He smiled ruefully. 'Don't fancy eating on my own, with it being Christmas. Let's try to salvage of what's left of the day, shall we?'

She hesitated for a few seconds, then nodded.

Downstairs, Angie sat at the table waiting for John to bring over the plates. He'd given her a smaller portion than normal and hoped she'd eat at least a little. His own plate was full, although he wasn't especially hungry.

'There you go, darling. Just eat what you want and leave the rest.'

She smiled, breathed in and picked up her knife and fork. John started on his own and tried not to look at her too much as they ate.

'How is it?' he asked. 'Obviously it's not as good as you'd cook it, but is it at least edible?'

'Yes, it's not bad. I'm sorry, John. You're right – I need to eat, or our baby will suffer. And I couldn't bear that.'

'Me neither. I'll support you, whatever you want to do to get better. I'm on your side. I love you more than you'll ever realise.'

'Love you too.'

He ate slowly so as not to pressurise her, but still finished before her. After taking his empty plate out, he returned with two glasses of fruit juice.

'Wasn't sure what you'd like to drink. Hope orange is OK?'

'Yes, thanks.' She took a small sip, then looked up at him, putting her knife and fork aside. 'Sorry, I can't eat any more. It's nice, though. Any other time and I'd have eaten the lot.'

'No worries. You've had at least half, if not more. So long as you're not sick afterwards, everything will be fine.'

She smiled again. 'I hope so.'

'Want any afters? Black forest gateau. A small piece?'

'Why not?'

She ate all of it apart from the cream on the top. It made his day.

'Why don't you switch the telly on, put your feet up? I'll do the washing-up and join you in a few minutes.'

'Thanks, John. For putting up with me, I mean. I'm trying my best to get myself right but it will take time. I promise I'll see the doctor again as soon as I can get an appointment.'

'That's no problem. Isn't that what husbands are for? I won't be long and then we'll have some quality time together. I'm looking forward to having you to myself for a change.'

<><><>

Angie sat in front of the TV, feeling tired and sick; she didn't want to watch anything. Instead she lay back and closed her eyes, feeling guilty for letting everyone down.

'All right, Angie?'

She jumped at the sound of his voice. 'Exhausted ... and ashamed of myself.'

'There's no need to be. You can't help it if you're ill. Isn't there anything on TV? It's Christmas Day, after all.'

'I'm not in the mood, John. I've lost interest. Don't want to stay in either. I'm all of a go inside. Mind if I go for a walk?'

'It's cold outside, and it'll be dark soon.'

'Doesn't matter.' She got up from her seat.

'Want me to come with you?'

'I won't be very good company.'

'Let me be the judge of that. Come on, then. Put a coat on, we don't want you catching a chill on top of everything else.'

'OK.'

Angie hated herself but she wanted to be alone. She knew what he'd want to talk about and she knew she'd get emotional again. That, she couldn't face.

She put on the sheepskin jacket that he'd bought her last year and they stepped out into the cold.

'Looks like the rain's kept off,' he said.

'So far.'

'Where shall we go?'

'No idea. Maybe the park? I need some fresh air.'

'Right, the park it is. It's a fair walk, though. You all right with that?'

'Perfectly.'

She took his arm, shivering.

'Cold?'

'I'll be fine once I've walked a bit. And John, please stop fussing over me. I'm all right, I won't break.'

'I know, but I can't stop worrying over you. Is that such a bad thing?'

'I suppose not. And it's appreciated, really – I promise you.'

He squeezed her hand and they walked for a time without speaking. Angie was aware of what would be coming soon enough, but for now she wanted only peace and quiet.

The park was full; children played on shiny new bikes and scooters, and people walked their dogs, trying to take off the weight they'd just put on.

'Shall we sit on one of those benches by the side of the lake? I've suddenly gone tired,' Angie said.

'Sure thing – I could do with a rest myself.'

They sat close together. For a second she put her head on his shoulder, but moved it when a man and his dog passed by.

The low late-afternoon sun broke through the clouds, but the cold remained and Angie quivered from the chill in the air. She moved closer to John, snuggling into his side. 'It's nice here, isn't it? Always wondered how the birds and suchlike cope with the bad weather, without the benefit of thick clothing. The water must be freezing.'

'Don't they have a layer of fat to keep them warm?' He laughed. 'I know a few people with that layer of fat, too. Bet they're nice and warm, but they'll sweat like pigs in the summer. I'd rather be as I am than like them—'

'This isn't the right time for us to have a baby.'

John turned to her sharply. 'What? Angie, there's no right or wrong time. The baby's here now and we must live with it.'

'That's easy for you to say – you haven't got to carry it around for nine months and then give birth to it. And then look after a baby.'

'What are you trying to say, Angie – that you wish you weren't pregnant?'

'I ... I think that might be what I'm saying, yes. How do we know having a child won't be a nightmare? Not sure I can go through with it, but ...'

'Well, you don't have a choice. Unless ... unless you're suggesting what I think you're suggesting?' He paused. 'Jesus, Angie – is that why you didn't want me to tell anyone? I can't believe I'm hearing this. What will our families think if you have an abortion? Just because according to you, it isn't the right time?'

'Are you blind, John? You've seen the state I've been in; I'm struggling with this already. I'm at my wits' end.'

'You've got to be kidding. I know you've been uncomfortable with all the sickness, but for God's sake, that's no reason to abort a baby. And if you do, believe me, you'll regret it for the rest of your life.'

'And if I keep the baby and I can't look after it properly, what will that do to the baby? It may scar it for life.'

'No, it won't. Because I'll be there to support you, and so will my mum and dad, and your dad too. You don't have to do this on your own, you know.'

'They can't be there forever, and neither can you. And what happens when he or she grows up? They might have all sorts of problems because of my failures.'

'You're being too hard on yourself. Everyone's nervous about having a baby, but you learn as you go along. We'll learn together, I promise you.'

Angie shook her head. She had hoped he'd show her a little more empathy. Obviously not.

'I've had enough of this. I came out for a walk to clear my head and to calm myself, and you've ruined it. Now I'm ten times worse. Do you actually give a shit how I feel? I think not.'

She stormed off.

'Angie!' he shouted after her, but she neither turned around nor stopped walking.

He caught up with her as she reached the park gates, and grabbed her by the arm. She wrenched it back.

'Come on, Angie – be reasonable, will you?'

'It's you that needs to be reasonable,' she spat back at him.

His eyes widened and he quickened his step to keep up with her. 'Slow down, will you?'

She wanted to run away and never come back. Instead, she carried on marching towards their house, and once inside ran up to the bathroom, locking the door behind her.

He banged on it, demanding entry, but she refused to answer him.

'All right, suit yourself. A fine Christmas this has turned out to be.' He stormed back downstairs.

Angie sat on the toilet seat and shuddered. There was no way out for her. Maybe she'd be better off dead.

Eventually, she opened the door and stepped out onto the landing, dreading having to face John. But she had to.

He was sitting on the settee, a glass of beer in one hand and a turkey sandwich in the other. He had his eyes glued to the TV.

She sat a little distance from him.

'Is it any good?' she asked.

'If you like period dramas, I suppose. Unfortunately, I don't, but it's better than staring at a blank screen.'

'Yeah, I guess so.'

'You feel any better now?

'I'm all right. I've taken another of those sickness tablets – my second today.'

'Good.'

'Listen, we haven't opened our presents. Why don't I bring them down, and we can open them now?'

'Sure. Whatever.'

She disappeared upstairs, returning a few minutes later with two bags. One she put by John's feet, the other by her place on the settee.

'Shall we, then?'

'OK … but first, this is for you,' John said, taking a small package from his pocket.

When she opened it, she gasped. A ruby eternity ring. She slid it onto her finger and stared at it in awe. 'It's beautiful.'

She gave him his present. By comparison to hers, the gold cufflinks seemed inconsequential, but he seemed to like them.

'Wow, smart – thanks.'

'Right, how about the others?'

'Yeah, why not?'

There were the usual chocolates, aftershave, smellies and slippers. Angie's dad had bought her a necklace and John a jumper.

'Want anything else to eat? I can make you a sandwich,' he said when they'd finished.

'I don't need you to keep tabs on my every move. If I want something, I'll get it myself, all right?'

'Only trying to help.'

God, he could be so patronising. Didn't he realise he was making matters worse? Be it on his own head, she thought.

Chapter 8

She woke suddenly. Her dream had been of her mother on one of her bad days – a violent row in which she'd faced a humiliating telling-off for not washing her hands before she ate her meal. She couldn't see why as she'd washed them a few minutes earlier after going to the toilet. Her mother had slapped her hard and made her cry. There weren't many such incidents, but when they came, they were loud and sometimes violent. Why did she treat her like this? Most of the time she'd been kind and loving, but when she lost her temper, Angie was terrified.

All of sudden she sat up, facing John.

He was awake too. 'Are you all right, darling?'

'I'm frightened.'

'What of?'

'Everything, that's the trouble. Hold me.'

He pulled her close. 'There's nothing to be frightened of. I'm here, aren't I? Always will be, no matter what.'

'Even if I'm ratty to you?'

'Especially when you're ratty to me.' He smiled, stroking her hair.

'What would I do without you, John?'

'Well, it's the same for me.'

'I don't understand why I'm in such a state over having a baby, though. Millions of women experience this, so it can't be all that bad – can it?'

'I'm sure it isn't, my darling, but for some reason you're just stressing yourself out. You have to find out why. That's where your doctor can help.'

'Will you stand by me no matter what?'

'Of course I will. You should know that by now.'

She melted into his arms, sure he felt sorry for her and what she was going through. But he was powerless to help. She lay awake for a while, but silence prevailed, her fidgeting stopped, and soon she'd returned to the land of slumber.

The next time she woke up, he was fast asleep, so she left him alone. Downstairs, she lay shivering in the cold; the horrible feelings of sickness had returned. She found her tablets in the kitchen cupboard, took the required dose and glanced up at the clock: five o'clock. God, so early again, and yet she wasn't tired. She tried to calm her nerves by breathing deeply, in and out, in and out, again and again until her fear receded.

She had no idea how long she'd been sitting there when the door opened, light from the hall filtered in and John appeared.

'Hey. What are you doing in the dark? I wondered where you'd got to.'

'I couldn't sleep. That's why I came down here. Must have dropped off in the meantime. I'm fine now, perhaps we should go back to bed.'

'It's eight o'clock – might as well get up now, since I'm awake, and have breakfast. Toast and marmalade. How about you?'

'Yes, why not?'

She did feel a bit better, but her apprehension returned when he gave her the plate with two pieces of toast.

She ate slowly, trying to ignore the fact that he was watching her every bite, and within ten minutes had finished. He seemed pleased.

'Drink?'

'Water please.'

She sipped it slowly.

'So, what shall we do today?'

'Don't know. What do you want to do?'

'I'm easy. Shops will be open – Boxing Day sales. Hey, we might get a bargain on some stuff for the baby! We could save money on a cot or a pram or something. What do you say?'

She slammed her glass down on the table. 'For God's sake! You have got to be joking! I haven't even had my first scan yet and already you want to buy baby stuff? I have seven months to go – anything might happen. We won't even know the baby's sex for ages yet.'

'Sorry,' he said, holding up his hands. 'Maybe I am a little premature.'

'You could say that.'

'Whatever you want. So shall we just stay in?'

'I don't know.'

As she lay in the bath, she felt the pressure building. Why did he keep going on at her instead of letting her decide on her own? Anger still smouldered inside.

The water was too hot and was making her queasy again; she ought to get out as soon as possible. Drying herself, she examined her belly in the mirror. How could she feel so different, and look just the same? It was only a matter of time until she turned into a whale, though, and she wasn't looking forward to that.

Back downstairs, she told John she'd decided to go out.

'No problem. But wrap up in something warm, it's perishing outside.'

'Yes, Doctor John.'

'I'm only thinking of you. What if you had a miscarriage? You'd feel ten times worse.'

'It won't happen, I'm not that stupid. Let's go to Dexford shopping centre.'

'When do you want to go?'

'Now.'

As they drove towards the town, the traffic was chock-a-block. Amazing that people still had money after the mad Christmas spending spree.

As soon as they reached one of the big stores, John made a beeline for the sale rail in the babywear department. Had he listened to a word she'd said? Angie didn't want to look at this rubbish, and walked off to look at shoes and suitcases.

They bought nothing.

Back in the car, John said, 'Well, that was pointless.'

'I can't help not liking anything. You don't want me to buy stuff for the sake of it, do you?'

'No, but there was so much stuff for sale, especially baby things. It seemed to me you didn't even want to look, let alone buy – no matter what they had available.'

'What's the point of buying stuff when I'm only a few weeks gone?'

'I'm not arguing. What's the point, when you won't listen?'

She was fuming. If he continued, she'd lose her temper, and then he'd really have something to moan about. But they were quiet for the rest of the journey home, and she hoped it remained that way.

<><><>

John walked into the living room with a plate containing two sandwiches, and a glass of water, which he put on the coffee table.

Angie looked at the plate then at her husband. 'What's the meaning of this?'

'Eh?'

'I asked for one sandwich, not two. What are you playing at, you fucking control freak!'

'I just—'

She picked up the plate and flung it at him, then threw the water after it.

'Thanks for that, Angie. I hoped you might want another sandwich. One isn't much with you having a baby.'

'It's got nothing to do with you what I eat. I'll decide myself, you moron. I'm very aware I'm pregnant, thank you, and I'm also aware what I have to do for myself and the baby. I don't need you to tell me time and time again. Leave me alone.'

She stood up and pushed him with her hands again and again, then slapped him hard on the cheek.

John looked up in astonishment, touching his cheek. 'Angie, have you gone mad? What's the matter with you? It's just a bloody sandwich.'

Angie shook her head and gave him a dirty look before disappearing upstairs.

<><><>

He fell asleep on the sofa, and when he woke, she'd gone. Her car had disappeared. He thought better of phoning family and friends, not wanting to cause a further outburst. She didn't want him mothering her, so he would just have to wait.

At ten o'clock he heard the door open and in she came, looking as miserable as when she'd gone out.

'Hallo, love. Are you OK?'

'What do you care?'

'I care very much – you know I do.'

'If you say so. I'm fine. At least, I haven't been sick.'

'Where have you been? I was worried about you and I didn't know what to do.'

'Just went to see Dad. We walked to the cemetery, put flowers on my mum's grave. And talked about old times when Mum was alive, looked through the photo albums, that kind of thing.'

'I see. I guess Christmas is a time to remember your loved ones, especially those no longer with us, isn't it? I'm sorry, Angie.'

'It's OK – I needed to get out. I felt like the walls were closing in on me here. Wish I knew what's going on inside my head.'

'That makes two of us. You're just not the same person, Angie. I hoped being pregnant would be the icing on the cake for you, but it's starting to seem like I was wrong.'

'I'll make an appointment to see the doctor tomorrow.'

'That's a good idea. It's not just the morning sickness, is it? There's something else …'

She smiled. But she still wasn't prepared to tell him the truth.

Chapter 9

Bang on eight o'clock on Tuesday morning, she tapped in the number, but had to wait in a queue before eventually getting through. She got lucky with an appointment.

'Nine o'clock,' she told him.

'I'll come with you,' he said.

'I'll be fine, John. I don't need wet nursing.'

'But …'

'No, John. I won't hear of it for such a trivial matter. So long as you're here for me when I need you.'

'That goes without saying. Well, can't I at least drive you there?'

'I can drive there myself. I'm not an invalid.' Her anxiety went up a notch. He was doing the same thing again, driving her mad.

'All right, I can tell when I'm not wanted.' He walked to the kitchen – to make breakfast, she guessed. Thank God he hadn't offered to do hers as well.

At the allotted time, she put on her coat.

'Sure you don't want me to come?'

She'd already closed the front door behind her.

Inside the car, she breathed in deeply, tried to pull herself together and drove off.

She was early and waited ten minutes before they called her. Dr Brodie gave her a smile as she sat down, but she didn't return it. Her heart raced as she pondered over what to say to him. Would it be worth revealing her worst fears? She wasn't sure.

'I ... I saw you last week, about morning sickness. You said for me to try over-the-counter remedies from the chemist. Well, I did that, but they don't seem to be making much difference. In fact, at times I've been worse than before.'

'I see. Have you been taking the recommended dose?'

'Yes, religiously.'

'In that case, as I mentioned the last time we spoke, there are other tablets I can prescribe. They're stronger than those you had from the chemist and hopefully they'll suit you better. Take them three times a day. Try to eat a little and often, and plenty of fluids. From what you've said you're able to keep some food down, but you may find that in the short term you'll lose a few pounds. But this won't affect the baby. However, if the situation gets worse, come and see me at once. In fact, unless it changes for the better, come and see me again next week.'

'OK,' she said, not looking at him.

Dr Brodie printed off the prescription and handed it to her. But Angie didn't get up.

'Was there anything else?' he asked.

'No, no – it's nothing. It's just me being silly.'

'Mrs Greaves, if there's something troubling you, you must tell me. That's what I'm here for. What else is worrying you?'

Angie's hands trembled as she thought about what to say. 'It's just that I feel down – depressed, even – and I'm not sure it's just the morning sickness. The sickness isn't helping, but I'm terrified.'

'Is it the actual birth, or the pregnancy itself?'

She shook her head.

'Something else?'

'Well ... the pregnancy is part of it, but it's to do with my mum and my childhood.'

'In what way?'

'My mum suffered terribly when she was having me. She was sick all the way through, but she had severe depression after I was born, and she never got better. Eventually she was diagnosed as having bipolar disorder. And she had it for the rest of her life until she committed suicide when I was ten. I ... I was there when it happened. I saw her jump off the top of a hill. It was ... pretty devastating.'

Dr Brodie handed her a tissue. 'My God, it's bound to be. Did you have any counselling?'

She sniffed. 'Not really. My dad helped me get through it, although God knows he had enough problems of his own, and eventually I was able to put it to the back of my mind – as much as you ever can with something like that, anyway. But the last few days I haven't slept well, mainly because I keep dreaming about it. I can't get it out of my head. And I don't know what to do to stop it, and now I worry I might get the same problem.'

'That isn't necessarily the case, Mrs Greaves. It's understandable that you'd be concerned, but I imagine the more you try not to think about it, the worse it gets. You need to let these thoughts come, rather than trying to push them away. That's what's causing your anxiety.'

'But lately I've been reading about bipolar on the internet, and found out that it could be hereditary and now I'm frightened I might get it too. And my baby.'

'Ah, I see. Well, yes, it's true that conditions like bipolar can sometimes be passed on to other generations, but it's by no means guaranteed. The latest evidence suggests that if one parent has bipolar, there is at most a thirty percent chance that the offspring will also get the illness. That means a seventy percent chance that they won't.'

'But if I did get it, it could affect how I'm able to look after my child. And what if my child got it too? My husband wants this baby so much, but if there was something wrong with it ...'

'Well if I remember rightly, most people with bipolar develop it in their teens and early twenties. Since you're in your mid-twenties, the risk has already dropped quite a bit. Of course, it is still possible you may get it, just like your mum did, but I don't think we should be too concerned at this stage.'

'But this is really scary. What can I do?'

'The best thing would be to discuss it with your husband. Explain the symptoms and the risks, and your worries about yourself and your baby, and take it from there.'

'I don't want him to know. He doesn't know about my mum. He'd leave me, I'm sure – and probably want me to get rid of the baby, too. And if I was on my own with the baby and ended up ill like my mum, how would I cope?'

Tears filled her eyes. Dr Brodie handed her another tissue.

'First things first, Angela. Let's get your morning sickness and your anxiety under control. Take these morning sickness pills, see how you get on, and come back to see me in a week's time. Then, if you're well enough, we'll discuss the next stage. And I would seriously think about telling your husband about your fears. I'm sure you'll find he'll want to know and be as concerned as you. Is that all right?'

She nodded.

'See you next week, then.'

'Thank you, doctor.'

She stopped at reception to book an appointment for the same time next week, then collected her prescription before going home.

The weather was overcast and grey and cold. A few flurries of snow fell, making her wonder if a snowstorm was imminent.

<><><>

John looked up from his book and smiled at her in surprise. 'Hey, that didn't take long.'

'I know. I was in and out in five minutes.'

'Did he give you some tablets?'

'Yes, some new ones. One tablet three times a day, after meals. I'll have a piece of toast with marmalade and a drink and take one after that.'

'I'll make it. Why don't you just sit down and relax?'

'No – I'll do it myself. Like I said, I'm not an invalid.'

'Suit yourself.'

She'd feared he'd get her going again but it appeared he'd learnt his lesson. She ate in the kitchen so he couldn't supervise her; as soon as she'd finished, she felt the need to vomit, but managed a drink of water and one of her new tablets.

'I thought you were having some toast,' he said when she came back.

'I did, in the kitchen, and I've taken my tablet.'

'OK. So how are you now?'

'Sick. Let's see what happens with these tablets, and if I'm no better I'll have to go back the doc's again.'

'Bit of a nightmare, this, isn't it? I hope it's not a sign of things to come. Then after the baby's born we'll be up to our eyeballs in nappies. I always dreamed having a kid would be the best thing ever. Now I'm not too sure.'

'You've changed your tune. Only a few days ago you were all for it. Came back down to earth with a bump, eh? Poor John.'

'Not really. But I haven't changed my mind. I want this baby so much – it's my own flesh and blood, after all. Or it will be when it's born. Hope you do too.'

'Well, the way I feel at the moment isn't making it any easier.'

'If these tablets work, you'll soon notice the difference.'

'With a bit of luck.'

'Want to do anything today? I mean there's no point stopping in, is there?'

'Haven't thought that far ahead.'

'Well, if you want to, just say, and we'll go.'

'Sure, whatever.' His nice-as-pie attitude was getting on her nerves. Sometimes she despised him. She switched on the TV and watched a vacuous daytime programme. It didn't interest her and she drummed her fingers on the arm of the sofa.

He noticed her boredom. 'Listen, if you're fed up, I've got an idea. Why don't we visit my mum and dad, give them their presents? Save them coming to us on Saturday. What do you reckon?'

She frowned, unimpressed. 'Why would I want to do that?'

'Because … I don't know … for something to do instead of sitting around here doing nothing?'

'And what about how I feel?

'No need to stay long – and no need to eat or drink anything. Will that suit you better?'

'It depends how they react.'

'They'll treat you with respect, as always.'

'I suppose.'

'So, shall we do it? Then if we don't see them on Saturday, we could go out together.'

That gave her food for thought. Or was he trying to manipulate her all over again? 'Ought you to tell them we're coming over?'

'I've already spoken to them; I said we'd go if you're well enough.'

'My, my, what a busy bee you've been. Got it all worked out, haven't you?'

'Like I said, I only did it so we could be together at the weekend. Don't blame me for that. But you don't have to go. If we can't make it, they'll understand. So, what do you think?'

'All right. At least it'll be over and we can forget about it.'

'Let's get changed.'

'Yes, let's.'

She was resigned to it, but feared what might happen when she got there. What if she made a fool of herself? Anything but that.

Chapter 10

As they drove over to his parents' house, John kept looking across at Angie. She was unusually quiet and even when he tried to coax her, she refused to elaborate apart from yes or no answers. He prayed she wouldn't throw a tantrum in front of his mum and dad.

'Here we are, then,' he said, smiling.

'Hope they won't be funny with me over Christmas Day. If they start, I'm telling you – I'll walk out.'

'Angie, they're not like that. You ought to know that by now.'

She shrugged.

John got their presents out of the boot and walked up the drive. His parents came out, waving.

'Hallo, John, Angie. How lovely to see you,' his mum said, hugging and kissing them both on the cheek. His dad did the same.

'Come on inside, take the weight off your feet,' Susan said.

George took their coats and they sat on the settee.

'Drink?' his mum asked. 'Tea, coffee?'

'Angie will have a mineral water, and tea for me, please.'

'Coming up.' A flicker of pleasure came in her eyes, but she didn't say anything, to John's relief. He knew Angie didn't want the attention.

When she returned, John reached for the plastic bag by the side of the settee and handed it to them.

'Sorry it's late.'

'That doesn't matter,' Susan said, 'these things happen. Congratulations to both of you – I can't tell you how thrilled we are. Our first grandchild! Can't wait!'

George smiled. 'We're so much looking forward to it,' he said. 'And how are you feeling, Angie? I gather you've not been too well with morning sickness. Your mum was terrible with that too, wasn't she, John?'

'I told her, Dad.'

'It was awful. I had that horrible sick feeling for three whole months – the worst three months of my life, it was. Could hardly eat and was sick every day. So I sympathise with you, love. But after that, I was fine. Eat plenty of fruit and vegetables and lots of plain food. None of these spicy hot foods – they'll play havoc with your stomach.'

Angie blushed. She hated being the centre of attention.

'Thanks for the advice. I've just got these new tablets – I hope they'll help, because I've been awful this past week. It's been so bad I nearly didn't go in to work.'

John put a hand on her knee, sensing she was becoming emotional again. He needed to change the subject fast. 'Anyway, we hope you like the presents. Why don't you open them?'

'Thanks, John,' Susan said. 'And I'll just get yours.'

John unwrapped two hardback books and two music CDs, then it was Angie's turn. As soon as she'd torn away a corner of the wrapping paper, John's heart beat faster. Inside the parcel was an assortment of babywear – matinee coats, sleepsuits, nappies – and a lemon-yellow teddy bear. Angie hurled them to the floor and ran from the room.

Susan's hand flew to her mouth. 'What's wrong, John? I thought it would be a lovely surprise.'

'Sorry, Mum. She gets very emotional over anything to do with babies at the moment. It's as if she wants to block out the fact she's having one. She's going through a difficult time and there's not much I can do to help.'

'That's a shame. She should be enjoying it. Has she seen a doctor about her mental state?'

'No, she's putting it all down to the morning sickness.'

'Well, let's hope that's all it is,' said George.

'I hope so. I've been at the end of my tether.'

Angie returned, not making eye contact, and muttered in John's ear, 'I have to go now.' She was already putting her coat on.

'All right, darling. Sorry about this, Mum. Angie's not well. I'll ring you later to let you know how she is.'

'Hurry up, John, or I'll be sick all over the carpet!' she shouted from the hallway.

He drove off, leaving his parents waving behind the car. Angie didn't look back.

John was furious. 'Go on, then. Why did you kick up such a stink?'

'I suppose you put them up to that, you manipulative bastard.'

He couldn't believe what he was hearing. 'Hey, that's a bit strong, Angie. For your information, I did nothing of the sort. I was just as surprised as you. They never said a word, honestly.'

'Why do it now, when I'm only a few weeks pregnant? They're as bad as you were the other day. Giving me baby things when I'm so unwell. At this stage who knows what might happen? What if I lose the baby because of the pressure I'm under?'

'Come on, that won't happen. No one's pressurising you. Mum and Dad bought you those because they love you, and they'll love their first grandchild, too. There's nothing sinister in it, Angie. They're just excited, and they want the best for us. They're as worried about you as I am.'

'I don't believe you. You're conspiring against me.'

'That's rubbish. Why would we?'

'I don't know!' she shouted, beating her hands against the dashboard.

John had to be careful; a flaming row in the middle of a main road would be dangerous. He had to calm her down.

'I'm sorry you're upset; that wasn't their intention. It was a silly mistake. They wanted to cheer you up, because of how ill you've been.

Mum can relate to what you're going through, remember, since she had a similar experience herself.'

'Whatever.'

'Can we forget about this and get back to reality? Angie, please don't shut me out. I'm your husband, for God's sake. All I want is to help you if I can. I hate seeing you like this, but honestly, it won't last forever. You will get better. We can get through this and at the end of it all we'll have a beautiful son or daughter.'

She didn't react and spent the rest of the journey not speaking.

<><><>

Back at home, he took hold of her hand, which she didn't snatch away. She turned towards him on the bed and moved into his arms. The tears flowed and he held her close.

How did she tell him she was sorry? For now, it felt good to be in his arms. Eventually, she moved back and looked into his eyes.

'How can you be so nice when I'm so horrible to you?'

'When you love someone, it's easy.'

She smiled. 'I'm not sure I deserve you right now.'

'Everyone gets ill, darling, even me. I can't blame you for that.'

'Is there something wrong with me?'

'Only that you're pregnant. As Mum said, after a few months you'll be much better.'

'But that's a long time. In the meantime, I've got to work tomorrow, feeling as sick as a pig.'

'You may not be. Once those new tablets get into your system, you might be fine.'

'Don't hold your breath.'

'If you're not, go back to the doctor. See what he suggests.'

'I don't think they're interested.'

'They must be – that's their job. I'll come with you.'

She became tearful again.

'What's wrong?'

She hoped and prayed he wouldn't laugh at her. 'I'm frightened, John. Frightened I'm not eating enough for the baby, frightened of how I'll look when I start to show. Terrified of the birth, the pain. I should have told you this before, I know, but I know how much you want to be a dad. And then there's bringing it up. I haven't a clue. What if I screw it up and the baby gets taken off us?'

'Hey, calm down. You haven't even had the baby yet. Take this one step at a time. You're filling your head with too much, and that's why you think you can't cope. Get over the pregnancy first, then think about looking after it. Let's just see how you are over the next few days, OK?'

She nodded.

'Come downstairs. It's cold up here.'

'All right.'

'We'll watch TV until teatime. What do you reckon?'

'If I must.'

They sat watching an old film, snuggled up to each other. She liked being with him. Her worries didn't melt away but most of them at least went to the back of her mind.

'So, what do you want for your tea? We have turkey, turkey or turkey.'

<><><>

After their meal they relaxed on the sofa. John had a couple of glasses of red wine and a shot of whisky in his coffee.

He kissed her a few times before bed. Alarms bells rang. If he tried it on again, she didn't know what she'd do.

'Listen, I'm going to bed now. I'm tired. It's been a long day.'

'OK. You sure you don't want to watch this comedy? It's your favourite.'

'I know. Any other time I'd stay up with you. But I need to look after myself, John.'

'OK, I understand. I won't be long.'

She was in bed within ten minutes, worrying, but she hoped that since he'd had a drink, he'd just keel over and fall asleep. Normally she looked forward to a night of love, but now she felt differently. Maybe if she pretended to be asleep, he might take the hint.

She was dozing when she felt an arm snaking around her, his lips on the top of her head and onto her cheek. One of his hands cupped her breast. She shuddered and gasped which spurred him on. Could she bear it if she had to? The answer soon came to her.

'John, NO!'

'Come on, darling – it's been over a week. I've never waited that long before.'

'John, I can't,' she said, pushing him away.

He frowned; she'd never rejected him before. 'Have you gone off me or something?'

She sat up. 'No of course not. I'm worried … and I still feel sick. I'm sorry.'

He looked hurt.

'It's all right. My fault, I should have realised, considering how you've been. I feel so guilty now.'

'It doesn't matter. It's not you, John. It's me. Normally I'd have jumped on you by now – you know I would.'

'Let's get to sleep, try to forget this happened. I bet you're whacked out.'

'I am, but I can't sleep. It's driving me crazy. My whole life is falling apart.'

'It isn't, Angie. Far from it. This just a little hiccup, that's all. You'll be OK, soon enough.'

'Hold me,' she begged.

He did and within minutes she slipped off in his arms. Her last thoughts were fears of losing him thanks to her behaviour. That must never happen.

Chapter 11

Tuesday morning soon arrived. John made the doctor's appointment for Angie as soon as the surgery opened. He needed to find out what was wrong with her.

They hurried into the surgery together, holding hands.

'Hope we don't have to wait long. I don't want to be late for work on my first day back,' Angie said.

'Me neither.'

'It's a shame it isn't Dr Brodie. He was so nice to me the last time,' she said.

Secretly, Angie had been relieved to find out it was a different doctor, but tried to look disappointed. At least she should be able to keep the details of her chat with Dr Brodie to herself.

'Never mind, this one might be good too, or even better.'

'We can but hope.'

Dr Strange was a plump woman of middle years, with an easy smile and blue eyes. She looked surprised to see John alongside Angie.

'Hallo, take a seat. How can I help?'

'I'm pregnant – only about six weeks, but I've been suffering badly with morning sickness. The other doctor gave me some tablets before the holiday. Those aren't helping much either …'

John prompted her. 'Tell her about the other thing.'

Dr Strange raised her eyebrows. 'Is there something else worrying you, Mrs Greaves?'

Reluctantly, she explained about the mood swings, the anger, frustration, anxiety and depression. The doctor listened intently.

'This happens to a lot of women. Pregnancy hormones can play havoc in your body in these first few weeks, and I'd be reluctant to prescribe anything this early into your pregnancy. The tablets Dr Brodie prescribed for the sickness do sometimes take a while to take effect, so let's see what progress you make in the next week, and take it from there. Have you made your first appointment with the midwife yet?'

Angie shook her head.

'Look, she's been in such a state this last week, she's not her normal self. She's been panicking over every little thing. I'm really worried about her. Can't you give her something now?' John said.

'What are your thoughts about that, Mrs Greaves?'

Angie blushed. 'Don't know. As long as they don't harm the baby, I'd think about taking antidepressants, but I'd hate to be hooked on them. Maybe a low dose would be OK.'

'Well, I won't prescribe anything until it's necessary. I suggest you continue taking the morning sickness tablets at the higher dose, and if you're no better by next week, we'll review the situation.'

Angie looked at John.

'I think you need antidepressants now, before the situation gets out of hand. But of course it's up to you and the doctor. I'm just telling you my own opinion.'

'I'll have to take the doctor's advice, John.'

'OK, fine. It's your call.'

Dr Strange smiled. 'I'll give you another prescription for a week's supply of the sickness tablets. Come and see me in a week. Take care, now – and don't forget to make that appointment.'

Outside, John wasn't happy. 'She ought to have given you those other tablets. They might have helped – you should have insisted.'

'I'm not taking anything else yet. Now stop going on. You'll make me cry, and I don't need that right now. Remember we've got work. What will everyone say if they see I've been crying?'

'All right, sorry. Of course it's up to you. Have a good day.'

'You too. See you later,' she said without looking at him.

John frowned. Why did she keep getting angry when he was only trying to help?

<><><>

The Sachs Gordon building stood only five minutes away from the surgery. John drove over, parked the car in his space in the underground car park, then took the lift to the third floor, looking at his watch; he was only a few minutes late.

Sarah Benson sat at her desk, busy on the computer. David Sanville was next to her, Joe Lyon next to him. David was the senior of the three, tall, in his forties with balding black hair. Joe, the baby of the office at twenty-five, had curly black hair and green eyes and wore a trendy three-piece suit.

John walked past them to his own desk.

'Hi, Sarah.'

'What time do you call this?' she joked.

'Had to take the missus to the doctor's,' he explained, 'and they were running late.'

David winked. 'Not been out on the razzle, have you?'

John gave a sardonic smile.

Joe studied him. 'Everything all right, John? Nothing serious, is it?'

'Yes and no.'

'Oh yeah?' David said.

It came out before he could stop it. 'We're expecting a baby.'

'What? Hey, John, that's great news! Did you hear that, guys? John's going to be a daddy!'

They gathered around and patted him on the back. 'This calls for a celebration. What say we go out for a drink lunchtime?'

'Don't know about that. To tell you the truth, I'm a bit cheesed off. Angie's getting terrible morning sickness.'

'Tell me about it, mate. My missus was the same with our three,' David said. 'How she got through it three times beats me. I hold my hat off to her, John, I really do. Treat her like a queen and she'll be fine.'

'She keeps crying and losing her temper. Is that normal? It's driving me insane.'

'Never mind, only another seven months to go,' David said, ignoring the question. 'And that's the least of your problems. Wait until the baby's born, that's when your troubles will start. The dirty nappies, the sick, the sleepless nights and food everywhere – and that's just the first year. And when they begin to walk, you've got to watch their every move. You'll be dead on your feet, mate.'

'John, don't listen to him. He's trying to wind you up,' Sarah said.

'Yeah, well, I won't take any notice.'

'I sympathise. All the best, mate,' David said.

'Thanks.' John logged into his computer.

The day passed quickly. The lunchtime drink never happened due to the volume of work they had on; he even had to do overtime. That meant Angie would have been waiting for him for over half an hour. His stomach flipped as he realised he hadn't phoned her; she'd be mad at him again.

He drove as fast as he dared over to the estate agent's.

She wasn't there.

'Shit!' What now? Where had she gone? The office was shut, as were the shops. She must have caught a bus.

He carried on home and saw the lights on in the house. Breathing a sigh of relief, he got out of the car and prepared to face the music.

He went inside, putting his briefcase down in the hall.

She was in the living room, watching TV. 'Hi, darling,' he shouted, 'sorry I'm late.' She ignored him. 'Had anything to eat?'

Still no answer. What should he do now? 'Look, if you won't talk to me, I'll make something for myself.'

'Why should I, after you left me in the lurch?'

'I didn't. I went to pick you up, but you weren't there.'

'And why wasn't I there? Because I was waiting out in the fucking cold for ages. I had to get the bus.'

'Angie, I got held up at work. I've been busy. Why didn't you phone?'

'Why didn't *you* phone, you selfish pig? And for your information, I did phone, but the line was engaged. Couldn't get through.'

'I was on the phone to a client for almost an hour, trying to figure out his accounts.'

'A likely story. You'll be lucky to get any tea, the way you're behaving.'

'Well, I'll make my own if that's the case.'

'Fine. But remember, John – don't push your luck. I'll only take so much and then I'll snap. Be very careful.'

John made for the kitchen and heard the oven humming. He opened it to see two fish steaks bubbling away. The steamer was on the go and there looked to be more than enough for two. He smiled, glad she'd thought of him after all.

They ate in silence, until the bad atmosphere made him too uncomfortable.

'Did you get that prescription?'

'Yes, in my lunch hour.'

'Been sick today?'

'No, not so far. But I still feel bad. Haven't eaten much either. Just a ham salad for dinner and now this. I'm not enjoying it – but I'll try to eat it, don't worry.'

'That's good news. This is the first day since this started that you haven't been sick. I'd say those tablets are kicking in. Try to look on the bright side, eh?'

'That's difficult when you feel ill all the time. Don't know how I got through the day. Luckily, I got to stay in the office, or I'd have come home.'

'Why?'

'Because I'm frightened of being sick when I'm out seeing clients. It's already happened once; I don't want it to happen again.'

'No, of course not.'

'It's all right for you – it's not your problem. You've done your bit and now the rest is up to me.'

'Yes, but only until it's born. After that it'll be a shared responsibility, and I intend supporting you as much as I can.'

'Oh, sure. How can you, when you'll be at work? Look at the next couple of weeks for instance, you'll be working all the hours God sends. So how can you help me then?'

'Can't help that, Angie. It's my job. I have to work. But when I'm here I'll do my share, I promise. I want to be involved.'

'I don't want to talk about it anymore. We both know what will happen.'

'You could always call on my mum – she'd love to help if you let her.'

'Great,' she said, rolling her eyes.

She put her fork down, having only eaten half of her meal.

'Nice dinner,' he said. 'Shall I do the washing-up while you put your feet up?'

'Whatever makes you happy.'

'Helping you makes me happy.'

'Don't be a creep.'

He made off with the dirty dishes, smiling.

Chapter 12

It had been another hectic day. It was now the first Thursday in February and nothing much had changed. Having to work late didn't please John – or Angie, who hadn't made dinner. Still, the takeaway was only five minutes away. A fish and chips supper was fine by him, but he worried there'd be more recriminations.

Armed with the two portions, he wondered whether she'd be able to eat it; it wasn't the most easily digestible food. Still, that was up her.

He put the paper-wrapped packages in the kitchen, then returned to the living room, where Angie sat watching the TV.

'Want them on a plate, or shall we eat out of the paper?'

'Out of the paper. Not sure how much I can eat but I'll try my best.'

He bought her food and drink on a tray and went back for his own.

She'd opened the paper and was eating with her fingers, slowly. He started on his own food, not taking much notice of what she did, in case she accused him of spying on her.

'I was in two minds over buying these, the way your stomach is right now.'

'Yes, but I have to eat something.'

'True.'

'So, that's what I intend doing. Here, let me give you a few chips. I don't want all these.'

He watched her pile chips on top of his own portion. Even he couldn't finish all those.

'So, how are you feeling now?'

'I'm still having problems, even with the higher dose of the tablets. And it's affecting me at work too.'

'Is it? How?'

He listened intently as she explained about her urges to throw up when showing customers around properties. He was shocked, but not surprised. He'd hoped that work would take her mind off it, but apparently not.

'John, I don't know what to do.'

'That's understandable. Unless the sickness gets worse and you can't eat at all, the doctors won't do much. As for this problem at work, have a few days off sick. Get a sick note off the doctor, and ask Duncan to excuse you from seeing clients for the time being. Or one of these days you'll throw up all over someone or in their house. How embarrassing will that be?'

'Don't remind me. It was awful when I went to that house and was sick in their bathroom sink. But I'm an estate agent, John – the main part of my job is seeing clients, negotiating with them. They've suggested sending Bethany out, but she's not qualified yet.'

'Well, that's their problem. They'll have to give you something else to do. If not, you'll be off work indefinitely.'

She shook her head violently. 'I love the job, and I don't want to take any time off. I'll go crazy here on my own.'

'It won't come to that if you look after yourself. Talk to Duncan, he seems a decent enough chap. You've worked there for years, and as far as I'm aware you've never had any time off sick. And you're good at your job. Your appraisals are always excellent, aren't they? They'll fall over themselves to accommodate you.'

'Maybe, maybe not.'

'Angie, come on. This is only going to be a temporary arrangement. Once you've got over these first three months, you'll be out on the road again seeing clients. You'll be back to normal ... well, except for your big bump.'

She rolled her eyes. 'I can't eat any more of this. Sorry, John, it's no good.' She pushed the food aside and took a tiny sip of her drink.

John finished his and took a muffin out of the fridge.

<><><>

She woke early on Friday morning, feeling queasy, but managed not to be sick, which was a relief. A light breakfast of toast and marmalade was all she could face. Then she took her tablet.

John peered around the door. 'Morning.'

'Before you ask, I had a good night. Still not well, but I managed to eat most of my breakfast and I haven't been sick yet.'

He smiled. 'Well, at least you've started the day on a more positive note.'

'That's one way of looking at it, I suppose.'

'Perhaps you'll be able to do your job without hindrance after all.'

'That what I'm hoping.'

Angie busied herself tidying up while John had breakfast. Soon they had to set off for work. As she searched for her coat, a wave of nausea came over her again and she had to rush to the toilet. She cried as she cleared up the mess, guessing John must realise what had happened.

When she came out, he was standing in the hall waiting for her. She noticed the concern in his eyes and went to him for a hug.

'What's the matter with me, John? What shall I do?' she said as he held her tightly.

'I've told you. Do what you think is best. For a start, phone in sick. Then make another appointment with the doctor.'

'I'm going into work. I've got to. It's what I do.'

'Angie, listen. Please don't go.'

'I'm not taking a day off just because I threw up. That's ridiculous. Now, move out of the way. I'm going, whatever you say.'

John stood his ground and she pushed him away as hard as she could. He staggered against the wall, startled.

She put on her coat and slammed the front door, then sped off. Not until she got onto the car park did she stop to look in a mirror. It was still early, and cold outside, so she waited in the car until someone came to unlock the office. She cleaned herself up, hoping no one would be able to tell she'd been crying.

Duncan waved as he parked alongside her. Time to go. She needed to act normal and hope he wouldn't notice.

'Hi Angie, you're bright and early. Are you all right?'

'Yes, thanks. Just wanted to get a good start, you know.'

'You still look as white as a sheet. You sure you're OK?'

'Yes, I just told you, didn't I?'

'Suit yourself, but if you're ill, you need to get well again. You're no good to us unless you can give one hundred per cent.'

If she'd told him she was fine, he ought to accept that and let her carry on.

He opened the office door for her.

'Thanks, Duncan. I'm going to check my emails and catch up on my paperwork first, if that's OK?'

'Sure, carry on. Oh, and by the way, I want to see you in my office in half an hour.'

'What for?'

'I'll tell you when the time comes.'

As soon as he'd gone, she slammed the door shut. What was going on here? Were they conspiring against her?

She logged onto her computer and started to work, but she found it hard to concentrate as adrenaline surged through her body. A fleeting suspicion of John phoning Duncan passed through her. He wouldn't do that – would he?

Nausea came over her again and she had to rush to the toilets.

As soon as she came out, Duncan came over.

'Angie, in my office now.'

'You said in half an hour. I've got lots to catch up on. I can't do my job if you're going to keep me locked in a stupid meeting.'

'Come in and shut the door.'

Fine. She was ready to have it out with him.

'Sit down, Angie.'

She stared at him coldly. 'Have I done something wrong?'

'Not exactly. A few of the staff and I have noticed how ill you look. Naturally it's to do with your pregnancy …'

'But I can still do my job, despite what everyone might think.'

'You think so? Sickness while you're pregnant can be serious. I know a woman who ended up in hospital because she couldn't eat or drink. They put her on a drip. Now I'm not saying that will happen to you. But I am aware you have been sick at work on several occasions. And a customer has phoned to ask how you are, since you were sick while interviewing her. She hasn't complained as such, but I don't think I can allow you to visit clients in your present condition.'

'That's ridiculous. It could have happened to anyone, pregnant or not. This is victimisation. Discrimination.'

'No, Angie, you're wrong. When someone can't do their job due to illness, I have to sort it out. And you should be telling me if you're not well. I've already seen you rushing off to the toilet today. I expect you to be honest. It's not fair on your colleagues or yourself.'

'But I'm all right. I've been sick a few times, but I can work through it – and I'm taking tablets …'

'Yes, but that's not good enough. I don't want you to be sick when you're out seeing a client again – it won't put the firm in a very good light. Take the next two weeks off and get yourself right. On your return we'll take it from there.'

'What about working in the office?'

'Angie, I'm not suggesting anything yet. Obviously I want you to carry on doing the job you're being paid for. But if that isn't possible, we'll have to find something else for you to do. Let's keep our options open, shall we?'

'What if I don't want to take two weeks off?'

'Angie, this isn't a request, it's an order. Now please go home and we'll see you in a fortnight, all right? Go and see the doctor, and get him to sign you off sick.'

'But I don't want to go on sick leave. I can't stay at home on my own, I'll be bored to tears.'

'Angie. Go home and rest.'

She stood up. 'Duncan, you'll regret this, I promise you.'

She stormed out, leaving the door open. She collected her belongings from her office and marched out past reception. Tears came into her eyes as she glimpsed the smug look on Bethany's face. She wanted so much to react, but she didn't. Bethany wasn't worth the effort.

Back in the car, Angie was frantic, but she wouldn't allow herself to cry. John was going to be unbearable, but there was no way to hide it.

<><><>

She lay on the bed, horrible thoughts sweeping through her head. Was it really worth having this baby if it was giving her so much trouble? She already felt like she was losing control over her own body and her own life; how much worse would it be once the baby was born?

She got on the laptop and searched 'natural ways to miscarry'. It seemed there were several possibilities: taking high amounts of vitamin C, doing vigorous exercise, eating cinnamon, parsley and some other herbs she'd never heard of. Then came a suggestion to have hot baths. Finally, there was the big one: having an actual abortion.

This might end her problems, but John wanted to be a dad; he would be devastated. If only she'd listened to her dad in the first place.

It was only ten-thirty. She picked up her phone, wondering if she might get an appointment this afternoon.

Chapter 13

She arrived at the surgery to see the appointments were running twenty minutes late. Never mind – with luck, she'd still get back home on time.

At four forty-five they called her name. She knocked and faced another female doctor she'd never seen before.

She explained her difficulties with work.

'So you're still feeling sick.'

'More than that. It's horrible. I'm taking the tablets as directed but although they are helping a little and I'm eating better, I'm still throwing up once or twice a day. It's a nightmare.'

'Well, we can't increase the dosage any further – you're taking the maximum amount. You may have to live with it for the next few weeks, or even for the course of your pregnancy, I'm afraid. It's a common complaint.' The doctor studied the screen in front of her. 'How has your mood been lately?'

'Well, I was coping, but now my boss has told me to take two weeks off because I keep being sick, and it's stressing me out. I don't want to spend two weeks at home on my own. It'll drive me mad. My boss suggested that you give me a sick note. He sent me home and told me not to come back until I'm better.'

'Well, there are options. We can put you on a low dose of antidepressants, as I believe Dr Strange suggested before. I can assure you there would be no risks to your baby. In the meantime, I'll give you a note for a week. Come and see me next week, and I'll assess you again then. Oh, and I see from your notes that you're due for your twelve-week scan soon. Is that booked?'

'Yes.' Angie said. 'It's on the fifteenth.'

'Excellent. Now, about the antidepressants. A low dosage for the next few months might help you overcome your anxieties – and when you feel better, you can come off them.'

'I don't know. If I could get over these sickness feelings and get back to work, I think I'd be all right.' She debated whether to speak to the doctor about the other thing, which might be the only way out, or face six months of hell.

'Here's your prescription and the note for your employer.'

Now or never. 'I … I wanted to ask another question. About … having an abortion. Could I …?'

The doctor raised her eyebrows. 'What makes you think you would want a termination?'

'I'm not cut out to be a mother. I'm dreading the birth, and I can't stop feeling sick, and the thought of looking after a baby scares me to death. I won't cope, and I won't be able to work, and I just won't be me anymore. And what if I go mad like my mum did?'

'Yes, I read the notes from your chat with Dr Brodie. But there's nothing to suggest your mum's illness has been inherited, Mrs Greaves. You're most likely just anxious, that's all. It's perfectly normal to feel like that. Have you talked this over with your husband?'

'No, I can't tell him about mum's bipolar. He thinks she died in a car crash; he'd be heartbroken if he thought I might end up the same as her …' Angie paused, then nodded. 'I just need it taken away and then I'll tell him I had a miscarriage. It's the only way.'

'Well, I can't make the decision for you, and I can't tell you what to do, but legally there's nothing to stop you at this stage of your pregnancy. But what I would say is that honesty is usually the best policy – I'd strongly advise you to talk it over with your husband first. And don't forget, there's plenty of help available without having to take such a drastic step. Antenatal classes, support groups, all that kind of thing.'

'All right, I'll think about it. You must think I'm cold and callous, but I'm not. I'm just more frightened than I've ever been in my life.'

'That's understandable. Pregnancy is an emotional as well as a physical experience. Next time, bring your husband, and we can talk about it together. I still think medication may be the answer, but you don't have to take my advice – it's your call. Please just have a think about it. You take care of yourself, now.'

Angie left, wondering if confiding in the doctor had been a stupid move.

<><><>

John finally arrived home after another gruelling day at work. He still had a mountain of self-employed accounts to finish for the end of the financial year. He wondered what reception he'd get when he faced Angie; frosty, he suspected.

Opening the front door, he left his briefcase in the hall, and went in search of her, but there was no sign of her in the living room or kitchen. Then he caught sight of her coming downstairs in her dressing gown, her hair covered by a towel.

'Hallo. Been washing your hair?'

'Yes, just had a bath. Got fed up of waiting for you, darling.'

'Sorry. It's that time of the year at work. Be glad when it's over. Especially with you in your present predicament.'

'Very funny. Your dinner is in the microwave. Just reheat it for five minutes.'

'OK, thanks.'

He brought his meal in on a tray and ate in front of the TV. Angie was watching a soap, feet curled beneath her on the sofa.

'So how have you been today?' he asked.

'As well as can be expected.'

'That doesn't tell me a lot.'

'No.'

'Will you elaborate?'

'Are you that interested?'

'As a matter of fact, I am. You know I'm worried about how this pregnancy is affecting you.'

'Want to hear the latest, then?'

'Of course.'

'Duncan told me to take two weeks off.'

He suppressed a smile. 'Oh dear. But it can't be helped. Maybe it's what you need to recover from this sickness thing.'

'I saw the doctor this afternoon, to get signed off. She said I'm taking the maximum dose for the sickness tablets and thinks antidepressants might help my anxiety. I said I'd discuss it with you.'

'You have been very anxious about having the baby, and looking after it and everything. If you took the morning sickness away, would it make you feel less anxious?'

'I don't know. Maybe, maybe not. It's a hypothetical question. I won't know until it happens. What do you think about the antidepressants?'

'You know what I think. As I said when we saw the doctor before, so long as there's no risk to the baby, I'd say go for it. I've been banging on about it for the last few weeks – you must be sick of hearing it. Millions of people take them these days, so it's nothing to be ashamed of.'

Angie sighed but didn't answer. 'Oh, and don't forget I have to go for my twelve-week scan on the fifteenth. You are coming with me, aren't you?'

'Of course. I've already booked the day off.'

Thanks,' she said, squeezing his arm. 'I wish I didn't have to take this time off. What will I do all day on my own? It'll drive me mad.'

'Well, take it easy for a start. That might help with your sickness problems. You'll find something to occupy yourself. Read a book or something. How about you get a couple on pregnancy and childbirth? Might put your mind at rest.'

'I doubt it. And I don't want to be doped up to get through this.'

'Well, you might only need to take a low dose. Then after a few weeks you can come off them slowly and you'll be fine.'

'John, can we stop talking about this now?'

'But we should talk. Having this baby is going to be one of the biggest events of our lives, something we'll never forget. And I want to treasure every moment. Why don't you feel the same?'

She grimaced. 'If you felt sick all the time, you'd understand. It knocks the shine off a bit.'

'I imagine it would. Wish I could help. It's very frustrating.'

'Never mind. You just get on with your lovely life and I'll get on with mine.'

He didn't respond; there was no way he could stomach another row.

She got up, her eyes narrowing.

'Where are you going?'

'Upstairs, John, away from you.'

He sighed. 'What have I done now, for God's sake?'

'Nothing. You're getting on my nerves. Rabbiting on and on about things I don't want to talk about. I can't stand being in the same room as you.'

John shook his head, bewildered by the way Angie had behaved just lately. This couldn't just be the sickness and her pregnancy; there must be something else, but what? Maybe a doctor could answer that one – but what chance did he have of getting her to open up and admit all her problems, whatever they were?

Chapter 14

Angie had a restless Sunday night, dreaming of strange things, but woke with a jolt to see the sun shining through the window. Her eyes screwed up as they grew accustomed to the light. Looking to her left, she saw no sign of John. She glanced across at the alarm clock that she didn't need today; eight-thirty already. Good God, she'd overslept. And John hadn't even bothered to say goodbye. Well, stuff him.

Panic spread through her; being alone in the house filled her with dread. What would she do? She had to calm down, take one step at a time. First wash and get dressed. Then food, if she could stomach it.

Breakfast consisted of toast and butter, which she forced herself to eat, followed by a drink of squash. Now she had to keep the food down and hope for the best.

Bitter thoughts came into her head: her treatment at work, her terror of being pregnant and being a parent. And then that same horrible sick feeling came on again. She couldn't live with this; she must put a stop to it before it was too late.

She drove to Dexford, and went to the health food shop. She bought three packets of high-dose vitamin C and some cinnamon, not wanting to risk any of the more obscure herbs for fear of the shop assistant realising why she wanted them.

On her return, she hid her purchases in a cupboard; although even if John found them, he'd never guess what they were for. How long before the vitamin C took effect – an hour? More? She needed a result as soon as possible, so best take the maximum dose and see what happened. The longer she waited, the harder it would be. Right now, the thing inside her was just a foetus – not a baby at all. That's how she must think of it.

At twelve, the phone rang – John. How jolly decent of him, after rushing off without a word. Still angry, she thought twice before answering.

'Hi. I'm just ringing to see how you are. Sorry I left without saying goodbye, but you seemed to be having a lovely sleep. Didn't like to wake you.'

'Doesn't matter – it was probably the right thing to do.'

'Any better now?'

'A bit.'

'What have you been doing?'

'Not much. Went into Dexford, shopping. Boring. I'd rather be at work.'

'You can't, Angie. Try to relax, take the weight off your feet.'

'Can you really see me doing that?'

'No, but think of yourself and our baby.'

There he was, talking about babies again. Well, not for much longer.

'I'm trying my best, but it's not easy. Please be patient.'

'I am. I know what you're going through and I just want to help.'

'I realise that. Putting up with me these days must be hard. How have you kept your temper?'

She heard affection come into his voice. 'When you love someone, that's what you do, Angie. Anyway, look, I'd better go – it's so hectic here, what with the February deadline coming up. I won't be back much before seven, I'm afraid.'

'Yes, I guessed as much. You'll have to have a warmed-up tea again.'

'That's fine.'

She felt guilty. Perhaps she didn't deserve him.

The tears flowed as she thought about the awful thing she was planning, but she had no choice. If he loved her, he'd get over it and get on with his life.

As she ate lunch, she thought about her next steps. She'd read something this morning about how strenuous exercise could cause a miscarriage. So, having taken the required dose of vitamin C, she dug out the tracksuit and trainers she'd last used two years ago during a fitness fad.

The weather was cold, but dry; out she ran, as determined as ever. Where she went wasn't important, as long as she pushed herself to the limit. She turned left onto the main road and carried on to a track that led to the canal.

A steady pace at first, to gauge her stamina. Not too bad; she was confident enough to run even faster. Along the canal the pain kicked in; she gritted her teeth but continued. Adrenaline pumped through her body as the agony became unbearable. Her legs were like rubber, her breath scorched in her throat, and she had to stop; there was a bench just past the next bridge.

Ten minutes passed before she got her breath back, and when she moved, her whole body ached. Her legs were like lead weights – and now she had to go back. At first, she walked, then sped up again. This time she ran at a more leisurely pace, conserving what little energy she had left. With the house in sight, she built up speed until she reached the front door.

Angie dragged her weary body upstairs and lay flat out on the bed. It had been such hard work, but there was no sign of a reaction, no hint of any blood, no pain anywhere but in her legs. Mortified, she cried with frustration. She had a sudden urge to go to the toilet, then spent the next hour running up and down the stairs. She felt sick, but that was nothing new.

Perhaps a bath would be a good idea.

She allowed the water to get as hot as possible and lowered herself into it. The pain was immense but she stayed there for five minutes, until the water cooled. Then she washed and dressed. Still nothing.

Although frustrated, she tried not to panic. This was only the first time, after all. She had several more weeks to go yet, and many other things to try.

<><><>

By the time John had finished work the following day, he realised he hadn't phoned or texted Angie all day. Shit, he muttered under his breath, fearing he'd be in trouble when he returned home. She'd been in an odd prickly mood last night, and asleep when he'd left this morning. Still, it was a genuine mistake.

As he got out of the car at seven-thirty, his stomach churned. None of the lights were on as he entered, which was strange. He flicked on the switch in the hall and went in search of her. Not in the kitchen, the living or dining room. Nor the downstairs toilet or the utility room. That left the bedrooms. She had to be there.

Their bedroom came first. The door was open, but the room was in semi-darkness. From the light on the landing, he saw her on the bed, lying in a foetal position facing the wall and wearing her dressing gown. She looked so beautiful lying there, so innocent, like the woman he had married. They had been so happy together, right from the start, and a baby should have been the icing on the cake. Just where had it all gone wrong?

Then, as he came back to reality, he noticed her legs. They were red and blotchy.

'Angie!' he shouted at the top of his voice. When she didn't answer, he tried again, even louder. This time, to his relief, she flinched.

She yawned, squinting as he flicked the light switch. 'Where's the fire?'

'I thought … I don't know what I thought.'

'No need to worry, I'm fine. I was tired and when you didn't come home, I had a bath and I must have fallen asleep.'

'And what's happened to your legs? They're bright red.'

Angie jumped. 'Oh, the water was a bit too hot. Didn't realise until I got in. It's nothing, the redness will be gone by the morning.'

'I hope so, or that's something else you'll need to see the doctor about.'

'Your dinner's in the microwave. Go and warm it up, I'll be down in a minute.'

'Thanks. Sorry I didn't get in touch today. I've been in and out of meetings; you wouldn't believe how frantic it's been.'

'Doesn't surprise me. I guessed I'd have to suffer this on my own.'

What could he say? He was telling the truth; surely she understood how it was for him?

'Angie, that's not fair. If it was an emergency or something really serious, I'd drop everything and come home …'

'Of course. But morning sickness is only a minor illness, isn't it? I mean, it's affecting my whole life, but that's a small matter.'

'I'm sorry. It's not an excuse. I'm just trying to explain how it is.'

'Better go and eat your dinner.'

It could have been worse, he thought, tucking into his food. Of course she wasn't happy, but that was to be expected. At least he'd managed to avoid a row again.

He was finishing the washing-up when she came down. She gave him a little smile, poured herself a glass of water, and went into the living room.

He sat by her and took her hand.

She didn't pull it away.

'How have you been today?'

'Would you believe it's been nearly two days now without being sick? I might have turned the corner. I still feel sick nearly all the time, but I've actually been doing a few things today. I even went for a run this afternoon, like I used to. Quite enjoyed it. I ran over five kilometres, went down by the canal. I'm not as fast as I was, but it felt good.'

'Angie, you must be careful. Can you imagine how you'd feel if something happened to the baby? You'd be devastated.'

'I suppose I would. But if you expect me to sit around all day like a stuffed dummy, think again. I'm not about to let this baby stop me doing things I want to do until I absolutely have to. Women have run marathons while they were pregnant – I hardly think a half-hour jog is going to do any harm.'

'I know. I just want you to look after yourself, that's all, and not take any risks.'

'I'm not stupid, John. And I object to you insinuating otherwise.'

'All right, I'm sorry. Forget I said it, all right? I don't need a fight, I'm beat as it is. A peaceful night is all I want.'

'Stop saying nasty things about me, then.'

John exhaled nervously, trying to bite his tongue. The atmosphere had changed and he wondered how to appease her this time.

Chapter 15

It was Monday 15th February – the day of the twelve-week scan. John was up before the alarm, his heart already beating faster at the thought of seeing his baby. He was fascinated to see how it had developed. But Angie didn't seem bothered. As he put on his dressing gown, he wondered about waking her, but as it was only six-thirty he let her be.

After eating his breakfast, he brought her a cup of tea and shook her gently by the arm.

'Angie, time to get up. We have to get to the hospital by nine-thirty.'

'Oh,' she mumbled, rubbing her eyes and yawning, 'what time is it?'

'Just after seven,' he told her, putting her tea on the small chest of drawers by the bed.

She sat up. 'All right, I'm coming,' she said. 'Another waste of time.'

'No, it isn't,' he said. 'Don't you want to see our baby? And even if you're not bothered, it's important for the doctors to see that he or she is developing correctly – they can spot all sorts of things on scans these days. I've been reading up about it.'

'I suppose,' she conceded.

'And don't forget we'll be able to see a picture of our baby! How good is that?'

She sighed. 'Great.'

He wished she'd be more enthusiastic, but decided it was best to leave her be and hope that in time her attitude would change.

By eight-forty they were ready to go.

'Have you got everything?' he asked.

'Sure have,' she said as she put on her dark woollen winter coat; it was freezing cold outside again.

'Wish this bloody weather would change,' she moaned as they stepped out. 'Don't think it's been above five degrees since Christmas.'

'I know, but there's nothing we can do about the weather. Never mind – another few weeks and it'll be spring, and by the time the baby's born it'll be summer. That'll be lovely,' John said as they got into the car.

Still shivering when they arrived at the hospital, Angie reached for John's hand as they followed the signs to the antenatal unit. They took a seat in the waiting room.

Within ten minutes, a nurse appeared and shouted Angie's name. She had a large jug of water and a couple of plastic cups.

'Hallo, Mrs Greaves. I'm Nurse Jordan. Have you had much to drink this morning?'

'Only a cup of tea before I came out,' Angie said.

'We need you to have a full bladder for the scan to work. Drink as much of this as you can, and don't go to the toilet until afterwards.'

Angie grimaced at John.

'OK,' she said.

'We'll call you in about twenty minutes, all right?

Angie nodded.

When the nurse had gone, she frowned at John. 'Can't say I feel like drinking right now, but I suppose I'll have to.'

'You will.'

It took a while, but finally she managed it.

'Ugh. I feel really bloated now, and if I need a wee, I don't know what I'll do.'

'Hold it in, as best you can.'

'What if I have an accident?'

'You won't.'

They sat around for some time, and finally Nurse Jordan came for them.

'Right, Mrs Greaves, we're ready for you now. If you'd like to follow me.'

'About time,' Angie murmured under her breath.

John hoped the nurse hadn't heard.

They went into a dark room with a large bed which had been
propped up at one end and covered in a paper sheet. There was a ma-
chine with a monitor at one side of it.

'All right, Mrs Greaves – if you'd like to lift up your blouse and
undo your jeans and lie on the bed.'

Angie did as she was told.

A man in a white coat who had been reading some notes in the corner came over. 'Hallo, Mrs Greaves. I'm the sonographer. I promise
you this won't hurt a bit. I'm just going to squeeze some gel onto
your tummy, then I'll pass this probe over your skin and take some
measurements of your baby. If you'd like to watch, you'll see the first
pictures of your baby on that screen to your right.'

The sonographer began his work and John watched, fascinated.

The image was blurry at first, but soon became clearer and they
were able to see their baby; arms, and legs, and head.

'Wow! How big is it?' John said.

'About seven and a half centimetres – that's a bit on the big side
for twelve weeks, so we'll need to adjust your due date by a week
or so. Now, I just need to do something called a nuchal transluceny
scan – it measures some fat on your baby's neck and helps us detect
abnormalities like Down's syndrome.'

Angie sighed. 'A waste of time, if you ask me. Will it take long? I'm
bursting for a wee.'

'Darling, it's better to be safe than sorry,' John said.

Once he'd finished, the sonographer said, 'All done. We just need to
take a couple of blood samples from your arm, and then you can go.'

Nurse Jordan came over and took the blood, putting cotton wool
and a plaster over where he'd taken it.

The sonographer smiled. 'Right, Angie. All finished. You should get
the test results through within three or four days – your GP surgery

will give you a call. Everything looks fine, but I should mention that the baby does have an increased nuchal translucency measurement, which is sometimes an indicator of Down's syndrome or other problems. Given your young age, it's probably nothing to be too concerned about. When the blood test comes back, your doctor will be able to tell you more about the risks and the options for further testing.'

John's face fell. 'But you said the baby looks fine.'

'Yes, Mr Greaves, it does ... but it's difficult to tell from the screen.'

'This is unbelievable,' John looked at Angie, whose hands were shaking as she fastened her clothes.

'I knew it,' she said, shaking her head. 'I'm not destined to have a baby. I should have had an abortion weeks ago.'

'Angie, don't be silly. I'm not even considering an abortion. We'll take what we're given, and deal with it when the time comes. I won't hear any more about it. This is our baby and no matter what happens, we will give it the best life we can, do you understand me?'

Angie nodded, lip trembling.

'Would you like a picture of your baby to keep?' the sonographer asked.

'Of course, yes. Thank you,' John said.

Angie didn't speak.

John took the grainy photo and put it in his jacket pocket.

The drive home was quiet, and John kept feeling tears prickling in his eyes. Glancing across, he could see that Angie was a quivering wreck. How would she deal with this latest revelation?

<><><>

When Angie got home, she felt numb. To discover their child could have Down's syndrome was a blow, another nail in the coffin; the thought of rearing a disabled child who might also develop bipolar disorder in later life made her even more determined to get rid of it. She must never tell John what she was planning, even though the baby's disability might be so severe that he would agree with her decision.

In his present frame of mind, he probably wouldn't, and she simply couldn't risk him saying no.

They sat down on opposite ends of the sofa, both lost in their own worlds. Angie waited for John to speak. She didn't want to hear what he had to say, as she knew how the conversation would end: with another almighty row.

'Well, this is a blow,' he said finally, rubbing his brow with the back of his hand.

'That's putting it mildly.'

'I never expected this. I thought it would just be a routine test and we could forget it and get on with our lives.'

'Life is never that easy, is it, John? Looking forward to caring for your monster child, are you? We'll be a laughing stock,' she wailed.

'Calm down. We don't know that for sure. All right, so the odds are a bit higher – it still may not happen. It's by no means a cast-iron certainty.'

'Yes, but the evidence points to it. And what about the blood test results? If they point to the same thing, what then?'

'We deal with it. But I can't accept you having a termination. As I said before, that's out of the question.'

'It's all right for you to say that – you're not the one who'll have to look after a disabled baby. I am. And the way I'm feeling right now, I'm not sure I can cope with it.'

'You will. Once it's born, you'll love it, maybe even more than a normal child. It's a mother's instinct. Believe me, it's true.'

'And what gives you the right to say that? What do you know about a woman's feelings? What do you know about children with disabilities? Nothing. It's just you surmising.'

'Anyway, there's no point arguing about it, because we still have to wait for the blood test to come back. And then discuss it with the doctor.'

Angie sighed. 'I suppose so. And in the meantime, if you dare tell anyone, I'll leave, John, and then you'll never find out what's happened.'

John shook his head at her. Let him think what he liked – she'd do as she wanted. It was her body; the baby was inside her and only she had the right to decide.

<><><>

Three days later, she got a phone call from the surgery.

'Mrs Greaves, we've had the results of your blood test through. If you'd like to make an appointment, the doctor will discuss them with you.'

Angie's heart sank. This couldn't be good news. She hurriedly made the appointment for that afternoon, deciding to see the doctor on her own. If John came, he'd try everything to stop her from having a termination, and she couldn't have that – not when her mind was already made up.

'Angela Greaves to Dr Harrison, Room 3 please.'

She got up, took in a deep breath and ambled over to the door, then knocked and went in to sit in the chair. The doctor was glancing at the computer screen, obviously reading Angie's notes.

'Hallo, Angela,' she said with a slight smile. 'How have you been?'

'Not too bad, but I still feel sick. Although I haven't been sick as often – it's once a day or less now.'

'Good. You're making progress. Next week should see further improvement, but it may not go altogether. It should become more manageable, though, which will allow you to resume your normal activities and return to work.'

Angie nodded.

'Now then, we've had the results of your blood test. You're aware that your twelve-week scan indicated your baby could be at a higher risk of having Down's Syndrome? Well, I'm afraid the protein levels in your blood are a little outside the normal range, which also suggests that your baby is at a higher risk of having the condition.'

'I see. How high is the risk?'

'About a one in fifty chance. Many women in your position choose to follow up a higher risk result with an invasive test – a sample of the placenta or the amniotic fluid – which will give you a definitive result one way or the other. Is that something you think you might want to do?'

Angie shook her head. What was the point in prolonging the agony, when she'd already decided what to do?

'I don't think so. But I wanted to ask something else, doctor.'

'Yes, of course. Fire away.'

Angie hesitated, took a deep breath. 'To be honest with you, I'd already decided on an abortion before this happened. Now this has made my mind up even more.'

Dr Harrison frowned. 'Are you sure? Have you discussed this with your husband? I must say, I'm a little surprised he isn't with you today.'

'He couldn't get away – but we've talked of nothing else. And we've decided a termination is for the best. He agrees with me. I can't have a baby now and since we now have this added worry about the possibility of the baby being disabled, it's out of the question. And we have our careers to think about. We can't afford for me to not be at work. Please can you send me to a clinic?'

'If that's what you want, then of course, it's your choice. I can't tell you to terminate, or not to terminate the pregnancy. But perhaps you should wait another week; the sickness may well have improved further by then, and you might feel differently. You're only twelve weeks pregnant, so there would be plenty of time to have the termination if you did still want to go ahead.'

Angie shook her head. 'Ever since I found out, I've been scared to death. I had hoped these feelings would go away, but they've grown even stronger. Could you make the appointment now?'

The doctor sighed. 'All right, if you're sure. I'll refer you. Now, are you having any other problems? Mood swings, depression or anxiety?'

Angie couldn't face going through it all again. 'Yes, although this sickness feeling is getting me down, and being off work isn't helping. I won't take antidepressants unless there's no other choice.'

'Well, if you're feeling down, counselling is available, and there are organisations out there that could help – I'll print you off a fact sheet and you can check them out. And I'll give you some information about Down's Syndrome and how the testing works. I'd like you to think about your options carefully, and some more information may help to set your mind at rest.'

'I don't need help. Just an abortion as soon as possible. Once it's gone, I'll be fine.'

'OK, Mrs Greaves. You'll receive a letter in the post in the next few days. Just ring to confirm the appointment. They'll examine and assess you first, before the op.'

'Thank you, doctor,' she said, trying to hold back the tears that threatened.

Back in the car, she breathed heavily, head pounding – but at least now something would be done to take away the pain. Soon she'd be out of this mess.

She'd have to face John, tell him she'd miscarried – he'd be upset, but he'd get over it – and then she'd go on the pill. And that would be that.

<><><>

The semi was the same house she'd lived in as a kid. She had lots of memories there, bad and good. Her father had been her rock after her mum's death; without him she wouldn't have got through the bad times.

She rang the bell and he answered at once.

'Hallo, Angie, lovely to see you! Come on in.'

Thanks, Dad. Just thought I'd see how you are.'

'I'm good, thanks. But how about you? You don't look well. Sit down, I'll get us a drink.'

'Just a glass of water, please.'

'Coming up.'

While he got the drinks, she looked around the room, which had been the same since before her mother had died – the same photos of her and her mum on the wall, the décor unchanged apart from the odd lick of paint.

He handed her a glass and sat opposite, smiling. 'Why do I get the feeling you want to talk about something?'

She burst into tears. 'I can't do it, Dad. You were right. I can't have this baby.'

'Because of what happened to your mum? I understand, Angie. You must be terrified, but deciding to get rid of your baby is a hard thing too, isn't it? Ask yourself, though – is it worth risking your own health?' He paused as though weighing up a decision. 'At the end, your mum became a very dangerous woman, you know. She pulled a knife on me more than once. And used it on occasions.'

He got up and opened his shirt.

She gasped.

A long, jagged scar ran across the top of his chest. There was another smaller one on his stomach; he turned around and Angie saw another on his shoulder.

She gasped. 'Oh my God.'

'I should have showed you these before now, but I didn't want you to think badly of your mum. It wasn't her – the illness was to blame. But there's not much they can do, even today, except put you on antidepressants. And once you're on them, you can't get off them.'

'I know, Dad. I'm scared. I didn't mean to get pregnant, nor for John to find out, but I kept being sick, and I couldn't hide it. And now something else has come up. I went for a scan and they told us the baby is at risk of having Down's syndrome.'

'Oh, God, that's terrible. How upsetting for you both. I suppose that's made you even more determined to have an abortion?'

'Yes, it has. The risk is less than it is for getting bipolar but it's still well above average. I can't take much more of this.'

He looked thoughtful. 'You know, it's funny you mentioned Down's syndrome. I'm almost sure one of my mum's sisters – Ellie, it was – she had a Down's child. Spent the whole of her life in an institution. Perhaps that runs in families, too.'

'Yes, it could. I have to accept I'm not destined to have any children, Dad. John will be heartbroken. Still, in a week or so it'll be over and after that I'll go on the pill. And he'll never find out.'

'You could always adopt, couldn't you? But you'll have to tell him the truth. Of course, if he wants to be a real father – to have a child of his own with you, I mean – he'll have to be told it might cause a problem in later life. It won't be easy, whatever you do.'

'I don't want to lose him, Dad. I love him so much, couldn't live without him.' Angie sniffed back tears.

Alan put his arm around her. 'Everything will be fine. Have the abortion as soon as possible, get it out the way.'

She nodded. 'I saw the doctor before I came here. She's sending me to a clinic for an assessment.'

'Ah, you've already done it. That's good news. Glad you've seen sense.'

'It's a case of having to. I've had these awful sickness feelings from the beginning, and now I just feel depressed and anxious all the time. It's been horrible, Dad. And what if I get what Mum had? How will I look after it?'

'Hopefully it won't come to that.'

She smiled sadly. 'I'd better get back. Got to cook the tea.'

He looked disappointed. 'So soon?'

'Don't worry, I'll come again when it's over, all right?'

'If you need moral support, I could come with you, since you insist on not involving John.'

'Thanks for the offer, Dad. I'll let you know nearer the time.'

He gave her a big hug. 'Love you, chicken.'

'Love you too.'

<><><>

She ate tea on her own because John was going to be late again. She had trouble eating as her appetite remained low.

Then she flopped onto the settee and switched the TV on. Her nerves were jangling again; what if he was at home when the phone call from the doctor came through? John should be at work – but if he wasn't, and he got to the phone first, and found out what she was up to, he'd go mad. And maybe their marriage would be in jeopardy, too.

He was all smiles when he finally arrived. 'Hiya, Angie. Phew, am I glad to be home! Thank God it's Friday tomorrow, then it's two days off at last. I'm done in!'

She glanced up at him, fed up of the moaning. He ought to be in her shoes, then he'd have something to moan about.

He ate his beef casserole in silence, as if he hadn't eaten for days. How she wished she could do that.

'This programme any good?'

'Not much.'

'So, what have you been doing all day?'

'Sitting around feeling ill and wishing I was at work.'

Still staring at the TV, he said, 'Oh, good for you. Glad you got out. Better than staring at four walls.'

She hurled the remote control at him. It landed on his plate and spattered gravy onto his shirt. 'You're not even bloody listening to me, you bastard, are you?'

'What the ...? Angie, we need to sort this out. I mean, we're having a baby, for God's sake. We should be happy, not constantly at each other's throats.'

She ignored him. Why should she speak to him, the ignorant pig?

He sighed. 'OK, fine. You carry on. This attitude will only make matters worse. God help us if it's the same when the baby arrives. Have you heard anything from the doctor's? That blood test should have been back by now.'

Luckily, he was still gaping at the TV and didn't see the colour rising to her face. She almost told him what she'd planned, just to see the look on his smug face. 'No. I'll chase it up tomorrow.'

After that they didn't speak. She guessed that annoyed him and she was right.

'Oh, sod this, I'm going to bed,' he mumbled and disappeared up-stairs.

Angie sighed with relief when he'd gone. These days she preferred her own company to his. He was so irritating.

By the time she went up she was exhausted. She tried to keep calm but found it difficult; the prospect of sleeping in the same bed as him filled her with despair. So she reached for a nightie and dressing gown and strode to the second bedroom – which he intended doing up for the baby, he'd said, more than once.

She found blankets and settled down. When he didn't come in complaining, she breathed a great sigh of relief.

Saturday morning, and he woke up with a start. Looking at his alarm clock, he was horrified to see it was nine o'clock. God, had he slept that long? Normally he was up by seven at the weekend. Work, as usual, had sapped his strength and made him oversleep. Every year it was the same and still nothing changed. How nobody ever went sick with stress, he'd never fathom.

The weather was dull and rain poured down. Looking out of the window, he saw Angie, in tracksuit and trainers, running towards the house. She was drenched, hair matted on her head, water streaming down the sides of her face. He couldn't believe his eyes.

He stood in the hall, waiting for her to open the front door. When she came in, she was shivering.

'Angie, what the hell are you doing?'

'Just went out for a run. I needed to get some fresh air.'

'In the pouring rain? Are you mad? What if you'd fallen over? Our baby's life could be at risk, and yours too.'

'I didn't do anything, John. When I started out it was dry, the sun was shining, and I only went to the park and back. No one was in any danger, least of all the baby.'

He shook his head. 'You want to get out of those wet clothes and dry yourself.'

She gave him an icy glare before running upstairs.

He didn't care what she thought. She had acted foolishly and had to be told.

Ever since she'd been pregnant, it seemed to have been one stupid thing after another. And he was powerless to stop it.

Fifteen minutes later, she came down the stairs in jeans and top, hair still damp but neatly combed.

She sat in the armchair and switched on the TV in sullen silence.

She was at fault, but maybe it would be best if he made the first move. 'Drink? Bet you need warming up after all that running in the cold.'

A flicker of anger came into her eyes. 'Mug of soup.'

'OK, coming up.'

When he returned, she was shivering again. Her hands went tightly around the cup and she sipped it every few minutes.

'So, are we going food shopping this morning, or do you want a rest after your Arctic marathon?'

'Very funny. I can't face food shopping. I'm not in the mood.'

'OK, I'll go on my own. Mind you, the way you're eating these days, we won't need much, will we?'

Her eyes widened. 'I can't help it, John. I'm not doing this on purpose. I want to eat, but when I feel like this it's impossible. It's not as bad now, but I'm still suffering.'

'Didn't stop you going out running, though, did it? Anyway, the morning sickness isn't all, is it? It's you, too. Always in a mood and most times you take it out on me. I try not to let it get to me, but ...'

'I'm sorry. I get so emotional and wound up over everything. And when I do, I lash out. But it will pass.'

'I'm not so sure of that. You need professional help, Angie, and only a doctor or a psychiatrist can provide that.'

'No. This is just because I'm pregnant. It will go in time.'

He sighed. 'I'd better make a list and get the shopping. Is there anything you want?'

'Not especially. Just buy stuff I like, and we'll see how it goes.'

<><><>

He got to the supermarket within fifteen minutes. Food shopping was a pet hate of his as Angie always complained he spent too much and bought rubbish. This time he'd stick to the list. She'd probably find fault in whatever he did, but so what? All he could do was try.

As he walked through the fresh fruit and veg section, he felt a tap on his shoulder; he turned around and saw Sarah. A big smile covered her face as if she'd enjoyed surprising him.

'Sarah, hi. Fancy seeing you here.'

'Yeah. I don't usually come here, but there's a few things I couldn't get at my usual supermarket. How come you're on your own? What's happened to Angie?'

'Oh, she's not well again. To be honest, it's been a nightmare ever since she got pregnant. She's had morning sickness, mood swings, she can't stop crying, and loses her temper over the slightest thing. It's a bit depressing.'

'Lots of women have problems during pregnancy, but that sounds worse than normal. That's a shame, John.'

He smiled. 'Sorry to bore you with my troubles …'

'Not a problem. I wondered why you'd been so quiet at work. I put it down to how busy we've been.'

'Well, I've tried to hide it, to be honest. You know what us men are like, and we hate bringing problems to work. Hopefully Angie will sort herself out eventually and we'll have a beautiful baby. And then I can forget all this nonsense.'

'I hope so too, for both your sakes.'

'Anyway, better get on, or Angie will wonder what I've been up to … Sarah. Please don't tell the others at work. I don't want it to be common knowledge.'

'No, of course not. But if you ever need someone to talk to, I'm a good listener. I might be able to help.'

He nodded and finished the shopping, wondering if he'd done the right thing in telling Sarah about his problems. He'd been careful not to mention the possibility of the baby having a disability. Perhaps it might never happen – he certainly hoped so.

When he got back, Angie had her feet up on the sofa. She was watching TV, and only glanced briefly at him as he brought in the bags. He gave her a slight smile, then got on with putting the shopping away.

Afterwards he sat down wearily opposite her, her feet almost touching him. He had no energy to start a conversation, but to his surprise, it turned out there was no need.

'John ...'

'Yeah, what is it?'

'I have a confession to make.'

'Oh yes, and what's that?'

'I had a phone call about the results of the blood test and I went to the doctor's on my own. I know I should have phoned you, but I panicked.'

'Angie ... how could you? I wanted to be there with you, you know that.'

'I'm sorry, I didn't think. And since then I've been bottling it up inside.'

'Oh, God. Was it bad news?'

'Sort of.' She told him what the doctor had said.

'Well, it's still not certain by any means, is it? All right, so the odds are higher than normal, but I'd still take them. Obviously, the doctors will monitor our baby's progress but I'm sure everything will be fine.'

'Why did this have to happen, though? I feel like I'm jinxed. And now I'm more frightened than ever. When will it end?'

'Did you mention all this to the doctor?'

'Yes. She wanted me to have counselling, but I don't want everyone knowing my business.'

'But if it helps you, it would be worth it. You should have let me come; we could have discussed everything together. Angie, you're not helping yourself by shutting me out.'

She looked away.

Chapter 16

The day of the abortion, Thursday 4th March, soon came, and Angie hadn't slept a wink. It was on her mind constantly. She'd already been for an assessment; they'd offered her counselling again, which she'd refused. The decision was made and nothing would dissuade her.

She stayed in bed while John got dressed, following his regular morning routine, secure in his ignorance. She kept up the pretence of being asleep until he'd left for work. Then she rose and had a bath, remembering her failed attempts at hot baths and the other ridiculous DIY methods of getting rid of the baby.

The taxi arrived on time. The driver beeped his horn and she walked out with a small case to the car. He must have wondered why she wanted a taxi when there was a car on the drive. Hopefully he wouldn't ask, because she didn't know what to say.

She got in the back.

'Where to?'

'St Mary's clinic, off Westcott Street. Know where it is?'

'Yeah, sure. Out of the town centre, on the way to Marlbury.'

'That's right.'

She saw him smile in the rear-view mirror and smiled back.

The traffic was lighter than usual so she would arrive in plenty of time. She tried to relax, taking in deep breaths, and even closed her eyes for a few minutes. Although it was only minor surgery, she feared the worst and longed for the op to be over.

Afterwards, she'd need to rest and would have the painful task of lying to John; telling him she'd miscarried would upset him. But if he found out the truth, all hell would break loose.

Her phone beeped. A message from her dad. *Good luck, you're doing the right thing.* She smiled and sent a reply. *Thanks.*

The taxi pulled up outside at a quarter to ten.

Climbing out, she asked, 'Any chance of a pick-up in about three hours' time?'

'Yeah, no problem.'

'I'll ring at lunchtime to confirm, OK?'

'Fine.'

As she walked in through the clinic doors, a wave of sadness came over her, thinking of this life only a few weeks old, soon to be taken away. But the alternative was unthinkable. If she ended up like her mother, all their lives would be ruined.

At the reception desk sat a middle-aged woman in a nurse's uniform. Angie gave her name and appointment time. Then waited.

Five minutes later, a dark-haired man in his forties came up to her. He wore white slacks and top and smiled at her over his round glasses.

'Mrs Greaves?'

'Yes.'

'I'm Dr Irwin; I'll be performing your procedure today. If you could follow me, we'll go through a few preliminaries first and then have you in surgery.'

She followed him into a room, where he opened a file on the desk.

'All right, Angela, this is just to make sure everything is in order before we begin. I want you understand what we'll be doing during the operation, and we have a consent form you need to sign. Once I've done this and you're happy, we'll take you to the operating theatre.'

Angie nodded but inside her heart raced like a train that would never stop. She trembled and felt herself perspiring.

As Dr Irwin went through everything, she couldn't take it in, but she acknowledged what he said, signed the consent form and waited to be taken into theatre.

'OK, we're ready for you now. Please follow me.'

The room was small and well lit, with a bed in the middle. Angie lay down as directed, her white paper gown rustling.

'All right, Angela,' a nurse said. 'We'll now give you an injection to numb you. Just a local anaesthetic, like they do at the dentist.'

The pain was sharp but soon over.

'We'll wait a few minutes for the injection to take effect,' the nurse said.

Angie realised she was trembling all over; tears streamed down her cheeks. The thought of killing the child that she and John had created hit her like a bullet. And what about John? Did he deserve this? All he'd done was to get her pregnant. And he longed to be a father. But now she was shutting the door in his face. She had no certainty that this baby would affect her the same way that her own birth had affected her mother. The possibility remained – but what if everything turned out fine? Even the prospect of Down's suddenly didn't seem to matter.

She cried out, 'No! No! No! Stop!'

The doctor looked startled and put down the silver instrument that was in his hand. 'What's wrong?'

Angie sat up. 'I … I can't go through with this.'

'All right, that's no problem, Mrs Greaves. Don't worry. I can stop the procedure now if you wish. Are you sure that's what you want?'

'Yes,' she whispered.

'The nurse will take you to the interview room. You can stay there for as long as you like. Don't worry – this happens regularly; there's no need to feel bad.'

'Thank you.'

She sat with the nurse.

'I'm so sorry for wasting your time. I thought I wanted to do this, but now I'm not so sure. This baby inside me deserves to live. And who am I to take its life away? I just want to go home.'

'Of course – as soon as the anaesthetic has worn off. And please don't feel bad. We're not here to judge you. Whatever your reasons for changing your mind, it doesn't matter. In a few months' time you'll have a lovely baby, and you won't even remember this.'

'I hope so. Can I phone for a taxi?'

'Yes. You can wait here until it arrives.'

'OK. Thanks again.'

Angie stayed put for fifteen minutes and then got a call to say the taxi was outside. When she got in the car, she recognised the same driver as before. Thankfully, he didn't ask any questions and knew the way home without asking her.

She slipped into the house and sat down in disbelief. For whatever reason, something inside her had decided she was having the baby now – but her fear of the birth, the pain and the chance of illness or disability remained.

She cried, wondering how she could possibly get through these long months. Picking up her mobile, she pressed for her dad's number. He answered straight away.

'Angie, are you all right? How did it go?'

She hesitated for a few seconds. 'Dad ... I couldn't go through with it. I'm sorry I failed, but ... well, to have my baby's death on my conscience would be unbearable.'

'I guessed you wouldn't. In some ways, I'm glad. I'd love a little grandchild. Let's just hope it doesn't affect you the same way it affected your mum. And that you have a healthy baby.'

'I know, Dad. But we'll have to take what we're given.'

'Maybe you should tell John the truth about your mum now. He probably has a right to know, and you know what they say: forewarned is forearmed.'

'No, never. It's our family's business, not his and if he finds out, there's no telling what he might do. He'd hold it against me, for sure.'

'Up to you, love. I suppose what he doesn't know can't hurt him. And if the worst happens, just plead innocence.'

'Yes, I suppose so.'

'Let's hope your sickness will pass and you can get through the next few months.'

'I'm scared, Dad. But all I can do is to take each day as it comes.'

'Come over any time, Angie. I don't see many folks these days and if it helps to talk, I'll be happy.'

'I will. Thanks, Dad.'

Part Two
Six Months Later

Chapter 17

John had been on tenterhooks for weeks during August. Four times Angie had thought she was in labour, only to be sent home on each occasion, so when she nudged him, in the early hours of Monday 29th August, he showed no sense of urgency. He was shattered and had to rub his eyes and yawn before turning to her.

'John, I'm getting the pains again. It's got to be labour this time,' she said, grabbing him by the arm.

'You sure?'

'Of course. Please, take me to the hospital, now.'

'All right. Can you get dressed?'

'I'll try my best. I'll shout if I need you.'

'I'll ring to say we're on our way.'

He disappeared.

When he returned, ready to go, Angie's face was screwed up in pain. She kept moaning as he helped her downstairs and into the car. He prayed this wasn't another false alarm. She'd got him down with her incessant whining over the past few months, especially over the Down's syndrome result, even though all their subsequent scans had shown no cause for concern. Now he really wanted the whole thing to be over.

The roads were quiet, the sun already warm. They arrived at Dexford hospital in under ten minutes.

They were taken to a side room, where Angie undressed. John took her hand. As the doctor examined her, her waters broke, which John hoped was the beginning of the end. His heart beat faster; excitement or terror, he couldn't tell which.

Angie panicked, and tried to get up. The midwives held her steady as she tried to squirm away from everyone. John was helpless as the doctors and nurses struggled to keep her calm.

'She's petrified of giving birth. Is there anything can you do?'

'Help me!' Angie cried. 'Please make this awful pain stop! I can't stand it!'

The midwife stroked her hair. 'It's very early days, Angela. I'll get you some painkillers for now; just try to relax, take in deep breaths.'

'I'm trying to … oh God, no!' she screamed.

John held her hand. 'Try to keep calm, darling. There's a long way to go yet. The doctors know what they're doing.'

'Fuck off.'

John apologised to the midwife.

'Don't worry, Mr Greaves. It's nothing we haven't heard before! She'll be a while yet – only a couple of centimetres dilated. I just have to go and attend to one of my other ladies. I'll be back soon.'

After she had left, Angie's contractions began to ease. 'I'm so scared, John. What if something goes wrong? What if they can't get the baby out?'

'They do this all the time. It's their job.'

'I know, but—OWW!!' She crushed his fingers between hers.

<><><>

They'd been at the hospital for hours. The new midwife who had just come on shift examined the traces and looked worried. 'Angela, I know this isn't what you want to hear, but your baby isn't making any progress, and that can be very dangerous for both of you,' she said. 'We're going to have to think about a C-section.'

Angie looked horrified. 'What – cut me open?'

'It's the safest way at this stage. If baby doesn't come out soon, there could be permanent brain damage. He or she is getting quite distressed.'

'I don't want an operation.'

John wasn't sure she was taking this in properly. 'Angie, do you understand what they're saying? If they don't do something soon, our baby could be harmed and you could die. All right?'

She nodded, wiping away tears with the heel of her hand.

'OK, let's do it. I'll read the form before she signs.'

A nurse fetched the form and handed it to John. He read, barely taking it in. 'That's fine. Sign it, Angie.'

Shaking and gritting her teeth, she signed with a scribble.

They were put in surgical gowns and taken to theatre. John saw her petrified face as the anaesthetist injected her spine, but he felt powerless to help. He wasn't sure either of them would want any more children after this.

He sat at the head of the bed, clutching her hand, willing himself not to look past the green sheet that shielded her belly. 'It'll soon be over, Angie. They said it would only take a few minutes.'

'It feels funny. I can feel my insides moving about.'

He smiled. 'That must be really odd.'

After a little time, she felt a sudden release, and the doctor lifted a red bundle above the sheet before handing it over to a couple of nurses in the corner of the room.

There was an agonising wait … and then a tiny whimpering cry.

One of the nurses came over. 'You have a beautiful healthy son, Mr and Mrs Greaves. Congratulations.'

She handed over the baby, now wrapped in a hospital towel.

John looked down at him. Matted black hair, chubby little face. He cooed, even opened his eyes which were sea blue.

There was a lump in John's throat. 'He's amazing,' he said, over-come. Tears trickled down his face. 'Angie, don't you dare pull my leg about the crying, OK?'

She smiled up at him. 'Dads are allowed to cry.'

<><><>

Angie was exhausted. Her eyelids fluttered, but were so heavy they kept shutting again. At last they opened. Her sight was fuzzy and she couldn't make anyone out. She just recognised John's smiling face, and held out her hand. It felt good to touch his warm skin.

He smiled at her. 'Hallo, Mummy.'

'John … I'm so tired … I can hardly move.'

'That's only natural, after all you've been through in the last couple of days. Want to hold him?'

'Later, when I'm better. I feel like my insides are going to come tumbling out if I move. Oh God, John. I thought it would never end. The pain was unbelievable, I thought I was going to die. Can't ever go through that again …'

She lay back, eyes full of tears.

'Come on, Angie, don't get upset. Forget all that and think about the future. We'll have the best time ever with our son, he'll bring us so much happiness. He's healthy, has nothing wrong with him at all. See? All that worry about Down's syndrome was for nothing. At last our little family is complete.'

'You think so? I hope to God you're right.' She saw the puzzled look on his face, but couldn't bear the thought of explaining further.

'The midwives said you might be in hospital for a couple of days. Everyone will want to visit.'

She closed her eyes. 'Oh God, no. Can't face them yet. That idea scares me to death.'

'Well, you won't be the centre of attraction – our son will. And no one will stay long. I'll say you're shattered because you've been through a lot. They'll be sympathetic.'

'Yeah, sure they will.'

'We can't say don't come. Not when it's their first grandchild. And you're just tired.'

'I don't care – tell them to wait until tomorrow.'

He sighed. 'OK, if you insist.'

'Now, I need to rest. Please go away.'

'Already? Don't you want me to stay and help with the baby?'

'No. I want you to go. Have you any idea how much having a baby takes out of you?'

'I suppose not. All right, if you insist. Until tonight, then.'

'No, not tonight. Tomorrow. I need a good night's sleep.'

'OK, one more peep at my son and then I'll go.' He reached over into the clear plastic cot to pick up his son.

'John, don't. You'll wake him. And I'm too shattered to look after him at the moment. Please just let him sleep.'

She realised he must be hurt by her comments. Well, tough. She wished he'd had to give birth, see how he felt.

'Until tomorrow, then.' He kissed her on the cheek, and left.

She breathed in deeply, glad he'd gone, wanting peace and quiet. Hospitals weren't pleasant, but she dreaded leaving this one because then she'd have to care for the child herself. The first two weeks should be fine with John at home. But what then?

She heard the baby crying. Dear God, what should she do? She looked away, hoping he would stop, but he didn't. She pressed her buzzer for the midwife; she couldn't bear to touch that child.

Chapter 18

When John got home, he wasn't sure how he felt: ecstatic over his new-born son, or worried over his wife's lack of interest in the baby and her attitude towards him. Was it just the trauma of the birth, or something else?

He phoned his parents and told them the news.

His mum squealed with delight. 'That's wonderful! How are they both?'

'The baby's well, as good as gold, but Angie's been through the mill. She was out of it earlier. Not bonding with the baby either – although to be fair, I think she's still getting over the anaesthetic. She's grumpy, too, and taking it out on me. Good job I'm thick-skinned.'

'She doesn't mean it, love. It's a very emotional experience. I remember after I'd had you, I couldn't stop crying. But after a few days it passed.'

'It gets to me a bit, though. Throughout the whole nine months she seemed out of sorts – apart from the sickness, I mean. I had to twist her arm to get her to buy anything for the baby. I even decorated his room on my own. She just never seemed interested in any of it. Hope it'll be different now the birth's over.'

'Try not to be so hard on her. She's suffered over the last few months and it's bound to take its toll. Are you visiting her later?'

'No – she told me to wait until tomorrow, because she's shattered and wants a good night's sleep. She didn't say a lot afterwards, just lay there dozing.'

'I feel for her. It's not easy. Will she mind if we come? We won't impose, but we'd like to see him, even if it's only for a few minutes.'

'Of course. We can go together in the afternoon. Visiting is from two till four, so I'll come for you at one-thirty, OK?'

'That would be lovely. Thanks, John.'

'Just don't take it personally if she's not up to talking.'

'We won't be offended.'

'Until tomorrow then.'

He didn't relish the prospect of ringing Angie's dad, but he felt sorry for the guy, being on his own. John had always got the impression Alan resented him for taking his little girl away, but luckily he didn't see much of him. He rarely called on them and Angie usually visited him on her own.

'Is that Alan?'

'Yeah, all right John. How's things?'

'Good, thanks. Just wanted to let you know Angie's had the baby.'

'Oh, great.'

John told him the story and expressed his fears about Angie.

'It figures. She always did take a long time to adjust to things. As long as they're both safe and well, that's all that matters for now.'

'I'm taking Mum and Dad to the hospital tomorrow afternoon. You're welcome to come too, if you're game.'

'That's kind, but I'll pass on that one. Angie hates crowds. I'll pop in on my own when it's quiet. Give her my best wishes, tell her I'll be in touch.'

And with that he rang off.

John wondered if this brush-off was intentional.

He made a few more calls, then went out to buy fish and chips. It was quiet without Angie; he missed her. He knew he'd have his work cut out with her when she came home, but he was determined to keep them together. For tonight, well aware that things would soon change, he'd be glad of the peace.

<><><>

Angie woke early the next morning. Her night had been restless, with dreams of her mother's death. She'd trashed the kitchen in a fit of temper. They'd had a blazing row, her mum and dad hit each other over and over again, before her dad grabbed hold of her, took her to their bedroom and shut the door behind her. Angie heard a thud as her mum dropped onto the roof ledge and then onto the grass. Her mum ran towards her car. She got in and drove off. Her dad followed in his own car, taking Angie with him, crying her eyes out. How she wanted to forget.

Now, sitting up carefully in bed, mindful of the stitches holding her abdomen together, she shuddered with fear. She peered into the cot; the baby was fast asleep. She felt nothing but a sudden urge to go to the top of the building and throw herself off the roof. But her shame wouldn't even allow her that release.

So instead she went to the toilet, feeling agonising pain in her stomach as she walked. She didn't understand what possessed people to have babies. But something must.

She washed her hands and returned to bed. As soon as she lay back, the baby cried. Angie sighed, picked up her phone and began to surf the net.

'Mrs Greaves, aren't you going see to him?' the nurse asked.

Angie lay stock-still, not wanting to touch the child. But what could she say?

'Sorry, I'm not feeling well. Could you, please?'

The nurse said nothing and did the necessary without complaint.

Angie couldn't force herself to face the baby yet.

After a light breakfast, she found a magazine to read. Bored out of her mind, she'd be glad to get out of here, except for the fact that once at home, she'd soon have to look after the baby by herself while John went to work.

Around mid-morning, she glanced up from her reading to see someone standing at the end of the bed.

Her eyes widened with pleasure. 'Dad!'

'Hallo, love. How are you?'

'Sit down, Dad.'

He sat at the side of her bed, smiling.

'So, Angie, I'll ask again – how are you?'

'Better than I was. The birth was horrendous, the pain unbearable – did John tell you I had a C-section? I never dreamt having a baby would take so much out of you. Why do women put themselves through such a frightful experience?'

'Well, I couldn't comment, since I'll never go through it. At least you came through unscathed. But I've heard whispers that you might be finding it hard to adjust and care for your baby.'

'That's a joke.'

'Not in my book, it isn't. I warned you of the risks. But you insisted on having the child.'

'I know. But I thought I'd be all right ... Dad, I can't even look at my son, let alone hold him. What's wrong with me?'

'Probably nothing. It's very early days. And I'm sure the nurses will be keeping an eye on you. Meanwhile, I have a keen interest in the lad, even if you don't. In fact, I intend picking him up if you have no objections.'

'Be my guest.'

He took the baby out of the cot, then sat down with him in his arms. Angie caught a glimpse of him, saw his blue-grey eyes open, looking around.

'Well, the lad's a belter. I reckon he looks like me, with his dark hair, and his eyes are the same shape as mine. Don't you think so?'

'Maybe, but he's only a day old and they often change.'

'True. You did. Blonde hair first, which came off and then it was brown. Now you're like your mother.'

'You seem pleased, Dad. That seems a bit ... hypocritical, after everything you said.'

'I still think you should have had the abortion, but it was your choice and I accept that. Let's just try to make the best of it and hope that you're both OK. If not, we'll have to face it when the time comes.'

'That's easy for you to say, since you're not in the thick of it. But I am. What if I'm incapable of having any feelings for him? Right now, I just feel as if he doesn't belong to me.'

Alan raised his eyebrows. 'That's not unusual. I'm pretty sure lots of women suffer the same thing. As long as you get the support you need, it'll pass within a few weeks.'

'How do you know that? And what if it doesn't?'

'Go to the doctor.'

She wasn't convinced. 'But if I carry on like this, it won't be fair on the baby. Maybe I should have him adopted.'

'Hey, hey. That's a bit drastic, you've only had him a day. John will never give him up without a fight, anyway.'

'Well, I'd do it behind his back.'

'Put those thoughts out of your head – it can't be done. Why not just give him a cuddle for a few minutes? You might feel different.'

He tried to hand the baby over to her, but she shied away as if the child was a monster from hell.

'OK, it's up to you, but at some stage you'll need to try.'

'No!'

'What would your mother say if she knew what you were contemplating? She'd tear a strip off you, for sure.'

'You should go now, Dad, before we fall out.'

'OK, if that's what you want. I'll leave the baby here for you, all right?'

He placed the infant down on the bed and walked out.

She was left to stare at the baby like a frightened rabbit. Oh God, what should she do? She couldn't leave him there, but...

He cried and her eyes widened; she had no idea how to pacify him. She leaned towards him and bile came in her mouth. Was she was going to be sick? Clenching her teeth, she moved ever closer, gingerly taking him in her arms to put him back in the cot.

She prayed he'd stop crying, but no.

Now what?

A nurse was walking past.

'Nurse, can you help me please? I'm not sure what to do.'

'Are you breastfeeding?'

Angie shook her head.

'All right, I'll have a feed made up. Be five minutes. Holding him might help. He won't break, love.'

'I'm not feeling well.'

The nurse sighed. 'OK.'

Angie hated letting the nurse see to him, but she couldn't face doing this until she absolutely had to. She closed her eyes, wanting the ordeal over.

'All done, Angie. But try to do it yourself next time. You really need to make the effort, even though it's hard. All right?'

'Yes, sorry. I know. I'm just so tired. When can I go home?'

At least there, John and his family would help, even if only for two weeks. But the nurse had gone, and Angie got no reply.

When lunch came, it broke the monotony of her existence. The baby was awake and quiet but didn't cry, which she was glad of. She even finished her dinner for the first time in months, and drank a litre of water.

She glanced at the clock above the door; only an hour remained before John's family descended on her. Another ordeal with no way out.

She lay down to rest, hoping they'd think she was asleep and go away. She heard noises around her more than once and voices too, but none she recognised.

Then John's booming voice sounded close by her. 'Angie, there you are.'

Her eyes fluttered open and shut; she yawned. 'Sorry, yes. Still tired, I'm afraid. Hallo.'

John's mum beamed at her. 'Hallo, Angie. May we look at our grandson?'

'Course, please do. He might need changing, though. There are nappies under the cot.'

John glared at her, then took out a nappy as his mum laid the baby down on the bed. She put the new nappy on and then sat transfixed with him in her arms.

'He's gorgeous, just like his dad.'

'Think he needs feeding?' John asked.

'More than likely,' his mum said.

George looked around the bedside table. 'Any feeds made up?'

'No, sorry. Ask one of the nurses,' Angie said.

'OK.'

He disappeared and John took over.

'He's fantastic.' John's eyes glistened as he smiled at Angie.

'Mm. Let's just hope he stays that way.'

George came back, holding a bottle. Angie hoped he wasn't planning on giving it to her. But he handed it to John, who already seemed to be a natural with the baby; just what she needed. The baby drank the lot, and John even remembered to bring up the wind.

'You've got a job for life there, son.'

John smiled.

'Thought of any names yet?' Susan said.

'Well, not yet. We'll get around to it, won't we, Angie?'

To his surprise, she nodded. 'I've been thinking about that. How about Alan or Adam? Adam was my grandfather's name.'

'How about Alan John? A bit of both families. We could call him AJ for short,' John said.

'Could do, I suppose. We'll talk about it when I come out,' Angie said.

'Any idea when that might be?'

'Maybe tomorrow.'

'Great – it'll be lovely to have you both home. Let me know what time, and I'll pick you up.'

'OK.'

'You want to hold her now?'

Angie hands began to shake. 'No, I'm tired. If nobody else wants to, put him back in the cot.'

'John, we'd better get going. We don't want to tire Angie out,' Susan said. 'Come on, George, let's go. John, we'll be waiting in the car – you two have a few minutes together.'

George smiled. 'See you when you're at home, Angie. Thank you so much for blessing us with our first grandchild – you've made two old codgers very happy.'

This was too much. She gave her in-laws a smile without looking at them, wishing they'd just piss off.

'So, how are you now?' John asked when they'd left.

'All right, I suppose.'

'Got over the anaesthetic now?'

'Still tired, but I'm hungry for the first time in months. I actually ate all my dinner, which is a blessing. Can't believe the baby's turned out to be so healthy after what I went through having him.'

'Yes, I know. Think we all were worried. Glad you've got a few suggestions for names, but Alan is a bit old-fashioned, and Adam is quite popular. So what did you think of Alan John, AJ for short?'

'Good. I wanted Alan because of Dad – I owe him a lot for looking after me when Mum died. And yes, AJ has a nice ring about it.'

'Wonder what he'll say when he finds out?'

'Don't know. He'll probably tell me not to be so silly and choose a more sensible name.'

'I offered to bring him here with us, actually, but he refused.'

'He came this morning on his own.'

'Oh, did he? That's nice.'

'Yes, it was. Listen, John, I've been thinking. I want to go back to work as soon as possible.'

'What? But you'll get paid maternity leave for the first six months. What's the point?'

'Because I need to get out of the house. I can't face being on my own with the baby.'

'But who'll care for him?'

'We'll have to hire a nanny. Sorry, but that's how I feel.'

John's mouth gaped open. But she needed him to know how she felt; if he wasn't happy with it, then tough.

'Listen, I'll just drop Mum and Dad off, and then I'll be back.'

'Fine. You can help me with the baby.'

'It'll be my pleasure,' he said with a smile.

Chapter 19

John couldn't believe what she'd said. To talk about returning to work so soon was unbelievable. Perhaps she only said it because she hadn't got over the birth, but what if she was serious? What could he do? Nothing.

He must have looked sour-faced, because when he opened the car door, his mum commented. 'Is everything all right, son?'

'What? Yeah, I suppose,' he mumbled, getting in.

'Something's happened, I can tell. You've got that concerned look on your face.'

'I'm fine.'

'Had a row, haven't you? You'll have to make allowances, John. She's been through so much – having a baby takes a lot out of you. Learn to turn the other cheek.'

'She meant what she said.'

'What did she say?'

'That she's going back to work within the next few weeks.'

'Oh, dear. Why would she do that when she has a newborn baby to care for?'

'No idea. Until she got pregnant, I thought she wanted a baby as much as I did. But ever since then, I've had to coax her into even discussing the subject. I'd hoped it would pass once she'd had the child. But it seems not.'

'She's still fragile, John. She's been through the mill, and probably doesn't mean any of what she says. Don't take it to heart. And even if she actually does as she says, she may not work full-time. If it's part-time, we'll help.'

'The ironic thing is, I'd love to stay at home, but it would be impossible, with all our debts. We need my salary.'

George intervened. 'Son, it may never happen. And besides, you'll have two weeks at home to support her. Once she gets into the swing of things, she might realise it's not as bad as she thinks.'

'Hope so.'

'Why not come around to ours for tea?'

'No, you're all right, thanks, Mum. I'm going back to the hospital. I'll grab something there. Perhaps if I'm there, she'll feel better and it'll take the pressure off.'

'OK, it's your call. The offer's there if you change your mind.'

'Thanks, Mum.'

After dropping them off, he returned to the hospital to find Angie lying back on the bed, her eyes closed as if she was asleep. The baby was asleep too, so he went for a sandwich and a drink, which he ate sitting by her bed.

Just as he finished, he heard the baby crying, so he picked him up and sat down with him, trying to rock him in his arms. He hummed a simple tune, but that didn't seem to make much difference.

Angie's eyes fluttered open.

John smiled. 'Just in time, eh?'

'Yes, he probably needs a feed. Ask the nurse for one when you see her.'

'Have you thought about breastfeeding? It would save all this hassle of making up feeds when you get home.'

She frowned. 'The milk hasn't come in yet – the nurse told me two to three days. What, are you trying to get out of the sleepless nights?'

'No, not at all. I'll still do my bit – changing nappies, getting him to sleep, all that stuff. You've no need to worry. I just thought it might save us time in the long run, and it might help you bond better.'

'Or it might make me feel like a bloody dairy cow.'

'Well, don't you think it's worth a try? If it doesn't work we can always go back to using bottles.'

She gazed into space, unwilling to engage further.

John shook his head.

'I don't know what you've got against it. It's the most natural thing in the world. Women have been doing it since the beginning of time. And a mother's milk is much healthier for the baby, don't you think?'

'Shut up, John. I don't want to talk about it anymore. All right?'

He adjusted the teat in the baby's mouth. 'OK. It's up to you, of course. Sorry if I went on about it.'

She didn't answer him, so he turned his attention fully to his son.

'Wow,' he said, some minutes later. 'Looks like he's drunk the lot! Want me to change him too?'

'If you want to,' she said. 'You're really over the moon about the baby, aren't you?'

'Of course, it's the best thing that's ever happened to me. To us, I mean.'

'Sorry if I'm being ratty. It's been a long nine months, so full of stress and worry – I don't know how I got through it all.'

'Me neither. But you did, and now we've got so much to look forward to. You'll be fine once you've got into the swing of things, I promise.'

John changed the baby's nappy like an old hand, then put him back into his cot.

They held hands for a long time, each locked in their own thoughts, until John realised it was eight-thirty. Time he went home.

'I'd better go now,' he said, a little louder than normal.

She opened her eyes and yawned. 'Shattered,' she mumbled.

He kissed her lightly on the lips. 'Give me a ring in the morning.' He had one final look at their baby, still fast asleep, and left.

<><><>

He got the call at ten o'clock the next morning. Angie didn't say much, except for him to bring the car seat and a couple of nappies.

He breezed into the ward to find her sitting on the bed, the baby still in the cot. She looked up, her expression blank.

'Ready?' he asked.

'Yes, of course. Put him into the car seat while I get my coat on.'

'OK. How's he been?' John strapped AJ into the seat gingerly and covered him with a blanket.

She ignored the question. 'Come on, let's get out of here. This place gives me the creeps.'

She sat in the back of the car beside her son, but stared out of the window. As John drove off, he sensed an atmosphere. They weren't speaking and he kept glancing in the mirror to see his wife's glum face. She didn't appear to be taking an interest in their baby at all.

When they got back home, Angie went straight to the bathroom, leaving John to bring everything in. Perhaps she just needed a little time to gather herself together. He took AJ out of the car seat and sat on the sofa, rocking his son gently.

She emerged after fifteen minutes.

'Well, don't you two look cosy?'

He smiled. 'You all right?'

'Mind if I lie down on the sofa? I feel so run-down.'

'Of course. I can look after the baby,' he said.

'Thanks, John. I'll make it up to you.'

'Don't be silly. I can imagine how much giving birth takes out of you. You rest – I'll look after everything else.'

<><><>

By mid-afternoon, she'd got up and suggested she go in the kitchen to cook the dinner. John didn't seem to mind, even though the idea was to get away from him and baby AJ. She wanted nothing to do with either of them. So she busied herself cooking, trying to drag it out as much as possible.

John was feeding AJ when she brought in the food.

'Want me to put yours in the oven to keep it warm?'

'Yeah, why not? He seems to be hungry, so I shouldn't be long.'

Angie had finished hers before him and left him while she made the tea and washed up. He brought out his empty plate soon afterwards.

'Thank you, darling,' she said. 'Why don't you sit down? Take the weight off your feet.'

'I will do now he's asleep. He hasn't been too bad – I expected much worse.'

'Good for you. I can see you love every minute with him. Why not sleep in the second bedroom with him tonight? I've put his cot in there. Can't face those sleepless nights at the moment. It'll do something to me, I'm sure – I'm aiming to be fit for work as soon as I can. Can't afford to be off sick, Duncan wouldn't be happy, considering all the time I had off during my pregnancy. Is that OK?'

She realised he was struggling to keep control of his temper, but if he lost it, she'd be ready. After all, he was the one who'd wanted children. She still couldn't understand how it had happened. She'd made sure he wore a condom every time and was certain one hadn't split. Perhaps God did work in mysterious ways.

John took AJ upstairs to his cot at nine, let him lie there quietly, and fell asleep.

When he came back downstairs and told her, she laughed. 'I always knew you had the knack.'

'Beginner's luck.'

'Could be, but practice makes perfect.'

'I'm not looking forward to sleeping on my own.'

'Come on, John. It's not forever. When he sleeps right through, we'll share a bed again.'

'That could be months away.'

'Don't fret. It's not as if I'm going to be jumping into bed with someone else, is it? And as long as you're the same, there won't be any problems, will there? Anyway, I'm going up now. If I were you, I'd make up a few feeds and put them in the fridge.'

'Hang on a minute – how about breast feeding? Come on, Angie, you have to at least try. Then when you've done it, I'll take him into the second bedroom – all right? Just think of the amount of money we'd save.'

Angie's mouth gaped open, but no words came.

'It's only a suggestion, Angie. If you don't feel up to it, you can try tomorrow.'

'See you in the morning.'

How lovely to have the bed to herself without John slobbering over her; not that she could do anything so soon after the birth, anyway. That would take weeks – and when the time came, she'd be on the pill, and would take it religiously every day. She couldn't afford another slip-up.

Chapter 20

Angie had gone to sleep quickly the following Wednesday night, exhausted and stressed. Her attempts at breastfeeding hadn't gone well, with John constantly breathing down her neck. He couldn't say she hadn't tried, even though she was on the verge of giving up; AJ didn't seem to like her milk and it had been almost impossible to get him to latch on to her nipple. It appeared he'd taken a liking to the formula milk.

She woke, depressed, at eight o'clock, already on edge at what the day might bring. A screaming baby and a moaning husband. Her longing for peace and quiet almost overcame her, but she had things to do. She wasn't looking forward to John going back to work; it was less than two weeks away now.

After breakfast she found him in the living room, AJ on his lap. How sweet, Angie thought, glad they'd bonded so well. It was just a shame work beckoned. When they got a nanny, hopefully AJ would take to her, too.

John looked up at her with a smile.

She returned it. 'You like being a dad, don't you? I'm pleased for you. Pity it's only for two weeks – although there's always the evenings and the weekends to look forward to.'

'Yeah, can't wait.'

'Good for you, John,' she said. 'I'm afraid I have to love you and leave you. Got an appointment at the register office and then I might browse around the shops. Oh, and I'll pop in to work to see my friends.'

'What, without the baby? Won't they think that strange?'

'It's not only a social visit. I want to ask about going back to work.'

'Angie. You only had a baby just over a week ago. You've had major surgery.'

'I'll be fine. I've always been a quick healer. And as long as I do nothing strenuous, it'll be OK. When you've got a minute, will you compile a list of nannies to interview for AJ?'

'OK, if I get time. Any idea when you'll be back?'

'When I've finished, I suppose. No need to cook anything, I'll grab a bite in Dexford.'

'If you're sure. But how are you going to get there? The health visitor said you're not supposed to drive until six weeks after the birth.'

'I'll catch a bus, don't worry. I'm going now.' She bent to give him a quick peck on the lips.

'Aren't you going to say goodbye to AJ?'

'Don't be ridiculous, how can he understand at nearly two weeks old?'

'Angie, your attitude worries me. He's your baby too. I know you're having trouble feeding him, but believe me, it will come. You don't seem to want to interact with him. What's the problem? Is there something you're not telling me?'

Angie glared. Why start on her now? 'There's nothing to worry about, I'm fine. Try to remember I've just had a baby and I was ill throughout the pregnancy and the birth. So, I'm not going to be in the best frame of mind, am I? See you later.'

'But …'

She wouldn't listen to any more of his whinging. Why couldn't he leave her alone?

For a moment after stepping outside, she stood quivering. A tiny part of her longed to stay with John. What her father had said about baby AJ and her mother haunted her; she should have killed him before he was born.

She caught a bus to Dexford and walked to the municipal buildings, where the register for births and deaths was housed.

The process was straightforward and the registrar didn't ask any awkward questions. After paying for two copies of the birth certificate, she was off again.

Now to face another ordeal – but either she did this or she got stuck at home with baby AJ. After walking around the block twice, she went inside. There was a new face on reception: young, pretty, curly black hair, bright red lipstick, blue eyes, showing her ample cleavage. She understood why Duncan had hired this woman. And where was Bethany? Doing Angie's old job, she guessed.

'Hallo,' Angie said. 'Sorry to disturb you, but is Duncan in?'

The girl smiled. 'In a meeting, I'm afraid. Do you have an appointment?'

'No, I came in on the off-chance. Any idea how long he'll be?'

'Hard to say, but the client's been with him for half an hour. I'm sure he won't be too long.' The girl glanced at the computer and said, 'He has no appointments until after lunch, but he'll be out most of the afternoon.'

'All right if I wait? My name is Angie, I work here – or did until I left to have a baby. I want to speak to him about a personal matter.'

'Oh, OK, I'll tell him you're here. I'm Penny. I've heard a lot about you.'

'Nothing bad, I hope.'

'No, quite the opposite,' she giggled. 'Take a seat.'

'Thanks.'

Angie sat on an uncomfortable plastic chair.

'Like a drink? Tea or coffee?'

'No, I'm fine, thanks.'

Duncan was with his client for over an hour, until suddenly a middle-aged man with a ponytail came rushing out of his office, clearly not happy. Duncan was red in the face, but noticing Angie, stopped in his tracks and smiled.

'Hallo, Angie. Come on through. Great to see you looking so well.'

'Thanks, Duncan.'

Angie sat down while Duncan closed the door behind them. He breathed in deeply and took the seat opposite.

'Tough customer. The bank won't lend him the money for the mortgage and he's taking it out on me. Unless he finds another provider, he'll lose the house.'

'What a shame.'

'So, what brings you here? And where's the baby?'

'At home with John.'

'Should have brought him in – we'd love to see him.'

'Yes, well, that's by the by. I wanted to ask if I can come back to work early. In, say, two weeks' time.'

Duncan sat back in his chair, put his hands behind his head. 'Well, you caught me on the hop there. But you're not supposed to be here for six months. And you'll be getting paid. Why on earth would you want to come back?'

'I'm not asking you to pay me twice, Duncan, but I have to work.'

'But what about the baby? Who'll look after him?'

'We're hiring a nanny. And I want full-time if possible.'

'You won't see much of your son.'

'That's my problem.'

'Yes, true. Sorry, Angie, but we can't have you back until the end of the six months. Penny has a contract until then and we'd have to pay that up to allow you back. It makes little sense.'

'Can't you keep her on and let me do another job?'

'There's not enough work. I'm sorry, Angie. Much as I'd love to have you back early, it's impossible. Find something else until then, if you must.'

Angie gritted her teeth. 'There has be a way around this! I need to work, don't you understand?'

'Yes, that's crystal clear, but there's nothing I can do. I'm sorry.'

Angie squirmed in her seat, panicking as the reality of the situation hit home. She began to weep, but when Duncan came over to comfort her, she shrugged him aside. 'Leave me alone!'

She got to her feet and rushed out of the office, with Duncan still shouting after her. She wanted so much to run away from everyone. But, realising that there was nowhere to go, she slowed down and stopped, not knowing what to do.

The supermarket around the corner was open, and she needed something to calm her nerves. Picking up a basket, she set off around the store, putting in a few odds and ends. The last item was a small bottle of brandy. She paid for everything by credit card, then found the toilets and went into a cubicle. There she unscrewed the top of the bottle and took a sip. The alcohol warmed her insides almost at once. It helped, but also made her instantly woozy after so many months of not drinking. After putting the bottle back in her bag, she pulled out a packet of mints, stuffed three in her mouth and came out.

She had only one place left to go: home. On the bus back, her head was spinning. She didn't want John to see her like this but she had no other choice.

Off the bus, she walked slowly, trying hard to concentrate. The house came into view, and she walked up to the front door.

Then the key wouldn't go in the lock. She feared for a moment that he'd changed the locks, but finally the door opened.

The pram was in the living room and a quick glance inside told her AJ was asleep. Otherwise, the room was empty, but John had to be somewhere. She needed to know where.

She found him in the kitchen, slaving away over a hot stove with his back to her. The smell of a meat pie came from the oven.

'I'm back.'

He turned around and glanced at her. 'So I see.'

He didn't look happy, and she still felt woozy. Had he noticed?

'Get everything sorted?'

'The register office was fine, but going into work didn't turn out well.'

'Really? Why not?'

'They won't let me come back. Not until six months' time. Can you believe that? I've got to get another job, John. I'll go mad.'

'There's no "got to". You want to. That's a different thing altogether. Do you care so little for me and AJ?'

'I do care. It's just … my emotions are all over the place.'

'Have you been drinking? I can smell something.'

'I needed a drink to calm me down. So I bought a bottle from the supermarket and had a little bit. I'll show you – it's in my bag. I'm a grown-up, John. I don't need supervision.'

'I know having a child can be hard for a woman, but this isn't normal. In the last nine months I've seen sides of you I never knew existed. What's the problem? Why don't you want anything to do with our son? It beggars belief. And what about when I go back to work? You'll have to look after him then.'

'Did you get that list of nannies to phone?'

'No, I didn't. I'm not doing your dirty work.'

'I told you to get me a list.'

'I've got better things to do than mess about on the computer for hours, so you can forget it. I've been up to my eyeballs with AJ, because somebody has to look after him, don't they? I've changed him six times, fed him, got him to sleep, washed his clothes, everything while you're doing nothing but trying to get back to work, you selfish cow.'

John never saw the punch coming. It hit him on the nose. And she came at him again, fingernails digging deep into the flesh of his cheeks. He shrieked, fear in his eyes, but she couldn't stop. For a few seconds, she wanted to kill him, but suddenly the rage left her. Ashamed at what she'd done, she ran upstairs to the bedroom in tears, slamming the door behind her.

<><><>

John was stunned. He remained on the spot, his cheeks burning where she'd scratched him. His nose throbbed and he tasted coppery blood.

She'd acted like a maniac – he never realised her capable of such violence. Normally, she was so placid. What had got into her?

In the downstairs toilet, he inspected the damage in the mirror. His nose didn't look too bad; he dabbed it with tissue paper and wiped away the blood. The scratches worried him more. Two on each cheek which had fetched blood. He washed his face and dried it with the towel.

People would notice. Perhaps they'd think he was at fault, but that wasn't true. He hoped the scratches would at least be gone by the time he went back to work. Best stay away from people for a few days, especially his parents.

An hour later, there was still no sign of Angie. He switched on the computer – resigned to the fact that Angie clearly wasn't up to looking after AJ once he'd gone back to work – and sought suitable nannies. But what would Angie do if she couldn't get a job? He shook his head and started a list.

The baby started crying again.

John sighed, then noticed that Angie was now sitting on the sofa, not moving a muscle. He hadn't seen her come in.

'He's crying. See to him,' she said.

He rubbed his eyes. 'All right, I'm coming.'

While Angie sat staring out of the window, he changed the baby's nappy and put a dummy in his mouth. AJ wriggled his legs and arms and blew funny noises, which made John smile.

'Thanks for that. What were you doing on the computer?'

'Looking for nannies, as it happens. Not that you care.'

'John, that's not fair. I don't want to hurt him, but I still can't bear being in the same room. He's your responsibility right now because I can't do it yet – and I might never be able to.'

'You're wrong. You'll be fine when you get better. But find out why and what to do about it.'

She crumpled right in front of him and he took her into his arms. He smoothed her hair with his hand.

'Help me,' she whispered.

'You know I will. But you need to see a doctor. You obviously have a mental health problem. What if you've got postnatal depression?'

'A proper little doctor, aren't you? Diagnosing my condition, if that's what it is.'

'Will you go to the doctor's? I'll come with you.'

She moved away, looking at him pensively. 'I don't know. You're the one trying to stop me from going back to work. Can't you see how important it is to me? I'm good at my job and I enjoy it. If I feel good about work, that'll help me be a good mother too. So I need to get a job.'

'Angie, you already have a job. All right, they've said you have to wait six months, but you're getting paid. Make the effort to connect with little AJ, enjoy bringing him up. It's not just a hard slog.'

'I can't. I need to work and I'm going to look for something else temporarily. Then when I'm back at Elliott's, I won't feel out of it.'

'Are you saying you won't try to get some help? Have you seen the scratches on my cheeks? I've never seen you like that before.'

'You got me so mad I couldn't help what I did. You don't understand.' She rubbed her hands together, blinked faster as if at odds with herself.

'Please, Angie. You've got nothing to lose.'

Angie knew he really did love her. But did she love him? Maybe, but at times she hated him – wanted to strangle him for trying to manipulate her again. If only he'd stop nagging her.

But what if he was right? Why couldn't she deal with AJ? She was frightened of what she might become, and what she'd do if he, too, showed the signs in later life. The signs she experienced with her mother. She couldn't forget those awful days.

'All right, John. Just don't expect too much.'

'Oh, thank God. You won't regret it.'

'But I'm still going to get a job and hire a nanny.'

His shoulders sagged again but she refused to budge.

'Why don't you pick him up? Touch him. Kiss him. Give him a cuddle. He's the most beautiful baby, Angie.'

'No doubt.'

John went to the cot, lifted AJ out and took him to the settee. 'Hey. Angie, sit here by us.'

Angie felt the heat flushing onto her face, but did as he asked. She looked at her son for the first time. But it was only a moment before, trembling with fear, she had to look away. Would this dread ever go away?

Chapter 21

The next morning, over breakfast, he soon brought it up again. 'Want me to phone for an appointment? Or will you do it?'

She glanced up in dismay. 'You do it. As early as possible, please, because I'm going out afterwards.'

'OK.'

He phoned on his mobile but took ages to get through.

'Nine-twenty – all right?'

'Perfect, then I'll be able to search for jobs when we're done.'

His face dropped but she didn't react. That was one thing he wouldn't stop her from doing.

When the time came to leave, she had to speak up. 'No need for you to come, John. I can handle this. You'd only have to bring the baby with you and you couldn't come in with me.'

'No problem. I did think of leaving him with Mum and Dad but we'd have to explain why – and I'm assuming you don't want them to know what's going on. And then there's these scratches. What do I say? No, we'll come with you, but we'll stay in the waiting room. After all, we haven't taken him out anywhere yet. It's a nice day, warm too. Let's take him out somewhere.'

'No. I'm going to look for a job.'

'Not for the whole day, surely. Why not go to the job centre this afternoon?'

Angie frowned. 'No, John. Now stop going on at me.'

<><><>

AJ was asleep in his pram when she emerged from the doctor's office.

'How did you get on?' John asked.

'I'll tell you in a minute, but first I've got to pop into the chemist's.'

Five minutes later she came out, clutching a paper bag.

'Shall we go the park, then?'

'Sure, if we must.'

'Want to push the pram?'

She nodded. They didn't speak again until they'd stopped by the lake and sat on a bench. Surprisingly, AJ was still fast asleep.

'Go on, then. What did the doctor say?'

'Not much.'

'Please, Angie, you were in there for over fifteen minutes. Don't keep it to yourself.'

'She gave me tablets but said I'm only to take them as a last resort. She thinks I have the baby blues but it should pass within a few weeks. The tablets are antidepressants, but only a low dose. I told her I find it hard to connect with AJ, and she said it's a common problem among new mothers. And if I can make the effort to get more involved, my mood should improve.'

He fought the urge to look smug. 'That's good. And what do you think? Do you agree?'

'Don't know. I felt fine talking to her but now I'm here, I'm all of a go inside.' Tears came into her eyes.

'Hey, don't get upset. You might have to take tablets to get through this sticky period, but it may not be for long. All right?'

She nodded.

He took her hand. 'Stop crying, Angie, please. You'll wake AJ.'

'Sorry. I do want to be a good wife and mother, John – but I'm not much of a success at either, am I? Anyway, I'd best be on my way.' She got to her feet.

'Well, surely not right this minute. He's gone back to sleep, and the sun's shining – why don't we sit here for a while longer?' John feared the worst, but he had to try to keep her spirits up.

'No. I'm going to see what temporary jobs are available at the job centre.'

'Can't you put that to one side for a few days and get acquainted with our son? Once you have, you might forget all about this job lark.'

'It's no use. I thought I could when I was talking to the doctor, but now it's a different matter altogether. Sorry, John. I'm doing my best.' She walked off.

'Angie, please wait. Can't we at least walk with you to the town centre?'

She didn't listen and marched off past the park entrance. By the time John and AJ got there, she'd disappeared.

<><><>

At half past three, the front door opened. She looked drained and took in a deep breath, closing her eyes when John came into the hall to greet her.

'Where on earth have you been? Everything all right?'

'Not really.'

'Did you go to the job centre? How did you get on?'

'Lousy. Not many temporary jobs – and those that are, I'm not qualified for. Nothing doing at the agencies either. Oh God, what am I going to do?'

'Well, it's not the end of the world.'

'I need a job or I'll be left here on my own.'

'Shall I ask Mum and Dad to help you when I go back to work?'

Her eyes widened as if she thought him mad; he dreaded what she'd say next.

'I won't let them do that. They'll take over and treat me like an idiot. I wish you didn't have to work. Can't you ask for more time off, while I get another job?'

'I could, but I'd soon use up my quota of holidays. And after that it's unpaid leave. We can't afford for me to be at home for long.'

She huffed and puffed.

He changed the subject. 'Had anything to eat?'

'What? No, I haven't had time.'

'How about a sandwich?'

'I'm not an invalid. I'll do it myself when I'm ready.'

'All right, no problem.'

'Where's the computer? I want to scout for jobs online.'

'Angie, can you please give it a rest? Carry like this, and you'll get even worse'

'Very likely.'

She switched the laptop on, logged in and started a search.

John shook his head in despair, but left her alone. As long as AJ remained asleep, he should make a start on the dinner. At least if he stayed in the kitchen, she'd have to see to the baby herself.

Half an hour later, she rushed in. 'John, he's crying and I think he needs changing.'

'Can't you do it? I'm up to my eyeballs here.'

'Let me take over, then you can sort him out.'

'No, Angie, you do it.'

'But I'm in the middle of filling in a job application.'

'Well, it will just have to wait. I won't do everything on my own, Angie. This baby is as much yours as mine. Take some responsibility and help me look after him.'

She gritted her teeth and stormed out.

He carried on washing up but when the baby's cries continued, he was puzzled. He left the crockery and cutlery on the draining board and charged into the living room. The baby was still crying – but where was Angie? He got the answer when he caught a glimpse of her car moving off the drive. Unbelievable.

Chapter 22

She had the urge to drive onto the motorway in the wrong direction and crash into the biggest lorry she saw. But she hadn't the courage to do that. She was afraid of everything these days, including – no, especially – tending to a defenceless little baby. John shouldn't push her because that's when she did bad things.

There remained only one place to go, so she turned off to the right. That house was rapidly becoming the only place she felt at peace.

She parked the car in front of the garage and sighed with relief. The door opened and out he came, all smiles, and took her into his arms, holding her close as she wept.

'Come on in, love.' He guided her inside.

'Thanks, Dad,' she whimpered.

'I'll make us a drink, shall I? A coffee with a dash of rum in it? That'll give you a lift.'

She smiled, wiping her eyes with a tissue. Alan returned with a mug.

'Here, get that in you. Then tell me what's bugging you. They say a problem shared is a problem halved.'

They sat together on the settee. He took her left hand in both of his, and she told him.

He listened intently, shaking his head every so often.

'It's not just the baby, Dad, it's everything.' she said. 'I have no interests, and they won't let me work until my six months' leave are up. I love my job and I miss it. That's why I need something temporary.'

'You said the doc gave you tablets. Have you taken any yet?'

'I'm not sure I should. Once you're on those things, you can't get off them. I could be hooked for life.'

'There's millions of folks on them, Angie. I was on antidepressants myself when your mum was ill, and after she died. It took me months to get well, but I did it in the end. If you need them, for God's sake take them. They help.'

'I never knew you were on tablets, Dad. And here's me thinking how strong you were.'

'Well, nothing's easy in life. Bringing up kids is difficult. Remember I had to bring you up on my own and go to work. And as I recall, you had a few tantrums of your own. It wasn't until you met John that your rebellious side mellowed.'

She smiled, remembering only too well what she'd put him through as an adolescent.

'What about me going to work, Dad?'

'I can't say. I'm thinking maybe you'll change your mind once you get into a routine with little AJ.'

'No, I won't. You're saying the same as John. But I need to keep myself occupied by working because it makes me feel good about myself.'

'Won't bringing up AJ make you feel the same way?'

'Who knows? At the moment it just feels like a chore and I dread it.'

'Why not do both? Work part-time for, say, three days a week and be with your son the other days?'

'Can I have another drink?'

'Sure, what do you want?'

'A rum and black?'

'OK, coming up. Think I might join you.'

He gave her the glass and sat beside her; put his arm around her and brought her close, like he did when she was a kid years ago. She leaned her head against his shoulder.

'Hey, when you were a teenager, we used to watch films together, me and you on a Friday night. Remember? Your favourite was Avatar, I seem to remember?'

'God, yes. Haven't seen that in ages.'

He put the TV on, but before long she'd slipped into a world of dreams.

<><><>

John was tearing his hair out. Where had she gone? Three hours had passed and there was still no sign of her. He tried phoning but got no reply. Then texting her. Still nothing. Then it came to him: her dad. As he was about to ring, his own phone beeped.

'Hi, John, Alan here. Just to let you know Angie's here with me. She's fine.'

'Oh, thank God. Can I have a word with her? I've been worried sick.'

'Sorry, she's asleep. Had a little bit too much to drink. Best leave her to sleep it off, and she'll be with you in the morning.'

'You sure about that?'

'Well, she didn't say she wouldn't. Don't worry – I'll make sure she comes home.'

'How's she been?'

'Upset at first. But I had a long talk with her and I think she's beginning to come to her senses.'

'Thanks, Alan, I appreciate it.'

'No worries. She'll be fine. She's promised to take those antidepressants. So that's a start, isn't it?'

'Yes.'

'How's the baby?'

'Fast asleep.'

'You and Angie will have to bring him over. I'm dying to see him.'

'You bet. I'll talk to her, try to arrange something.'

'That would be good. Speak soon, John. Sorry about all this trouble, but let's hope she's on the mend.'

'Let's.'

John breathed a sigh of relief. He'd been imagining all sorts. The way she was going, he'd be on tablets himself.

<><><>

He brought AJ downstairs and sat in the armchair, watching breakfast TV. It helped to pass the time while he fed him.

Halfway through the feed, he heard a car pull up outside. Then the front door opened and in she walked, looking at the ground.

He turned the TV off. 'Thank God you're back. I haven't slept a wink. Look, I was out of order about you looking after the baby. I'm sorry.'

'That's all right – it's my fault. I shouldn't have reacted, but I couldn't help myself. It was silly of me to run off without a word. I panicked, didn't know what I was doing. It won't happen again.'

'Doesn't matter, so long as you're OK. I know you're suffering right now, and I just have to make allowances until you're better. You don't look very well, actually.'

She smiled ruefully. 'Got a hangover. Dad always gives me too much to drink and it goes straight to my head. I'd have come back otherwise, but I wasn't capable of driving. I keep telling him, but he thinks two large shots of rum will do me good.'

'So what did he say?'

'Not that much. Just trying to talk me into taking the medication. So, that's what I'll do. I'll take them in a few minutes.'

He nodded. 'You'll feel the benefit once they're in your system. I think we should hold fire on the nanny, see how you get on, on your own. If you have problems, then we'll discuss what to do next.'

Angie's anger resurfaced. 'No, John! That's not what I'm going to do – and you know what? Dad agrees with me!'

John shook his head. 'I'm not having that. You're being paid for six months to look after AJ, and that's what you should do. You do any other job and you'll be taxed to the hilt. Working for next to nothing would be plain ridiculous.'

'You can't stop me.'

'Anyway, you've got to get a job first – and that won't be easy.'

'Won't it? Just you wait and see.'

'I'm not going to interfere. But think of the baby. You want a stranger looking after him? Who knows what it'll do to him?'

She grinned. 'You know nothing. He won't bond with anyone at his age. He's only a few weeks old.'

'You'd be surprised.'

<><><>

On Monday morning, John had to return to work. She dreaded being alone with the baby, but she had no choice.

Her heart sank when his alarm went off.

'Wish you didn't have to go,' she said, taking hold of his hand.

'So do I. I hate leaving you here on your own.'

'I'll be fine – don't fret.'

'At least we're sharing the same bed again.'

'I know. Just remember we can't have sex until my stitches have healed.'

He winked at her. 'There's still plenty we can do,' he said, pulling on his dressing gown.

John kissed her on the lips and went to the bathroom. She remained in bed, afraid. If AJ woke up after John left for work, could she cope? She knew what to do, but whether she could bring herself to do it was another matter.

She stayed in bed, eyes closed, hoping her problems would disappear. She smelled toast, then heard John coming up the stairs. He pushed the door open with his foot.

'Hey, I brought you breakfast,' he said, giving her arm a shake.

She rubbed her eyes and, blinking, saw him standing there with a tray full of food. There was cereal, milk, tea, toast and marmalade.

Angie sat up. 'Wow, John, you're spoiling me.'

He put the tray on her lap. 'Just a thank you for allowing AJ in our room and me back into our bed. But I'd better get a move on. Got to be out of the house in half an hour. I bet I've a mountain of work to do – God knows when I'll be home.'

She didn't react, but seethed inwardly. Insensitive pig.

After finishing breakfast, she went downstairs. John appeared to be in a rush.

'Have you woken AJ?' he asked.

'No, I thought I'd let him wake himself.'

'He needs feeding and changing, Angie. And a wash. Better make a start, darling, or you'll be snowed under.'

'Yes, John. I know. You've spent the last two weeks ramming it down my throat, telling me how hard it is.'

'I'm only trying to help. I want you to succeed at this. It'll make a big difference, don't you see?'

'You think?'

'Yes, I do. Come on, you said those tablets you're taking have helped – and that's after just a couple of days. If you can get through looking after AJ today, it'll be the icing on the cake.'

'John, I'm frightened I'll do something to him without knowing it. I get in such a flap when I'm stressed. What if I lash out at him and hurt him? I'd never forgive myself.'

John smiled as if he didn't believe her. 'You'd never do that. Because deep down, you love him as much as I do. I've seen it in your eyes.'

'I hope you're right, because if not you'll have it on your conscience for life.'

'Rubbish. Now, I really can't stay any longer. Time to go. You'll be fine, I promise you. But if you want to ring me, you can.'

She tried not to let him see her shaking as he kissed her on the lips and said goodbye.

The front door slammed shut.

AJ started to cry.

Calm down, she told herself. She needed to take her tablets to stay focused – but first her little son wanted her. She picked him up and laid him on the bed, found a nappy and took off his sleepsuit. The dirty nappy was half on and half off, and spilled its contents over the bed cover. He kept wriggling about, making her job harder. She threw the nappy on the floor and tried to put on the new one. It took her ten minutes to get AJ sorted … and as soon as he was in his cot, he cried again. Hungry, no doubt.

She rushed downstairs to the fridge, took out a bottle and, while it was warming, took a tablet. Relief crept through her veins.

Having tested the milk, she rushed up the stairs and found the baby still crying. She held him to her breast and took him to the bed.

He gobbled up his feed in double quick time, and she brought up his wind easily. Having wiped his mouth, she laid him in his cot. A smile briefly appeared on her face as she felt a flicker of self-confidence. But then she remembered the mess on the bed cover. She needed to change it and put it the washer.

As she reached the bottom of the stairs, she heard him crying again. Now what? She brought him downstairs and tried to settle him in the pram.

Within five minutes, he was asleep. She'd done it.

The feeling of elation didn't last long. At a loose end, with little to do except moving the bedcover from the washer to the tumble dryer, she found herself itching to go out. She felt ridiculous – trapped in her own house by a baby. This was why she needed to work. She'd told John time and time again, but he wouldn't listen. If anything happened, he'd get the blame; she hoped he realised that.

She wanted a drink.

Just one brandy to steady her nerves.

She swallowed it in one gulp, felt the liquid warming her insides and at once she calmed down. Better than those stupid tablets, she thought.

The phone rang. There was only one person it could be.

'Angie, how are you doing?'

'All right, everything is under control. I've fed him, changed him, got him to sleep. He's been fine. No problems.'

She heard John's sigh of relief. 'See! You did it! I'm so glad. We're lucky, Angie, he's such a good baby. It will be wonderful watching him grow up.'

'Yes – I'm finding that out.'

'So now I don't want to hear you moaning over not having a job.'

Angie gripped the phone tighter.

'If I must.'

'That's a good girl. Speak to you later.'

As she put the phone on the table, the tension rose again. She'd get a job if it killed her.

Chapter 23

John put on his coat and said goodbye to his colleagues. Yet again, he was late leaving work. He ran down the stairs to the car park at the back of the building, wondering how Angie was getting on. He'd spoken to her at lunchtime and noticed she'd been a little tetchy, probably annoyed at him for ringing her again, so he'd left her alone for the afternoon. Now, driving home, he felt guilty – had he done wrong? Or would she say he didn't care?

When he opened the front door, silence greeted him.

He walked through the hall to the living room. She was sprawled out on the settee, fast asleep. But where was the baby? And the pram?

His heart beat faster. Dear God, what had she done?

He dashed to the kitchen and saw the pram by the door, with AJ sound asleep inside. He checked to make sure he was breathing normally, and relief swam over him. But the room was in a mess: dirty dishes in the sink, dirty nappies on the side. No dinner in the oven. And a bottle of brandy by the bread bin. Unopened the last time he'd looked, but now only three-quarters full.

He pushed the pram into the living room, switched on the light and walked across to where Angie lay. He moved close, smelling the alcohol on her breath.

He tugged her arm. 'What the hell are you playing at?' He shook her harder.

She opened her eyes. 'Get off me. Leave me alone.'

'I can smell it on you. Have you no shame? You're supposed to be in charge of our son, and you've been hitting the bottle again.'

'I ... I only had a small brandy, that's all. AJ wouldn't drop off and it made me nervous. I didn't have it until he'd gone.'

'I don't believe you. You've had more than one drink out of that bottle – I've seen it. What's the bloody matter with you?'

Angie looked close to tears. 'You don't understand what I've been going through. I—'

'What are you talking about? Looking after a baby isn't that difficult, for God's sake. I managed it, didn't I? I mean the doc's given you those tablets, and you said you've been feeling better. And now you're back to square one again. So why the sudden change?'

'I ... I took an extra tablet this morning.'

'Well, that hasn't done you a bit of good, has it? Right, I'm getting rid of all the alcohol in the house, for a start. What if something happened to him while you were asleep? How would you feel?'

'It didn't happen, and it won't.'

John took out all the bottles from the drinks cabinet and poured the contents down the sink. It wouldn't stop her if she was that way inclined, he knew, but he needed to feel there was something he could do.

<><><>

Late that night, while John watched TV, she set about filling in a job application for a temporary shop assistant at a DIY store. Six months' work would suit her and get her out of the house. It may not happen, since she had no experience of working in a store, but if she impressed them enough at the interview, they'd train her. She now had three jobs in the offing, although she didn't hold out much hope of getting any of them.

'I'm going to bed, Angie. Lock up, will you?'

'OK.'

By the time she slipped into bed beside him, he was snoring, fast asleep. She smiled, but prayed to God that AJ wouldn't wake up or she'd have to deal with him herself. All day was hard enough, without the nights as well.

She closed her eyes, but sleep didn't come, no matter what she did to summon it. And he was spark out without a care in the world.

Then AJ woke. She was tempted to elbow John, but something made her get up herself. She picked AJ up and held him close. But it made her shudder; she moved him quickly away from her body as though he was infectious. Downstairs, she put him in the pram while she fetched his feed. He finished it in ten minutes. A quick nappy change and rocking him for only five minutes got him to sleep again. Climbing back into bed, she realised the whole process had only taken half an hour. She felt proud of herself, although she'd loathed every minute.

The next morning, Tuesday, she woke early; AJ was still asleep, and John too. Her clock said five-thirty. She didn't want to get up yet, but she felt her heart thumping away. She needed to walk, to try and get her head straight for the forthcoming day on her own.

She made herself a black coffee, then walked back and forth from one end of the room to the other, breathing deeply in and out, trying to calm herself until, hearing John coming down, she sat down and picked up her cup.

'I wondered where you'd got to,' he said with a slight smile.

'Couldn't sleep, so I came down for a drink.'

'Hey, AJ slept right through for the first time! How amazing! You know, he really is a good baby. We're so lucky.'

She snorted. 'He didn't. He woke in the middle of the night, but I was awake anyway, so I saw to him.'

'You're a star, Angie. I never heard a thing. How about breakfast? I'll cook you bacon and egg if you like.'

'Thanks, but I'll have a bowl of porridge. Lost my appetite.'

'OK – let's hope it doesn't turn into something serious.'

'Don't worry, I'll work it off if I need to.'

'That's what I like to hear. Dedication to duty. I'm impressed.'

'Well, I might disappoint you again, the way I am.'

'As long as you lay off the booze, I don't care.'

'John, that was a one-off – my first day alone with him. I was scared. But I won't do it again, I promise.'

'I hope I can trust you.'

'What are you saying, that I'd neglect my son? You're wrong. I'm terrified of harming him, so I check and double check everything I do.'

'OK, I'll take your word for it. The subject's closed. I'll never mention it again, so long as you pull yourself together and get over whatever it is that's getting to you.'

Her hands shook as she picked up her cup of coffee and she spilt some on her dressing gown. The pressure was overwhelming; she feared failure as much as she feared harming the baby. But AJ seemed happy so far. She'd done all right with him.

'No need to keep phoning me today, John. I'll be fine. If I get into trouble or he's not well, I'll soon ring you,' she said as he made to leave.

'Sorry. I just wanted you to know I do worry about you being ill. I realise you're finding it tough right now. OK?'

'Thanks.' She kissed him on the lips.

Once he'd gone, she closed her eyes, not sure if what she felt was relief or dread. First she checked on the baby, got him out of the cot, brought him downstairs, changed his nappy and washed him. A change of clothing followed and she gave him his feed. Again he took the whole bottle, much to her surprise. After that she put him down in the pram while she cleared up.

Then she switched on the television and watched the last few minutes of breakfast TV. God, how boring life had become. No way could she stay in all day. She considered her options; as long as he slept or kept quiet in his pram, she might be able to go to Dexford for a mooch round the shops. She only had to hop on the bus. It would pass the time and she'd easily be back for lunch.

She had her coat on and had the pram ready when her phone rang. She gritted her teeth in anger, assuming John was checking up on her. But it was only ten o'clock.

It was Susan. God, what did she want?

'Sorry to disturb you, love, but we're in your neck of the woods today and wondered if we could pop in to see AJ, say around two o'clock.'

Angie's heart sank. 'I'm out shopping shortly but I'll be back by lunchtime.' She took a deep breath and sighed it out. 'Yes, that will be fine. See you later, then.'

'We're going for a meal at the Scott Arms at twelve. You're more than welcome to join us, if you want to.'

'Thanks for the invite, but I'll pass on that one. There's no telling what AJ might do and I wouldn't want to spoil your dinner.'

'No matter – we can do it when he's older.'

'Yes, I'll look forward to that. See you later, then.'

Why were they doing this? She had her suspicions, but no proof – yet.

After lunch, she got AJ fed and then dozed off – until the doorbell ringing brought her back to reality. She dragged herself to the front door, her heart thumping, to see their beaming faces staring at her.

'Hallo, come in. I'm afraid AJ is fast asleep right now, though.'

'Doesn't matter – he'll wake up soon enough,' George said.

They followed her into the living room and sat next to each other, while Angie sat in the armchair usually reserved for John.

'I'm surprised you've come when John's not here – wouldn't you rather have come in the evening?'

'Well, we were just passing, that's all. You don't mind, do you?' Susan asked.

'Not at all. Can I get you a drink? Tea or coffee?'

'Tea will do fine. Thanks.'

'OK, back in a minute. Have a peek at him if you want while you're waiting.'

Angie made the drinks, unhappy that her in-laws should invade her privacy like this. But they were entitled to see their first grandson.

She came in with their drinks, then fetched her own.

Susan smiled, eyes twinkling. 'He's lovely.'

'He is that,' George agreed. 'There's a lot of you in him, Angie. He has your hair, doesn't he?'

'Yes, that's what my dad says.'

'I bet he's over the moon, too.'

'He said it's great to have a baby in the family again. I wish Mum was alive – she'd have doted over him.'

Susan patted Angie's arm. 'She would. We certainly do!'

'We all do,' Angie said, smiling.

'And how are you getting on? I gather you've not been well. John said you've been a bit ... down in the dumps?'

'Yes, a bit. Just a touch of the baby blues, I think. It's a bit difficult to deal with now, but I'm on tablets for it.'

'That's good news. You'll get over it in a few weeks, I'm sure.'

'I hope so. I'm lucky AJ's such a good baby – I haven't been as stressed out as I thought I might be.'

George chipped in. 'If you need a rest ... well, now we're both retired, we have lots of spare time on our hands. We'd love to help you out. If you want to go out somewhere, or you need a hand with the chores, you only have to say.'

The more she heard, the more she suspected John had put them up to this.

'That's kind, but it's not necessary. AJ's been good, so I'm fine.'

Susan smiled. 'Don't be so bashful, Angie. We all need help at some stage in our lives. You don't have to accept our offer, of course, but I'd hate to think what might happen if you got into trouble ...'

Angie had had enough of their patronising attitude.

'Did John ask you to come? Only he's never said a word.'

Before either of them could answer, AJ cried to save their bacon.

Angie sighed. 'I'd better go sort him out.'

'Of course. Anything we can do to help?'

'Get him out if you like – he might need his nappy changing.'

Susan had the baby in her arms in no time and was soon cooing at him. 'Oh, isn't he beautiful, just like his daddy! Would you mind if I fed him, Angie? I'm out of practice, but I remember what to do.'

'Sure, be my guest.' Angie handed her the bottle.

'Thanks – I appreciate it.' She checked the temperature on the back of her hand. AJ took to the teat straight away and soon got the milk in him. 'Wow, he is a hungry boy, isn't he?'

'Yes, he's been eating well ever since he was born.'

George smiled at his wife. 'That's like his dad, too.'

Angie gave a slight smile, wishing they'd go. But they weren't budging, even now the feed was done.

Susan cast her eyes around the room. 'Now, is there any housework needs doing? Anything at all – we're not proud, are we, George?'

'No – we realise how difficult it is, when you're on your own with a baby.'

'I've said no. If I needed any help, I'd ask for it.'

Susan smiled an awkward smile. 'Anyway, our offer stands, day or night. We're available.'

'Yes, that's kind of you. I'll bear it in mind, thanks.'

'Shall I get him asleep for you before we go?'

'OK. Put him in the pram. He likes to play for a while. Sometimes he goes on his own.'

'Wow, that's good,' George said.

Susan turned away from the pram. 'You can all come to ours, any time you like. How about Sunday lunch?'

'Maybe. I'll ask John when he comes back from work.'

'That would be lovely, we'd be thrilled to death.'

When they'd gone, she burst into tears. Why did he do this? Plotting and planning, wanting her to be something she'd never be. She picked up a cup from the coffee table and threw it against the wall, smashing it into tiny bits. Another two cups followed. She screamed out loud. AJ cried. Her own fault, but she knew no other way to vent her frustration.

Sometimes she hated her husband so much.

Chapter 24

All day, John worried about what he'd done. But it had been with the best of intentions; Angie struggled with AJ, so this was the only solution.

Opening the front door, he sighed quietly, put his briefcase down and wondered what awaited him. The living room door was open, the TV blared away and he guessed AJ was in his pram. Angie looked around, then up at him.

'And how's he been today?'

'Can't complain,' she said.

'What did I tell you?'

'You did. I even remembered to put a ready meal in the oven. I'm pleased with myself. Wash your hands and I'll dish up. Spaghetti Bolognese. Your favourite.'

'Ooh, lovely. Things are looking up, darling.'

'Aren't they just?'

John had a peep at AJ, finding him awake and playing with a rattle. He breathed out deeply, glad everything was fine.

As he took his seat at the table, he noticed bits of crockery lying on the carpet and marks on the wall. He was about to mention it when Angie appeared with the food. She raised the plate, then dropped his boiling hot dinner over him. He yelped and his hands scrabbled at his face. 'What the hell did you do that for?'

'For going behind my back without telling me.'

'You what?'

'You know what I'm talking about. I don't need to spell it out.'

He should have guessed. 'Have you gone mad? You nearly scalded me.' He pulled a tissue out of his pocket and wiped his face and shirt. Most of the food had ended up on the carpet.

'Nearly? More's the pity.'

'Well, thanks very much.'

She shoved the table towards him. 'Your mum and dad paid me a visit.'

'So what? They're entitled – they're his grandparents, for God's sake. What's wrong with that?'

'Everything.'

'Look, Mum phoned me at work, asking if they could see AJ. I said to ring you first, in case you were going out. I would have warned you, but I've been really busy.'

'You're lying, John. You planned this with them, didn't you? Told them God knows what. And when they came over, they couldn't do too much for me, because I'm a lunatic who can't look after myself or my kid. Have you any idea how they made me feel? About two inches tall. I'm an inadequate mother – that's what they think. Patronising me over how I'm bringing him up. I nearly threw them out, I can tell you. It was so embarrassing.'

'Angie, they were only trying to help. They love AJ, and you too. If you'd let them help, it would take the pressure off you.'

'That's a joke. It's had the opposite effect. Now I'm worse than ever.'

John sighed, and his tone softened. 'I don't want you to go to work. I need you to be with me and AJ.'

'That's ridiculous. Even if I stayed here all day, you wouldn't be with me, because you're at work. I want a proper nanny to take care of him.'

'There's no point in discussing this now. You haven't even got a job yet, and until you do, you either muddle your way through, or accept Mum and Dad's kind offer. Please.'

'I can see whose side you're on.'

'It's not a question of sides – it's doing what's right.'

'I'm sick of this. And I'm warning you, you ever do that to me again and I'll leave. If you get any more great ideas, ask me first – or keep them to yourself.'

She walked away, leaving her dinner cooling on the table.

'Where are you going?'

'Out. If you're hungry, have mine. I've suddenly lost my appetite, for some reason. And as for the baby, you deal with it. I've had enough of the lot of you.'

<><><>

He didn't go after her, which was a blessing. He wasn't that stupid.

Where to now? Not her dad's; maybe Gail, her old friend from school. She felt like getting drunk and letting her hair down, as she did before she met John.

She stopped in a layby and rang Gail on her mobile. They hadn't spoken in ages – come to think of it, she didn't even know Angie had a baby.

'Hi, Gail, how are you?'

'Angie! What a surprise! I'm OK, thanks. You?'

'Good – listen, I just wondered if you were free tonight. Fancy going out for a drink? We could catch up with all our news. I've got loads to tell you!'

'Angie, I'd love to, only me and Richard are off on our holidays to-morrow, to Benidorm for a fortnight. Tell you what, when I'm back, I'll ring you. Got loads of juicy gossip for you too, believe me.'

'But I ... OK. See you in two weeks. Have a nice holiday.'

'Thanks. See you soon.'

The line went dead. 'Shit! Shit! Shit!'

Not giving in, she rang several other old friends, but to no avail.

Tears streamed down her face. Nobody had time for her now; everyone had it in for her. Even though she shouldn't be driving yet, she decided to get as far away as possible.

Within minutes, she turned onto the motorway, still unsure of what to do. In the fast lane, she put her foot down, driving at well over the speed limit. The speedo hit one hundred miles an hour and she giggled, filled with an urge to see how much faster the car would go. And if she crashed head-on into another vehicle … she wondered if death would be instantaneous.

The sight of blue lights flashing brought her back to reality. She slowed, glanced in her mirror and caught sight of the police car coming alongside, telling her to pull over. Oh God, just what she didn't need.

An officer strode towards the car, indicating for her to wind her window down.

'Sorry to disturb you, madam, but do you know how fast you were travelling just then? You were well over the speed limit.'

'Oh, I'm sorry, officer, I didn't realise, I apologise, I won't do it again.'

'Please get out of the car.'

She did.

'Breathe into this,' he said, holding the breathalyser out towards her face.

'But I haven't been drinking, officer.'

'Just blow into the bag.'

The officer looked at the breathalyser. 'Seems you're right. Can you show me your driving license?'

She took it from her purse and handed it over.

'Right, Mrs Greaves. I have to caution you. Your car's speed was measured at 82 miles per hour. Since your license is clean, I'm giving you a verbal warning this time, but if you are caught again, you will be liable to a £100 fine and three points on your license. Driving at that speed is very dangerous. You're putting yourself and others at risk. I advise you to keep to the speed limit in future.'

Consider yourself told off, she thought. John would be so mad at her again if he found out; thank goodness she'd escaped with a warning.

She guessed she hadn't been out for that long. As she stopped on the drive, she noticed the lights were still on. John wouldn't be happy, having to do it all himself.

He'd cleaned the place up, and now he sat in the armchair, reading a magazine. She glanced at the empty pram, guessing AJ was upstairs in his cot, fast asleep.

She made herself a cup of coffee and switched on the TV – better that than sitting in silence. He ought to be careful how he treated her, or she'd go somewhere from where there'd be no return.

'Did you have any trouble getting AJ to sleep?'

'No – ten minutes and he was out like a light.'

'Good.'

'We're lucky with him. When I heard all the scare stories from the guys at work, I expected the worst, but I reckon he's done us proud.'

'Yes.'

She picked up the laptop from the coffee table and began her nightly ritual of looking for jobs, without any real hope. John carried on reading in silence.

<><><>

A peck on the cheek was all she got in the morning.

'See you tonight,' he said. 'Why not take AJ out later? The weather's good, it'll be nice in the park.'

'Yes, I may do.'

The day passed slowly. She did take AJ for a walk in the park, but didn't stay for more than half an hour as it clouded over and rained. Back home, staring at four walls and seeing to her son bored her to tears – literally. If only she'd thought to call in at the off-licence while she'd been out.

The phone rang at one o'clock; John, she assumed, checking up on her. But she got a big surprise.

'Is that Angie?'

'Yes.'

'This is Helen Blewitt from Betterbuy Stores. You applied for the part-time job. Could you come for an interview?'

'What! Yes, of course. When?'

'Is tomorrow at two o'clock convenient?'

'Of course.'

'Wonderful. I look forward to meeting you.'

'The same here.'

After she'd ended the call, she yelped with joy, but quickly realised she had a problem: what to do with the baby. She didn't want John to find out yet, nor his parents – which left only her dad. That would be fine, surely? AJ wasn't any trouble. In fact, he might sleep right through. She felt giddy with excitement. She sailed through the afternoon, and was even pleasant when John rang.

Next, she had to ring her dad.

'Hallo, petal.'

'Dad, I need to ask you a favour…'

'Now, let me think. You want to leave the baby with me while you go out.'

'How did you guess?'

'You get to know a person after you've lived with them for twenty-five years. So, am I right?'

'In a way, you are. Can you keep an eye on him tomorrow while I go to a job interview?'

'Job interview already? That was quick.'

'Well, I've been trying really hard. But it's just for six months, to get me out of the house.'

'Is that wise? I mean, who'll look after the baby, for a start? I hope you haven't got me in mind. I'm too old to do that sort of thing on my own.'

'No, Dad. I'll hire a nanny.'

'Well, they don't come cheap. And you'll miss AJ. He needs you for these first few months.'

'Don't you start. I've got enough of that with John and his parents.'

'OK, it's your life. You have to sort it out yourself.'

'But can I bring him over tomorrow afternoon for an hour?'

'I suppose so. I've never turned you down yet, have I?'

'Thanks, Dad. What would I do without you?'

Chapter 25

She left the interview room in a daze. When the job offer came, it was unexpected – and to start next week was scary. That gave her very little time to find a nanny. She'd be working mornings from eight until one, and every other weekend. Not ideal, but it wouldn't be for long; she'd be back behind her desk at Elliott's within a few months.

As she drove to her dad's, she guessed he'd be horrified, but she was confident of talking him round.

She tiptoed into the living room, where she found him sitting with AJ on his lap. He was giving him his bottle, lost in another world.

'Make us a drink. There's coffee in the cupboard.'

'Dad! "Hallo" might have been nice.'

'Come on, love. My hands are full, and I'm gagging for a drink.'

'All right,' she conceded.

She came back with the drinks, noticing the time. She needed to go home soon and face the music with John.

'I say, he doesn't hang about, does he? Never seen a baby drink so fast, he'll be getting a stomach ache. He's been as good as gold, by the way. A real pleasure.'

Angie smiled.

'So, come on then. How did the interview go?'

'Good – they offered me the job.'

'Did they now?'

'I start next week.'

'Wow, that's a surprise.'

She nodded. 'Yes. It was.'

'So, are you pleased? Over the moon, I suppose.'

'Not exactly; excited, nervous – it's hard to say.'

'Well, you know my feelings about it, love, but it's up to you. I'm not going to interfere.'

'Good. You won't, unless you want a fight.'

'All right, I'll keep my thoughts to myself. As I've always said, you only learn from your own mistakes.'

Angie drank her cup of coffee, hoping the conversation was over. Her dad meant so much to her, and she wanted to leave on good terms.

'Sorry, Dad – I must dash.'

'Keep me informed, won't you? I hope it works out for you.'

'So do I.' Her heart was racing.

On her way home, she thought of nothing else but how John would react. But if this was what she wanted, she must stick to her guns and fight for what she believed in.

<><><>

John came home early, having visited a new prospective client, a chain of dental practices, where he did a presentation of his firm's services and prices. It had gone well; Sachs Gordon stood a good chance of winning the contract. He was in good spirits, until he opened the front door to find Angie gone. Where had she got to this time?

The house was a mess; left for him to put right, obviously. Well, he didn't see why he should be left to deal with it. He had other things to do.

He tapped away on the computer, writing up notes and observations from his meeting. Half an hour later, she came in, carrying AJ in his car seat. She looked surprised, even shocked, to see him.

'What brings you here at this time?' she said.

'The meeting finished early, and it wasn't worth going back. So, I decided to work from home.'

'I've been over to Dad's. He absolutely dotes on AJ.'

'Bet he's thrilled to have his grandson named after him.'

'Yes, and he loves spending time with him. It was great to see them together. I might take him over more often.'

He smiled, then turned back to his computer.

'John, I've something to tell you.'

'What's—' And then the baby bawled. 'Shit. I'll go.'

Twenty minutes later, he sat down again.

Angie was doing something in the kitchen; when she'd finished, she came in, looking nervous. She blushed when he looked at her.

'You all right?' he said.

'Fine, couldn't be better.'

'Great – the tablets seem to be working, then? You're more positive now, aren't you?'

'Am I? I just take it one day at a time. Most days I still cry or want to run away and never come back.'

He gasped. 'But why? I thought things were settling down for you, with AJ and everything.'

'Maybe so, but that butterflies in the stomach feeling never gets any better. I'm frightened, John. I'm a failure, a bad mother, a bad wife, a bad worker. And I don't know how to get better at any of it.'

'You're not a failure. Those feelings will stop once you realise how lucky you are.'

'They won't. They'll only stop when I do something about it. That's what I was going to tell you before AJ started crying: I've been offered a job.'

'You what! A job? This is ridiculous. And pointless, too, since you're already getting paid by the estate agents. I told you that before.'

'It's nothing to do with money – it's me going out to do something useful.'

'So, did you accept the offer?'

'I did. I start a week today.'

'But what about AJ? We'll never get a nanny by then. There's always my parents, I suppose, although it depends how many hours you're doing …'

'Five mornings a week from eight until one, and every other week-end.'

'My God, you're joking.'

'I'm not. Did you get me that list of nannies?'

'No.'

'Oh, thanks very much, so I'll have to do it myself now.'

'Angie, I've been at work all day. When was I supposed to have time?' He sighed. 'Well, I can't stop you – but I won't encourage you either.'

'You bastard!' she screamed. 'You never give me a thought, do you? All you're interested in is me being a good wife and mother. But that's not me. I want to be independent and fulfil my dreams. I'll never be a stay at home mum, John – I've made that clear more than once.'

'I'm not arguing with you. Just let me know what's going on. I mean, I'd jump at the chance to be a stay at home husband, but it's impossible. We couldn't live on just your wage.'

'You don't say.'

'All right, I'll leave you to it.'

'OK, but now I've apparently got to find a nanny myself, can you look after AJ?'

'Of course. It seems to be mostly my job anyway.'

Out of the corner of his eye, he watched Angie on the laptop, taking details, emailing nannies and writing down phone numbers. It made his blood boil, but he didn't speak. If anything happened to AJ because of her selfishness he'd never forgive her.

Chapter 26

A_{fter} John went to work on the Friday morning, Angie interviewed another prospective nanny over the phone. By lunchtime she had spoken to four professional and experienced women, but only one of them was available to start work in time for Angie's first day at the shop.

When she told Alison the good news, she was pleased and promised to start at eight o'clock on Monday. Angie intended paying her out of her own money so John couldn't complain. But she'd wait until the weekend to tell him.

The atmosphere remained tense for the next two days, and she knew that when he learned what she'd lined up, he'd be in an even worse mood. It took her until after Sunday lunch to pluck up the courage.

'Just so you know, I'm starting work tomorrow.'

He rolled his eyes. 'Right. I wondered when that was coming. You've left it late to get someone to look after AJ, though. Shall I ask Mum and Dad if they can help?'

'No, there's no need. I've found a nanny, and she's starting tomorrow morning.'

He looked crestfallen. 'Really?'

'Yes. Sorry. You probably think I'm a selfish bitch, but this is for everyone. If I'm stuck here on my own with AJ, I'll go to pieces. It's so claustrophobic and I'll feel like the walls are closing in on me.'

'I'm so sad it's come to this. I always dreamed of having kids, but so far it seems to have done us nothing but harm – first when you were pregnant, and after he was born too. The only positive is that AJ has been far less trouble than I imagined. But I wish you could get over this anxiety.' He wiped a tear from his cheek.

She'd never seen him cry like this before; it struck a nerve.

'I can't help how I am, John. I'm sorry. I long to be like other mothers but it's not to be.'

'There are lots of things you can do, even if you don't take this job. Baby groups to join, support groups, websites …'

'Been doing your homework, I see. You never give up, do you? Trying to convince me to stay at home. It won't work. I've made my decision and I'm sticking to it. Now please leave me alone.'

His fresh tears made her guilt worse. But she wouldn't change her mind, no matter what he did.

'Oh, fuck you!' She stood up quickly and her chair fell over backwards. 'Take him upstairs when you're ready. I've had enough of both of you.'

She stormed up to their bedroom, where she undressed and found herself a book that she could pretend to be reading if he came up after her.

He didn't come up until eleven; the light was off, but she saw him put the baby in his cot before getting into bed himself. There was no touching and for that she was grateful. Now all she had to occupy her mind was her first day at work.

She set her alarm for six o'clock, hoping this would leave her enough time to get ready and pass AJ over to Alison.

<><><>

As soon as she got up, she realised John wasn't there.

She glanced in the other rooms but saw no sign of him. Only on looking out of the living room window did she discover that his car had gone.

AJ started crying. Typical. John was supposed to take over until Alison arrived. Still, she couldn't allow him to bellow in pain.

She went back upstairs, picked him up and laid him on the bed. The stench was awful, and there was dried sick on his sleepsuit. His nappy was full and the contents were spreading up his back and down his legs. Gagging, she pulled out a change of clothes for him.

It took fifteen minutes to clean him up; now she needed to feed him before Alison came. But when she tried to put the teat in, he spat it out again and again. He'd never refused a bottle before, and now he felt incredibly hot. The boy wasn't well. This was all she needed on her first day.

She took him downstairs, put him in the pram and phoned the emergency doctor, who advised her to take AJ to his own GP when the surgery opened at eight. She'd need to let Alison know; she must be on her way by now. But her mobile wasn't answered and neither was the land line. Angie swore under her breath, but AJ was crying again and she needed to get him ready. Her anger at John was acute; leaving her in the lurch was unforgivable.

When they got there, she got an appointment for half an hour's time. She hated waiting but had no choice. At last they called her.

'He's been sick, and his nappy was really runny this morning,' she said.

The doctor nodded. 'OK. How many times?'

'I'm not sure – it happened in the night.'

'Let's have a little look at him.' Angie held him close while the doctor examined him. 'He's boiling – must have caught a bug. I'll give you some medicine to get his temperature down and his stomach right. See how he goes, and if he's no better within two days, bring him back at once.'

'I don't know where he's caught it from, he's hardly with any other people. I'm baffled.'

'These things happen. It's surprising how easy it is for babies to pick up these bugs. He should feel better in a day or two.'

'Thank you, doctor.'

Having got his medication, she drove home. As soon as she got in, she realised she hadn't phoned work; she should have been there at eight-thirty, but it was now well after nine. Alison must have found the house empty and gone home. Shit. She put AJ down while she tapped in the number on her phone.

'Hallo, this is Angie Greaves, is Mrs Blewitt there, please?'

'Yes, speaking.'

'Hi – I'm really sorry. I'm ringing to tell you I've had to take my son to the doctor's. He's got a bug. I've got to speak to the nanny when she arrives, and then I'll be in.'

'You needn't bother. We don't need timewasters on our staff.'

'You what? But why?'

'Goodbye, Mrs Greaves.'

Later, when she'd pulled herself together, she gave AJ his medicine and wondered whether John had orchestrated the whole thing. If he had, she'd throttle him.

<><><>

John had gone to work early to avoid meeting AJ's nanny. He wanted no part of all that. Once at work, in before everyone else, he dwelled on what he'd done. He supposed she'd shout at him when he got home, but she'd still have what she wanted, which left a bitter taste in his mouth. So when the phone rang later that morning, the last person he expected was Angie.

'What the hell have you done? He was throwing up all over the place this morning. Did you have anything to do with that, by any chance?'

John scratched his head. 'What? You've got to be joking. Why would I want to make him ill? When I brought him up to bed last night he was fine, had his feed no problem. If you don't believe me, that's your problem, but I promise you it's the truth.'

'Whatever. Anyway, you'll be pleased to know everything went wrong for me today. I couldn't go to work because of him being ill. And I wasn't at home when the nanny arrived. As a direct consequence, I've lost the job I wanted – and the nanny.'

'Well, that's got nothing to do with me. If things didn't work out as you'd intended, I'm sorry. But I won't be shedding any tears.'

'You bastard!' she shouted and switched off the phone.

He might have expected this, given he'd left her to deal with a sick baby on her own, but at least she'd have calmed down when he came home.

The rest of the day passed far too quickly as home time loomed. With so much bad feeling between them, he wondered if he could take any more. Only his love for his son kept him going.

As he said goodbye to his colleagues, he almost stopped off for a drink, but decided against it. He needed a clear head to deal with Angie's tantrums.

His heart beat faster as he opened the front door. The baby was crying, so no doubt he would have to go to him. He half expected to see Angie sitting there, allowing AJ to cry without lifting a finger. But no – there she was, rocking him in her arms.

'How is he?' he asked.

'As you can see, still poorly. No thanks to you.'

'Rubbish. As I've told you, I had nothing to do with Alan being ill. Why would I do something so callous? I'd never use him to stop you doing what you want. I'm not like that. I might not agree with it but if you're that passionate, I've no objection – you carry on.'

'I don't believe you, with that smug look on your face. I'll get another job, don't you worry – and another nanny.'

'If you say so.'

'Better get your own dinner. With AJ sick, I haven't had time. All right?'

'Sure, no problem. I'll soon rustle something up. Have you eaten?'

'John, how do you imagine I'd make myself something with the baby ill. My God, do you think so little of me?'

'Shall I take over? Then you can rest, since you're been so busy.'

She glared at him, got up and handed him AJ.

'There you are. I've had more than enough for one day.'

'Has he eaten? Had his medicine?'

'Yes, to both questions. Don't worry, I've taken good care of him, despite what you think. Perhaps I've not bonded with him like you but I'd never harm him.'

'No one's saying that, Angie, but ...'

Too late. She'd walked out.

Later, while he fed AJ, she sat at the table, eating beans on toast and playing with her phone. His stomach growled. He'd been glued to the sofa under the baby for an hour and a half.

'A cup of tea wouldn't go amiss if you can spare me two minutes,' he said.

She got up from her seat to go to the kitchen. Wonders would never cease. He manoeuvred AJ gently onto the settee so he could have his nappy changed. When he turned around, Angie stood right in front of him, a pot of tea in her hand. He wasn't prepared for what happened next.

'Tea!' she screamed and threw the red-hot liquid over him. Mercifully, it missed the baby.

His arms took the brunt of it. He screamed in pain and tried to brush it off. But the damage was done.

His flesh was red, burning like fire. He ran to the kitchen, holding his arms out, and thrust them under the cold tap. Tears came into his eyes, but after several minutes the pain slowly eased. He dabbed his skin with a towel, wincing; he would have to keep his sleeves rolled up.

He reached up for the first aid box, and found some bandages. He tied them around his arms with difficulty, still in severe pain.

When he returned to the living room, she acted as if nothing was wrong. AJ lay in his pram, fast asleep. At least she'd managed to do something useful.

'What the fuck did you do that for? That tea was scalding hot. My arms are red raw and swelling.'

'To teach you a lesson. You ever meddle with my life again, you'll get much worse than that.'

'Not that again. I've told you, I'm not responsible for AJ being ill, and if you can't see that, well, I feel sorry for you.'

'I'll get another job.'

'All right, get one. You've got to stop hurting me. I'll end up in hospital if you keep this up. And what the hell am I going to say if someone sees my arms?'

'Keep them covered up. You shouldn't keep doing these horrible things. You provoked me, John – it is any wonder I lashed out? It's your own fault. I realise I have problems, but you've been so insensitive. I wish you could be in my shoes for one day. Then you might understand.'

John shook his head. 'And how can I look after the baby with my arms in this condition?'

'Come on, it's not that bad. You're just laying it on to get back at me.'

'You're unbelievable.'

'So are you. Trying to control me – well, I won't be controlled. Be very careful, John. I'll go – and if I do, I'll take AJ with me.'

He wouldn't listen to this any longer. 'I'd be grateful if you'd keep quiet now. You'll wake the baby.'

'It'll be my pleasure.'

<><><>

They lay together but apart in bed, John fuming over what she'd done, trying to ignore his sore arms and Angie's lack of sympathy. Then her hand touched his shoulder, another wrapped around his waist. She kissed him on the back of the head and moved him towards her. Despite the rows and bitterness, he got aroused by her unexpected tenderness. They made love as if was their first time and afterwards held each other tightly.

'I love you,' she whispered in his ear.

'I love you too,' he replied, revelling in this most tender moment. Afterwards, while she slept, he lay awake, wondering how long this reconciliation might last.

Chapter 27

A loud cry came from the cot. Angie sighed, looking for John; not there. Meaning she had to see to AJ herself.

She felt sick to her stomach but she picked him up, changed his nappy and carried him downstairs. John sat at the table, eating his breakfast. He had taken the bandages off his arms. They were red and ugly blisters covered them; she guessed he must be in pain. But she didn't feel sorry for him after what he'd done to her.

'Good sleep?' he asked.

'Not bad,' she said. 'But I imagine I'm in for a hectic day. AJ only woke up twice, not too bad considering he's unwell. I'll give him his medicine and hope he'll take his feed too.'

'OK.'

'I wish you could be at home with me.'

'So, do I, but you know that's impossible. We have bills to pay, and the mortgage ... but hey, once we've paid that off, we'll be laughing. Before you know it, we will be together.'

'Oh, sure, maybe when we retire. That's thirty years off yet.'

'That's life, Angie. But we can go on holidays, jet off to exotic places – and we have the weekends, too.'

'It's impossible with a baby.'

'No it isn't. Why don't we ask my parents or your dad to babysit, if we fancy a night out?'

'That doesn't solve the problem, though, does it? The fact is, unless I get a job sometime soon, I'll be on my own with him five days a week. It'll drive me crazy. And it's still almost six months before I go back to Elliott's. That's an eternity.'

'It'll pass quicker than you think. And anyway, isn't it fascinating to watch him develop and grow? And you'll be with him throughout that journey. You should be thrilled to have that opportunity.'

'Maybe so, but I'm not, John. I'm trapped in this house with him – it's my worst nightmare.'

'How you can say that? He's your son!'

AJ started to cry.

'Why don't you get off to your accountancy world, that's the best place for you since you care so little about me.'

Anger flickered in his eyes but he kept quiet. Instead, he put his empty plate in the sink and disappeared to the hall, returning in his coat with his briefcase under his arm.

'I'm off,' he said.

'What's the matter with you now? Feeling sorry for yourself, are you? God, it's me that's got the worry with him over there.'

'If you say so. The trouble with you is that you think every little mishap is a major crisis. You need to put it all into perspective. AJ is a healthy, normal baby – and you ought to be grateful for that.'

'You haven't got a clue. You should take the trouble to find out before you keep slagging me off. Just piss off and leave me alone.'

It was if last night's sex had never happened.

<><><>

The pain in his arms remained, but he was too embarrassed to go to the doctor. He'd need to keep the sleeves of his shirt rolled down now the bandages were off; he should probably keep his jacket on, too, to be on the safe side. He hoped his colleagues wouldn't find it odd, and that today wasn't as warm as yesterday had been.

He was in early, said good morning to David and Joe and sat down at his desk. After checking his emails, he glanced up, spotted Sarah, and smiled.

'How's it going?' she asked.

'AJ's caught a bug and isn't well. We had a bad night,' he explained.

'I thought you looked a bit run-down. Has he been to the doctor's?'

'Yes, Angie took him. They've given him some medicine. He's improved a bit this morning, so we'll see how he goes during the day.'

'Glad to be at work, then?'

'In a way. I'll ring her at lunchtime. If I fall asleep give me a nudge, will you?'

'Hey. Don't sleep on the job.'

He grinned. Sarah always had the knack of making him smile.

Come twelve o'clock, he phoned Angie at home, but got no reply. Either she was out or not answering the phone. He tried her mobile too but had no joy. His heart fluttered.

'Hey, John, coming the pub for a pint?' Joe asked. 'We're going to the Pheasant.'

'Yeah, I could do with a bite to eat. You carry on – I'll be with you in two ticks.'

This seemed like a good plan. He needed to take his mind off Angie and the baby and anyway, he hadn't brought any lunch.

He found them sitting at a table near the bar. David and Joe squeezed closer together and Sarah too, allowing him to sit at the end.

'Got you a pint in,' she said.

'Oh, thanks, I'm parched. I'll just order my dinner, won't be a moment.'

Upon his return, he sipped his drink and smiled at them. The heat was sweltering. Outside, the temperature was in the mid-twenties and the atmosphere unusually humid for mid-September.

As he ate his burger and chips, he felt worse. Sweat trickled down his cheeks. Everyone else was in shirtsleeves, and he sensed their eyes on him.

'Hey, John,' Sarah said. 'You all right? You look hot – why don't you take off your jacket?'

'Yes, I will in a minute.'

He blushed, unable to bear it any longer. As soon as he did, exposing a couple of inches of wrist, they gasped.

Sarah looked concerned. 'John, what the hell happened to your arms? They're all red and blistery.'

'Yeah, I know. Had an accident. Lifting a bowl of boiling water out of the sink. I slipped and it spilled all over me.'

'My God, that must have been painful, mate,' David said.

'A little.' He gave a rueful smile.

'Have you seen a doctor?' Sarah asked.

'No, there's no need. I soaked my arms in cold water and that helped. Can't believe I was that stupid. Got so much going on these days, with the baby and everything.'

'How's Angie?'

'Oh, up and down. Bringing up a kid isn't easy, you know, even when he's as good as AJ. I think she feels a bit isolated having him on her own ... I think she's got a touch of postnatal depression, to be honest.'

'It does get better, mate,' David butted in. 'But you wait till you have another one – it's ten times worse and twice the work.'

'God, can't even think about that yet.'

'Hey, you put any cream on those burns?' Joe asked.

'Not yet. I might buy a tube later. I had bandages on them but they were so uncomfortable I had to take them off in the toilet.'

After the interest had died down, John remained subdued and embarrassed. Had they believed his explanation? He'd told them a lie, but he was sticking to it.

Sarah walked with him from the pub. 'So, fatherhood has been a disappointment? That's a real shame.'

He shrugged. 'Yeah. But AJ is great – it's amazing how he's constantly changing.'

'You and Angie ought to go out more, get someone to babysit. I bet your folks and Angie's would love to have him. Why not come out with me and Jack? You had a good night the last time we went out. Talking football all night, weren't you?'

'Something like that. Yeah, we enjoyed it; ironically, we were talking about babies, I seem to remember, weren't we? And not long after that, Angie found out she was pregnant. I'll speak to her, see what she has to say. I can't promise, since she's always shattered at the moment.'

'Any problems, and I'll talk to her for you.'

'OK, thanks.' He smiled.

<><><>

Friday tomorrow at last, Angie thought. What a horrendous week. Although AJ soon got well, caring for him for five days was stressful. She went out, stayed in, visited her dad and John's parents, but still her anxiety prevailed. How much more could she take?

When John came home, he smiled but she didn't return the favour.

'How things?' he asked.

'The same as normal. Crap.'

'Well, at least we've got the weekend to look forward to.'

'We won't be together as long as he's here.' The words were out before she could stop them.

John looked dumbstruck.

'What? Did I hear you right? Well, I'd say we won't be a family without our son.'

'If you say so.'

He sat in the armchair, rubbed his eyes and sighed.

Angie could see how shocked he looked, but it brought no reaction. Instead, anger festered over how little empathy he had for her. She saw red, but said nothing for now.

She disappeared into the kitchen and checked on their meal. It smelt delicious. Pity she wasn't hungry.

John held AJ in his arms when she returned.

'Is he due a feed?'

She nodded. 'An hour ago, but I thought it best to let him sleep. So, if you want me to feed him, I'll leave mine in the oven.'

'OK. Got any feeds made up?'

'No, haven't had time.'

He got up and headed for the kitchen. 'Have you been giving him that special milk?'

'Yes, and the sickness and runs have gone.'

'Great.'

This time, AJ took longer to finish his feed. John had eaten his dinner and pudding by the time Angie started on hers. She ate it in silence, then headed for the living room.

When he returned from doing the washing-up, he sat down with a subdued expression on his face. Maybe she should tell him first.

'I've come to a decision, John. You're not going to like it.'

'What's that?' he said, looking straight at her.

'About AJ.'

His eyes widened.

'I can't deal with him anymore. There, I've said it, admitted it. I guess I'm not cut out to be a mother. I have no maternal instincts whatsoever and the more I try, the worse I am. Every bit of bringing him up is a chore and if something doesn't change soon, I'll hurt him. That's why I want him put up for adoption.'

Chapter 28

John never saw this coming, not in a million years. To give their beautiful son away on a whim? That would be unthinkable.

'What are you talking about? Adoption? Over my dead body.'

'I'm not joking. I've been thinking about it for a while. It's the only solution, under the circumstances. We have to do what's best for him. He'll never get the life he deserves here, not with me.'

'You speak for yourself. I won't give him up! He means everything to me – as he should to you. What the hell's the matter with you? Go to the doctor's, ask her to sort you out with counselling or whatever else it takes. If I let you do this, you'll regret it.'

'You're wrong, John. As long as I'm here, I worry I'll do something terrible to him. I can't take that chance. Don't you understand that?'

He made a conscious effort to calm down. Shouting would only make her worse. 'No, I don't. It's postnatal depression, darling. If you'd done what the doctor advised, you'd probably be on the mend by now. You won't get better unless you have counselling as well as taking the antidepressants. You're too hasty by far – it's only weeks since you had him. That's too soon to make such a momentous decision.'

'I've been looking at adoption agencies on the internet. They seem nice. Imagine how many couples can't have a child? How heartbreaking is that? We could make one of them so happy. He'd be perfect and he's as good as gold. Let me show you on the computer!'

'Angie, for God's sake. Listen to yourself. And even if this wasn't a mad idea, I'm not interested. AJ is ours to be loved and cherished. I'll never give him up, no matter what it costs.'

'But what if it costs you our marriage, and causes us to break up? Is it worth keeping him if you lost me?'

'Don't ask me to choose between you and the baby. The baby doesn't have a choice, but you do.'

'Have it your own way, but don't say I didn't warn you.'

'I'll not be held to ransom. If he's so awful, we'll come to another arrangement.'

'Like what?'

'I don't know. But in five months you'll be at work, anyway – and I presume you'll be full-time again. That's when to make arrangements for a nanny or a childminder. Not now.'

'So you refuse to consider my suggestion?'

'Yes. Not when he has a family and grandparents to love him. Have a long hard look at yourself, darling. Remember: if you had him adopted, you couldn't change your mind. And you'd never see him again. That would break your heart.'

'No it wouldn't.'

'I'm not discussing this any further. He's my baby too, and the answer's no.'

She shrugged, but gave him a sneering smile that made his heart flutter. He worried she'd still go ahead without his knowledge or consent. Fine – let her try. He'd kill her.

<><><>

The next morning, he woke early, still worrying over what Angie might do. She was so unpredictable. But she had taken care of AJ and there were no signs that she'd harmed him, despite her saying she loathed looking after him. Although she'd sounded serious last night, he was sure she would never intentionally hurt him. He sensed she loved him and was only sounding off out of frustration.

Both mother and son were asleep when he popped his head around the door half an hour later. He leaned over and gave her a peck on the cheek and whispered, 'I'm off darling, see you later.'

'Mm,' she mumbled, turning over in her sleep.

He was the first to arrive. He had his own key, so he opened up and sat staring at an empty screen until he caught sight of Sarah.

'You're bright and early,' she said.

'Yep.' He didn't smile.

'How's your arms?'

'All right.'

'Are you always this chatty in the morning?'

'Sometimes.'

'Are you even listening?'

'What? Sorry. Had another rough night with AJ.' As he tried to smile, he found he had tears in his eyes. He hoped Sarah hadn't noticed, but the concern on her face suggested otherwise.

'What's wrong?'

'Nothing.'

'John, you can do better than that. Something's upset you. And my guess is it's to do with Angie.'

He grimaced. 'How come you're always so perceptive?'

'Because that's what women do. They notice things.'

'I don't enjoy talking about stuff.'

'You and every other man. So, will you talk to me or not? I'm not being nosy – I'd just like to help. You're my friend. Come on, spill the beans before anyone else comes.'

He told her almost everything, having to stop twice to regain control of himself. She listened, her eyes widening with shock.

'That's terrible. One thing, though. Did you really spill hot water over your arms? Are you sure it wasn't … you know – deliberate? What did she do to you, John?'

He sighed. 'I really thought I was convincing. OK – she threw a jug of boiling water over me. She's never been violent towards me before she got pregnant and yet now …'

'I knew it. It's hard to take this in, John. She needs help. I suggest you persuade her to go back to her doctor and ask if she'll refer her to a psychiatrist.'

'That's easier said than done, when she won't listen to me. How on earth do I convince her?'

'Has she family who might support her?'

'Only her father; her mother died when she was ten, in a car crash. No brothers or sisters.'

'And is she close to him?'

'Yes, he brought her up on his own after her mum died. She dotes on him.'

'That's the answer, then. Speak to him – maybe he has some influence over her.'

'It's worth a try. I find it hard to understand her. I mean, we both wanted kids, but ever since she got pregnant, she's had these mood swings and tantrums. God knows how she'd react if AJ really played up. This wanting to have our son adopted is the final straw. I'm at my wits' end.'

She squeezed his arm, being careful to avoid the blistered areas. 'Lots of women have trouble bonding with their baby – you'd be surprised. She might come round.'

He smiled. 'Thanks for listening, Sarah. And you're right. I'll ring Angie's dad. Sorry if I've bored you with my problems.'

'You haven't. Isn't that what friends are for?'

'I need to get on with some work before I fall apart.'

'Yes, well, that new account for the dentists needs sorting. It's a mess. No wonder they changed over to us.'

'Too right. They've had me tearing my hair out.'

'Speak to you later.'

As he worked, he pondered over what to say to Alan. Was it worth talking to him? He wasn't sure, but he had nothing to lose.

He waited until late in the day, fearing Angie might be with him. How embarrassing would that be?

It took ages before Alan answered and the tone in the man's voice wasn't friendly. But he'd got this far, so there was no going back.

'Sorry to ring you, Alan, but I wanted to talk to you about Angie.'

'Why? Is there something the matter with her?'

'Yes ... no ... I don't know. She's not been very well lately. She's depressed, she's had problems connecting with AJ and she's getting worked up about it. And now she wants to him put up for adoption – can you believe it? I'm worried to death. She can't do anything without my consent, of course, but how do I get her to change her mind? I wondered if you might have a word with her.'

Alan didn't answer at first but finally said, 'That's not any business of mine. I prefer not to interfere. And besides she might not listen, anyway. She's very headstrong, as you well know; once she's made a decision, there's no talking her out of it. I know she's unhappy, she told me she finds the baby hard to cope with and she misses work. But I never imagined she was that bad. I'm sad she's considering giving up my grandson, but it must run deeper than that.'

'You've not seen her?'

'Not since last week, so this has come as a bit of a shock. It's drastic ... Tell you what I'll do – if she mentions this, I'll try to dissuade her. She normally tells me everything; it's not like her to keep it to herself. Thank you for telling me. I promise you it will go no further.'

'OK, thanks. I appreciate it.'

When he rang off, John didn't feel any better. Her dad was vague and he seemed to be saying that he wouldn't help unless she brought the subject up herself. What use was that to anyone?

He left work, wondering what would happen when he got home. Upon his return, she appeared to have everything under control.

'How's AJ?'

'Fine. I'd say he's over that bug, thank God. Eating like a horse again.'

'Great. Been anywhere today?'

'Yes, took him to the park and shopping – he slept while I walked around the shops, got me a new skirt and a top.'

'Oh good, you must show me afterwards.'

'I will, John. Can you pop through and see how the dinner's going? Should be ready.'

'Sure. If it is, I'll dish up, shall I? You look as if you're done with him.'

'Another five minutes and I've finished.'

'OK. I'll bring the plates in.'

They made small talk during dinner. Angie didn't mention adoption; perhaps she hadn't meant what she said, or had just been letting off steam. He breathed an inward sigh of relief.

'Fancy going out this weekend? The forecast is nice. We could go for a walk by the river at Liverton, have fish and chips for lunch and take a look round the shops. What do you say?'

She thought for a moment and said. 'Yes, if we could find someone to babysit.'

'Don't you want to take him with us? It'd be good for him to be out in the fresh air.'

'He'll be in the way. And what if he's sick or something?'

'I don't believe this. We're not together as a family if he's not there.'

'What's the point? He won't know where we are. You're living with your head in the clouds, John. The painful reality is he'll spoil everything until he's older.'

'I don't agree. We can't leave him out – I want to watch him grow up. I'm fascinated. If he can't come, I won't go.'

'Don't bite my head off. This isn't just about what you want. We need to have quality time alone together or we'll end up drifting apart.'

'Yes, but not yet. He's only a few weeks old and you want to palm him off on someone else. Makes no sense.'

'It makes perfect sense. We need a life of our own without him. And I need a break. It's all right for you, you're not here, you only have him at nights and weekends while I'm with him twenty-four hours a day, seven days a week. It's bound to get tiresome. This is too much for me, I'm going insane.'

'Come on, Angie. He needs his parents with him.'

'That's why he has to be put up for adoption. If I'm there, he'll not be in a happy environment. Isn't it better for him to live with parents who can love and cherish him?'

'I'm not discussing this anymore. I won't have him adopted. I'll bring him up on my own, if I have to. Mum and Dad will support me if I ask them.'

'You've got this worked out, haven't you? Plotting and planning behind my back. Trying to push me out because I have a few problems. You are so self-centred, you make me sick. I'll walk out, John. Let's see how you get on then, shall we? You'll soon think the same as me.'

He shook his head, picked up AJ and went upstairs, his whole life in turmoil. Why was Angie doing this to him?

Chapter 29

Angie was busy on the computer, making a list of adoption agencies she intended ringing on Monday morning. Later, in bed, while John slept and snored like a pig, she lay awake, unable to keep still. She got up and went downstairs; after lying on the settee for a couple of minutes, she had to walk around the room, trying to rid herself of the awful anxious feelings in her head. She wanted a drink but there was no alcohol. She considered taking an extra tablet, but decided against it for fear of turning into a zombie.

In frustration she made for the kitchen and opened the cupboards and drawers, pulling out the contents, smashing crockery, throwing things here, there and everywhere. Glasses smashed into tiny pieces. Tins were thrown askew and the contents of the fridge were strewn around. She laughed; causing such destruction made the adrenaline surge through her and gave her a high.

John appeared in the doorway. 'Angie! What the hell are you doing?'

'Having a smashing time,' she giggled.

'This isn't funny. Have you gone off your head, darling? Stop this now, you hear me?'

Giving out his orders as usual. She glared at him and threw a box of eggs on the floor. He grabbed her by the arm and tried to manhandle her out of the kitchen. But Angie, livid, managed to pull her hand free and punched him in the face, a broken china cup in her hand. She jabbed it into his nose. Blood spurted everywhere, and he cried out in pain. When he put his hand to his nose and moved it away, it was covered in blood.

'Oh my God, look what you've done!' He coughed and took out a handkerchief, dabbed the wound.

'Good – you deserve it.' She walked out.

Back upstairs, AJ was crying. Hungry, no doubt. She had to get his bottle but John was still in the kitchen. He had his back to her, obviously dealing with his bloody nose. The fridge door was still open; she took a feed out and dropped it into a jug of warm water.

Within half an hour she'd fed and changed AJ and got him to sleep again. Even though she loathed this chore, she was pleased with herself for doing it without a hitch. John was still in the kitchen, clearing up the carnage, but why should she help? He'd provoked her to such an extent that she couldn't stop herself from lashing out. His fault, not hers.

<><><>

After a difficult weekend, John woke on Monday morning exhausted but determined to go to work. He didn't want to face Angie across the breakfast table. No, he'd talk to her tonight.

What worried him was the sight of his nose. Swollen around his eyes and scabbed on the top – everyone was bound to notice. Of course, he couldn't tell the truth. But they would either ask or wonder.

Sarah, in early as usual, was first. He wore his glasses but although they helped, it was still noticeable.

'Hey, what happened to you?' she asked, aghast.

'Don't ask.'

'But I am asking. Have you been in a fight? Or did someone attack you, or what?'

'Yes, sort of. I was in the fish and chip shop and this guy accused me of jumping the queue and when I said I wasn't, he punched me. Didn't half hurt, I can tell you. And then he scarpered. Thought he'd broken my nose, but I think it's just bruised.'

She narrowed her eyes. 'That sounds like a tall story to me.'

'Why? It's the truth.'

'No, it isn't. This is you trying to protect Angie. Why don't you admit it?'

John hesitated for a few seconds. 'OK, but I won't go into details.'

'Why did you come in, John?'

'I'm fine. It only hurts when I touch it.'

The lads ribbed him a little, but he took in in good heart.

The work was routine after that, and nothing he couldn't handle. Good job too, after the weekend he'd had with Angie. Could he face another day like that?

<><><>

When Angie got up and went downstairs, there was no sign of John – he must have left for work already. He was a star in some ways, having cleaned up the mess from her tantrum for instance, but not in any others that were important to her. Perhaps it was good they hadn't spoken, or she may have faced another row.

And she had AJ to deal with. Eight o'clock, and he wasn't yet awake. Very impressive. But not impressive enough.

She took out the final bottle and went back upstairs. No doubt he would wake soon, but at least this time he allowed her to wash and dress and do her hair.

By ten o'clock she had him ready. She ate toast and marmalade and had a coffee, then put on her coat, strapped AJ in the back seat and drove off.

She knew straightway where she was going – without invitation. But it was a risk worth taking. The journey was uneventful, the roads quiet; seeing a car on the drive of the impressive detached house, she breathed out with relief.

She took AJ out in his car seat and rang the bell. They were about to get a shock. Susan answered, her eyes widening at the sight of Angie standing there with the baby.

A slight smile came on her face. 'Oh, what a lovely surprise! Won't you come in, love? We love seeing AJ?'

'Wondered if you'd mind having him an hour or so. I arranged to meet my pals from work at lunchtime as one of them is leaving, and I thought I'd have a look around the shops first. Do you mind? He's been fed and changed. I've brought fresh clothes, nappies and two bottles of his milk – keep them in the fridge. I'll bring in the wheels too, for when he needs a nap.'

'Of course, we'd be delighted to. Shall I take him off your hands while you fetch everything in?'

'Yes – thanks. Won't be a minute.'

She put the pram and baby bag inside the door as Susan came into the hall.

'Sure, you won't stop for a drink?'

'No, no, thanks, must dash. Won't be long.'

'All right, we'll speak later.'

'Yes. Bye.'

Before John's mum could speak further, Angie got into the car and drove off at high speed.

Heaving with relief, she drove towards home, all the time fearful John might ring. Thankfully, he didn't. She walked inside and straight upstairs.

Within an hour she had everything packed, ready to go.

She shed a tear as she locked the front door. John was her soulmate but wasn't there for her when she needed him. Only one man had always put her first - her dad. She didn't even phone him, because she knew he'd welcome her with open arms.

<><><>

At three o'clock John got a phone call. His mum.

'John, I don't know if you're aware, but Angie dropped off little AJ with us this morning. She asked if we'd look after him while she went out with colleagues from work. Only time is moving on and she still hasn't come back for him. I was just worried something might have happened to her.'

'Oh, I see. No, I had no idea. Have you tried phoning her?'

'Yes, but her phone appears to be switched off.'

'What about her dad? She sometimes goes over there.'

'No reply there either.'

'I don't know what to say, then. She could be anywhere; you know what it's like when girls get together. I'm sure she'll turn up. Are you all right to have him for a bit longer until she comes back? I mean, if it's a problem, I'll pick him up myself. I could come out of work early if need be.'

'We're fine, and we haven't got to go anywhere, but she only left two feeds, which we've used. His next one is due in about an hour.'

'Tried ringing the house?'

'Yes – no reply from there, either.'

'Very strange. All right, Mum, if she isn't there within the next hour, ring me and I'll come to you. I'll buy another box of his milk on the way, all right?'

'I was amazed when she appeared at the door with AJ. She very rarely comes here on her own,'

'Probably fed up of being stuck in the house, I should think. I told her to join a baby group, but she didn't seem that keen.'

'Has she been all right? She looked a little upset when she was here. Wouldn't even have a cup of tea.'

'She's still depressed, but no more than normal. Thanks for letting me know. I'll be in touch.'

He wiped his brow, not knowing what to think. She was unstable, sure, but why had she left AJ with his mum and dad? His heart skipped a beat – this was all he needed.

Just over an hour later, he rang his mum again; still not a word from Angie.

He went in to see his boss.

'Sorry to be a pain, Stu, but I need to leave early. Angie's left the baby with my mum and dad, but she hasn't come back for him and we don't know where she is. I'll have to fetch him.'

'That's odd. Of course, mate, you go – hope nothing bad has happened to Angie. Any problems, ring me at home. You've got my number, haven't you?'

'Yeah. Thanks, Stu, I appreciate it.'

John rushed out as Sarah and the others gaped at him, puzzled. He would tell them tomorrow.

Luckily, his parents didn't live far away; it was only a fifteen-minute journey in the car. He was there in twelve. No other car stood on the drive besides their own, so Angie still hadn't returned, by the look of things. He ran up to the front door, adrenaline pumping through him.

'Has she come back yet?'

'No, not a word.'

'Is AJ all right?'

'Yes, he's fine. Your dad's got him. What happened to your nose?'

'Don't ask. It's a long story.'

He rushed through to find his dad. AJ lay contentedly in George's arms; John came over and waggled his fingers at him. He wriggled his little arms in response, which brought a smile to John's face.

John pulled out his mobile and tried his home landline. Nothing. And when he rang her dad's number again, no reply.

'I don't know what to do.'

'Why don't you call the police or Dexford hospital? I can't imagine she's been hurt, but you never know,' Susan said.

'Not yet, Mum. Best try to keep calm – it's only been six hours. She might still be celebrating with her friends, who knows? But I'm sure she'll have an explanation for me.'

'Let's hope so,' his dad said.

'We'd better get going. If she comes back here, tell her I've taken AJ home.'

'Sure you don't want to wait for her, then you could go home together?'

'No, I'm not waiting any longer. I can't believe she'd be so irresponsible, not to come back when she said. I'll speak to her.'

'John, don't have a row with her. She deserves to let her hair down once in a while, especially when she's been so down about everything. And we didn't mind looking after him – quite the opposite, in fact.'

'If she has a feasible explanation, there won't be a row. Right now, I'll just be glad to have her back. Can't tell you what a strain this is on me.'

'We'll ring straight away if she comes here. I promise.'

'Thanks, I'll see you later.'

As he drove, he wondered if she'd be home when he got there. He didn't know what he'd do if she wasn't.

Chapter 30

'Hallo, Angie. This is a surprise. Where's AJ?' her dad said.

'Oh, he's with John's parents. Don't worry, he's in capable hands.'

'OK, you'd better come in. Want a drink? Sit yourself down.'

'Just a coffee, thanks, Dad.'

Five minutes later he returned with the drinks. She hoped he hadn't put a drop of rum in, as she needed to keep a clear head. But he had.

She took a sip and then left it by the armchair.

'Dad, I want to ask you something.'

Surprise came over his face. 'Go on.'

'Can I stay here with you for a while?'

'Eh? You mean move back in? But why?'

'Because John and the baby are driving me mental.'

'Pardon?'

'Because ... looking after AJ is just too much for me. I've tried my hardest, but it's no good.'

He snorted. 'I never imagined a baby was such hard work. Feed him, change his nappy and put him to sleep. Even I could do that.'

'It's not that easy. I have to care for him twenty-four hours a day. And I'm not bonding very well and ... I resent him spoiling my life. But when John takes over, he really gels with him. And he doesn't understand why I'm like I am. He's not sympathetic to my needs. When I asked go back to work early, he got so mad. I've had enough, Dad, I had to leave. You're the only person I can turn to now.'

'Hey, come here.'

She moved to him, went into his arms. Cried and felt safe there, as she did after her mother had died.

'Everything will be fine. You just need some breathing space to get yourself together again.'

'But I'm not cut out to be a mum.'

'That's not for me to judge. As I've said before, there'll always be a home here for you. Stay as long as you like. But ask yourself, do you really want to live with your old dad? I mean you're young, your whole life is still ahead of you. In the long run it won't do you any good – much as I wish that wasn't true.'

'I need you, Dad. You look after me better than anybody.'

'Yes, but that won't always be the case. And what then?'

'I'd die without you.'

'You wouldn't. Life moves on. You must take care of yourself, love. I won't be here forever.'

'If I hadn't left home, this wouldn't have happened. John could have had a baby with someone else. I had a new job, Dad, but AJ was ill and I couldn't go. That would have made a difference, but the baby spoilt everything as usual.'

'So, what will you do with yourself if you stop here? You'll be bored out of your mind.'

'I won't, because without the baby I'll get a job. And in five months, I'll be working at the estate agent's again.'

Alan sighed. 'Well, it's a shame it's come to this, but I can't tell you what to do. No pressure, honestly. But does John know you've left him?'

'No, but he will do when he gets home and sees my stuff has gone.'

'Well, I'm not telling him. You can do that yourself. Want your old room?'

'Please.'

'I'd better get it ready for you – no one's used it since you left. I'll make your bed and air it up. Bring your stuff in.'

'Thanks, Dad.'

She put her suitcases on the bed and surveyed the room she'd lived in for over twenty years. Nothing had changed. The same wallpaper and paint, except it now needed a fresh coat. The flowered curtains were the same, too; she wondered when he'd last washed them.

Suddenly the phone rang. Alan looked at her. 'That's John. You get it.'

'No way. I'm not speaking to him.'

'Well, me neither.'

So, it rang and rang and finally stopped.

'You'll have to talk to him at some stage.'

'But not now.'

'I bet he's worried sick. Why don't you text him, at least tell him you're alive and well?'

'I will later.'

'Angie, it's cruel to keep him wondering.'

'All right, Dad, don't go on.'

She took out her phone from her handbag. There were more than a dozen messages, all from John and his parents. She typed a brief message to him: she was staying with friends, she said, until she got a place of her own. She deleted all the messages without reading them.

Then she unpacked and wondered how John was getting on with the baby. Not well, she guessed. How long before he got reinforcements in, in the form of his parents? They wouldn't miss her and neither would he once he had his helpmates.

<><><>

When John turned into their road, he expected to see Angie's car parked on the drive. But it wasn't there.

He carried AJ inside and put the pram in the living room. AJ had slept right through the journey, which was good, as John needed time to find out where Angie had gone. Downstairs looked exactly the same as when he'd left that 'morning; now for upstairs. As soon as he saw the open bedroom door, he knew the answer.

The wardrobes were open, as were the drawers by her bed. Most of her clothes and toiletries had vanished, along with jewellery and knick-knacks.

She'd done what she'd threatened. And he was devastated. Tears filled his eyes as he thought of AJ with no mother and himself without a wife.

He checked his phone again. She'd sent him a text to say she was alive and not hurt, but there was no indication of which friend she was staying with. He'd never find her, unless she wanted to be found.

Then he wondered if her dad knew where she was … although he guessed Alan would deny all knowledge of her whereabouts. He wasn't answering the phone, but Alan was his best hope. If not for baby AJ, he'd have paid him a visit. Maybe he should ring him again. But the man still wasn't answering his calls.

John shook his head in despair. He was no longer angry, only sorry for her. What a terrible plight she was in. But what could he do? He'd tried ringing and texting again, but her phone was switched off.

And now he had AJ to consider, too. Starting from tomorrow. For now, he'd ask his parents to have him but in the longer term – if it came to that – it would be too much for them.

But first things first: dinner. He didn't relish cooking or going down the chippy with AJ. He settled for a tin of soup and some bread.

Not long afterwards, AJ woke. After feeding and changing him, John held the baby close to his chest and felt the full force of his love for the boy. He looked forward to seeing him grow up and sharing in his life. If not for Angie leaving, he'd feel happy. But she wasn't here – and may never be again.

Best not to dwell on it.

He needed to ask his family about tomorrow and the rest of the week. He picked up the phone.

'Hallo, Dad.'

'Everything OK? Heard from Angie yet?'

'As a matter of fact, I did …'

'Oh, that's great news. How is she?'

'She sent a text saying she hates being a mum and needs to get away. But she doesn't say where she is, except she's with friends.'

'She's been through it. It's too much for her. Leave her be for now – she'll be back when she's good and ready. Be patient, son.'

'If I could just talk to her, I might convince her to come home.'

'Or you might make matters worse and you'll never see her again.'

'But what about AJ? I'll have to find a childminder or something. I don't know where to start.'

'No, you won't. We'll look after him for you. We've got lots of time on our hands, which we'd love to spend looking after our grandson. In fact, we'd be offended if you didn't accept our help.'

'I'll pay you the going rate.'

'Don't be ridiculous. We don't want paying. We want to look after him because he's our grandchild. Just tell us when you're bringing him over.'

John relaxed. They were falling over themselves to help him in his hour of need.

'You mean that?'

'I wouldn't offer if I didn't. And I'm speaking for your mum, too.'

'Thanks, Dad. It's a big help. OK, so I'll drop him off at half-seven. And I'll fetch him at six. God, that's an eternity, isn't it? Five days a week. I can't expect you to do that.'

'You can and you will.'

'It won't be for long. She'll be home soon, I hope.'

'Yes, with luck.'

'OK, see you in the morning. Thanks again, Dad.'

'Great stuff, son – we'll look forward to it.'

Once they'd gone, he was angry at Angie, for forcing him to have his parents mind his son while he was at work. He wanted to ring her but knew she wouldn't answer. Maybe that wasn't such a bad thing.

Chapter 31

Angie felt sad. The guilt and failure at being unable to be the wife John wanted played on her mind. But it was no use; she'd never cut it as a mother.

She realized her dad was watching her as she stared into space.

'Do you regret coming here?'

'No – not at all. I've let him down, but that's my own fault. I should have done what you said, then I wouldn't be in this mess. But I wanted to be a good wife and thought if I had his baby, we'd be happy. I thought I could manage. I was wrong.'

'Well, I'm not going to say I told you so, love. Why didn't you tell him the truth about how your mum died?'

'I thought I'd lose him if I did. When I got pregnant, I knew I'd made a terrible mistake. I've ruined his life as well as my own.'

'Yes, but now a child is involved. You'll always be his mother, but without getting John's agreement to an adoption, it won't happen. Perhaps John might meet someone else who'd take on AJ.'

Angie shuddered at this. 'That would be hard to take. I love John, and I can't bear the thought of him being with someone else – but I can't live with his child.'

'Then you have a big problem. Have you thought about starting afresh? Get as far away from them as possible. Move to a different part of the country.'

'But I'm happy here. It's where I work, where my friends are, where you live and where Mum is buried.'

'Then all I can do is to give you a roof over your head.'

'I'm not asking for any more than that, apart from your company and your advice.'

'OK, so we know where we stand. Want a bite to eat? I haven't forgotten how to cook. What do you say?'

'A cheese sandwich will do fine.'

'Coming up.'

'And go easy on the butter – my stomach is delicate.'

He nodded.

He did as she asked, but the bread was thick with butter. It made her smile.

'I can't promise to finish these.'

'Try your best. Oh, and here's a drink for you.'

'Thanks, Dad.' She took a sip and grimaced. 'Have you put a tot of whisky in this tea?'

'A small one. I'll make another one, if you don't want it.'

'No. Doesn't matter.'

He sat beside her, put his arm around her shoulder and squeezed.

'It feels good to be here. Only wish it was under different circumstances.'

He nodded, then took a gulp of his drink. He cleared his throat. 'Angie, I'm sorry to bring this up, but there's something I have to tell you.'

'Pardon?' She frowned.

'Ever since your mum died and you left home, I've been on my own. I've mourned for her ever since, but now I need to start living again. I have needs, Angie, the same as everyone else.' He coughed again. 'Thing is, love, I've met someone. We get on well and I've been thinking about asking her to move in. Right now she stays over two nights a week ...'

Angie slammed her mug down. 'You kept that quiet, didn't you? What about Mum? You've always said she was the only one for you!'

'I'm not cheating on your mother. How can you say that? I've grieved for too long – it's time to move on. I'm only fifty and I don't want to spend another twenty or thirty years alone. I deserve a little happiness, wouldn't you agree?'

'I suppose,' she conceded.

'She's coming over tonight. We're going out for a meal and then she's staying the night. Why not come along? It'd be good for you two to meet.'

'You must be joking. I don't like playing gooseberry. It's too soon to do that stuff yet. No, you go on your date – and if she stays over, I'll lock myself in my room until morning.'

'Don't be ridiculous, Angie. I've wanted to introduce you to her for ages, but what with AJ coming on the scene, and you being ill, I held off. But now you're set to stay here, it's the perfect opportunity. Tell you what: we'll stay in instead – I'll open a bottle of wine so you can chill out.'

'Don't you dare tell her about me and John. She'll turn her nose up at me and she'll just judge me when she hasn't got the facts in front of her.'

'She won't. She not like that. You'll be surprised how nice she is. Actually, she's a psychiatrist – that's what she's gets paid for, to talk to people and help them with their problems.'

Angie spluttered into her tea. She needed to avoid this woman at all costs.

<><><>

Two hours later, the doorbell rang. For a second, she feared it was John.

Alan leapt up from his seat. 'That'll be her!'

'Oh God, I'll go upstairs.'

'No, you won't. Please let me at least introduce her.'

'Dad … no.' Tears came into her eyes, and she had the urge to run away again. But she was trapped.

Her dad went out to answer the door. They didn't come in straight-away, and Angie could hear them talking. Her hands shook.

The attractive woman behind him when he came in had short black hair and green eyes. Plump, she wore jeans and a smart top and looked about fifty. She smiled at Angie and held out her hand.

'Hallo, Angie. How lovely to meet you. I'm Rachel.'

'Hallo.'

'Mind if I sit by you?'

'No.'

'I'll get us a drink, shall I?' Alan said.

Angie studied Rachel's face. 'So. You're dad's girlfriend.'

'I am, and you're his beautiful daughter.'

'Not sure about the beautiful bit.'

'You look a lot like your mum.'

'Yes. When people see photos of me now and mum when she was my age, they say we're very much alike.'

'Yes, that's very true.'

'I had no idea Dad was seeing someone. Never thought he'd be going on dates again.'

Rachel laughed. 'Yes, you get a bit out of practice. But we're both in a similar position. I lost my husband three years ago – a heart attack – so your dad and I had something in common from the start. He made me laugh for the first time in ages.'

She smiled. 'Yes, he is funny when he wants to be. A bit accident-prone, too, I think you'll find.'

'I've noticed.' Rachel smiled.

Alan came in carrying a bottle of sparkling white wine, which he put on the table. He filled three glasses to the brim.

Rachel drunk half of hers immediately. 'Sorry, I'm a bit nervous,' she said.

'Be careful, it might go straight to your head,' Alan said.

'That's what I'm hoping for,' she giggled.

'Angie's staying with me for a few days, aren't you, love?'

'For as long as you'll have me.'

'That's great,' Rachel said. 'I'd love us to be friends. I never had a daughter, only two sons, so I never had the chance for a bit of girly talk. It gets boring in a house of men where the only conversation is football, cricket and rugby. Can't understand what the attraction is, but I can leave all that talk to your dad now!'

'Dad, since when did you ever talk sport?'

'I do when I'm with Rachel's sons.'

'Trying to get your feet under the table?' Angie teased.

His face turned pink. 'I do like football actually.'

'Well, you're a dark horse, aren't you? That's a side of you I never knew about.'

The conversation continued in a similar vein for the rest of the evening. Pleasantries and small talk, so as not to offend. Rachel seemed a nice enough woman; likeable, but she'd never take the place of Marion.

At ten o'clock, Rachel looked at her watch. 'Well, I'd better go. Work in the morning.'

'But …'

'Sorry – another time, Alan.'

'Don't leave on account of me. This is the twenty-first century, after all.'

'No, Angie, it's fine. You don't want a strange lady sharing your father's bed. When you're a bit more used to the idea, I might change my mind.'

'OK – it's your choice. Nice meeting you, Rachel. If you make my dad happy, I'm happy too.'

'I hope I do. And he makes me laugh. I'll see you again, Angie. I'm so glad to have met you.'

She gave Angie a peck on the cheek.

Once she'd gone, Alan had a silly smile on his face.

'That went rather well, didn't it?'

'Maybe, maybe not. I felt pretty uncomfortable.'

'Yes, we all were, but you've only just met. Did you like her, though?'

'It's too early to say. You've done all right for yourself, Dad. Hope it works out for you.'

'Thanks, love, that means everything. Hope you and John find a way around your problems, too.'

'That's not likely, but I guess it's the thought that counts.'

Angie felt strange sleeping in the bed she'd slept in for all but the last five years. It was nice to be home, but she missed John.

<><><>

When John got into work, he looked for Stuart, to let the man know the state of his home life, but there was no sign of him. As he walked to his desk, he saw Sarah.

'Hi, John, how's it going?'

John shrugged. 'Could be better.'

'Things still not going well?'

'That's an understatement.'

'Oh, and why's that?'

He wasn't sure about telling her but his need to confide in someone was too great to resist.

'What are you doing lunchtime?'

'Nothing much. Or at least I've got nothing planned.'

'Come across to the pub, then, and I'll explain. Hope you're a good listener.'

'I am. And I'm flattered you've put your trust in me.'

'See you at one o'clock, then.'

'Sure thing, John. Chin up, eh?'

Out of the corner of his eye, he saw Stuart walk in.

'Stuart, can you spare me a minute, please?'

'Yeah, sure. Take a seat.'

John closed the door behind him. Stuart took off his coat and sat opposite him.

'How are you doing, mate? Has your wife turned up?'

'In a manner of speaking. No idea where she is, but she sent me a text.'

'I feel for you, John – so soon after the baby, too. If we can help, please let me know.'

'As a matter of fact, I do have one small request. My parents will be looking after my son while I'm at work. I wondered if I could come in later – say 9.30 – and leave earlier at 4.30? I'll work my lunch to make up the time.'

'Not a problem with that but I'm concerned you're having no lunch. Promise me you'll take at least fifteen minutes – we all need a break.'

'All right, I promise. Hopefully it's only for a few weeks, until I make more permanent arrangements for AJ. Although my parents will look after him for now, as they're in their sixties I don't want them to do it for too long.'

'OK, mate, it's up to you.'

'Can we start tomorrow?'

'Sure, I don't see why not. Keep me informed of any more developments.'

'Of course.'

'Good luck, John, I hope Angie sorts out her problems.'

'Thanks for your support, Stu, it means a lot.'

John left the office, not motivated at all. But he had a family to keep, and needed the money.

At one, after phoning his parents about AJ, he caught sight of Sarah coming towards him.

'You still want that drink?' she asked.

'Yeah – actually, I need more than one, but I don't want to get into trouble.'

She laughed.

The pub was only across the road.

'What can I get you to drink?'

She thought for a moment. 'Just a Coke, please.'

'How about food?'

'A burger and chips.'

'These are on me.'

'There's no need, John.'

'There is, since I need your shoulder to cry on.'

She smiled. 'I've got a few spare tissues handy.'

'Thanks.'

Sarah found a table towards the rear of the room while John ordered the food and brought the drinks to their table.

'There you go,' he said, sitting down opposite her.

He had a pint of lager, half of which he drank at once. 'God, was I thirsty,' he said.

'Hey, watch how you're drinking that. Don't think I can carry you back to work!'

'Don't worry, I'm only having the one. I'm not that stupid.'

'So, what's going on with you and Angie?'

'She left the baby with Mum and Dad and did a bunk. And then sent me a text message saying she couldn't carry on and needed time to herself, and not to contact her. She's gone to live with some friends or maybe her dad – I'm not sure which. It's a big blow.'

'That's so sad. Lots of women suffer before and after pregnancy, but it feels like she's suffered more than most. I'm sure things will improve, though.'

'I don't know. Right from when she found out she was pregnant it's been a nightmare. The morning sickness lasted the whole nine months and she ended up in hospital with it, remember? And since AJ was born, she's never taken any interest in him. She said she wanted to go back to work to get out of the house, but they wouldn't let her because they'd already set someone on for the six months. And when she couldn't find a temporary job, she wanted me to agree to … to have the baby adopted.'

John's eyes filled with tears. Sarah squeezed his hand across the table.

'Come on, John. That's terrible, of course, but I reckon this is just because she's sick. I sure she'll be back to normal before you know it. She'll soon realise what she's missing, you can bet on it.'

'I'm not so sure. She went to the doctor, but refused to take any more antidepressants than she's been prescribed. And … and she's been violent with me. She did this to my nose, by whacking me with a broken mug. She's hit me more than once, and she trashed our kitchen.

Every cup, plate, saucer and glass smashed to bits. She's ranted and raved at me over the most trivial of things. I can't fight back, Sarah, she's a woman. I'm at my wits' end.'

'Oh my God, John, that's awful. I can't believe she'd do these things – I mean, whenever we're out together, she's lovely, friendly and funny. I feel for you.' She gasped and clapped a hand to her mouth. 'She's never harmed the baby, has she?'

'I feared that, too, but she hasn't. Although she has no interest in him, she's always done what she needs to do for him.'

'Deep down, she loves him, I'm certain. All this violence and anger is probably just a cry for help.'

'But I'm doing my best. Whenever I'm there, I do the chores. She only does stuff when I'm not there. What else can I do to help her? I've done my best – can't do any more.'

'Do you ever go out together?'

'Sure, before she got pregnant. But since then … rarely, because she was ill, and then AJ was born …'

'That's so sad – you always seemed like the perfect couple. AJ should have been the icing on the cake, shouldn't he?'

'That's what I thought, yes.'

Sarah noticed tears welling in his eyes and decided to steer the conversation in a more practical direction. 'So, what will you do with the baby when you're at work?'

'Mum and Dad are minding him, but five days a week is a lot to ask. They're both in their sixties – in good health, but at their age, you never know what might happen. I'll hire a nanny or a childminder, but that option doesn't sit well with me.'

'Lots of people do it, John.'

'I suppose so. But it will be hard for me to bring him up on my own.'

'At least you've got him. What if she'd taken him with her? Who knows how often you'd see him? Be grateful for that, John.'

'Yeah, you're right. If I lost him, I'd be devastated.'

'As I've said, she'll come home. She'll soon get fed up of staying with her friend and since she's not working, she'll be bored to death.'

'When you say it like that, I feel better. I always said you'd make a perfect counsellor.'

'Funny you should say that ...'

'Hey, get off with you. Sarah, you won't say a word, will you? Not even my parents know what's been going on. It's not nice – it's taken a lot of courage to speak to you. Not sure I could confide in anyone else, even Stuart.'

'I'm flattered you chose me. Wonder what I've done to deserve it?'

'You're a good friend. One of the best, Sarah, and I don't say that lightly.' He began to cry again.

'Hey, John, come on now. Pull yourself together for little AJ. He needs you now, more than ever. You ought to see the doctor yourself if you're that low.'

'Yeah, I might do that.'

'First thing in the morning.'

'Err ... Yes. I'll ring the doctor's when I get home.'

The food came and while Sarah wolfed her food, John found he wasn't hungry.

'You not eating?'

'Not hungry. I've lost my appetite.'

'If you don't want your chips, I'll eat them – I'm starving.'

'Help yourself.'

A few minutes later, John glanced at his watch. 'Time to go back.'

'Yes, unfortunately. That burger was lovely. We must come here more often. Maybe invite the other guys, too.'

'Yes, but not to talk about my problems. We keep this to ourselves.'

'If you say so. And John – stop worrying. Give her time and she'll come running back,' she said, squeezing his arm.

'That's what I keep telling myself.'

'Why don't you bring AJ around to mine one night? I'd love to get acquainted with him.'

'Oh, that's kind. Won't your fella mind?'

She rolled her eyes. 'Nah. He's out twice a week, football training. I get cheesed off on my own in front of the telly.'

'Make sure he's OK about it first.'

'I will.'

Back at work, John sensed the others were looking at them. He wondered if he'd done the right thing by confiding in her.

Chapter 32

The following morning, Angie woke early, having heard her dad snoring away, as loudly as ever, in the next room. Dawn was fast approaching as she looked out of the window. The sky was blue without a cloud in sight; another fine day was coming. Pity this didn't make her feel any better. The appearance of Rachel on the scene had knocked the shine off her plans.

Depressed, she sat in the living room watching breakfast TV, a bowl of cereal on her lap. Her plan to stay with her dad had gone up in smoke. She knew she had no right to spoil his relationship, even though she didn't approve. He'd be disappointed, but at least he had Rachel.

He came downstairs, in jeans and an old T-shirt, obviously planning to spend the day in his shed, where he restored old furniture. He made a fair amount of money from it, as he was highly skilled; Angie had seen him in action and was in awe of his talent.

'You're up early, Angie. Couldn't you sleep?'

'I slept for a bit, but I woke up at four. Had a bad dream – although you snoring didn't help.'

'Oh dear – sorry, love. I'll stick a peg on my nose in future.'

'You haven't changed. It's like a pneumatic drill.'

He smiled, his face flushing. 'That's what Rachel says, too.'

'I'm not surprised.'

'If you want breakfast, there's plenty of stuff in the cupboards. The fridge and freezer are well stocked too, although I might need to go to the supermarket soon now you're here.'

'Wanted to talk to you about that.'

'Sure. Listen, I don't need any money off you. Business is booming, I have more work than I can handle.'

'No, it's not that ... Dad, I can't stay here now Rachel is on the scene.'

'Oh, love, honestly, she isn't put out. She likes you. You don't have to go. Look, I know I tried to talk you out of staying with me in the first place, but I've kind of got used to having you around now. Why not wait until you've sorted yourself out? You'll be so lonely living on your own.'

She shook her head. 'No, Dad. Rachel isn't Mum, is she? We'd all be uncomfortable with the arrangement – it's only right I look for somewhere else. I was pondering over it last night. And it's not only that; for as long as I'm in the same town as John, we might bump into each other. I can't face seeing him and the baby. I'm going to look for a job somewhere else.'

'I don't think there's any need for that, love. Why not find a flat close to us, so you can pop in and we'll come to you as well. Do you really want to be on your own, with no one to turn to? That won't be good for you, especially right now, when you're not at your best. You need someone around to support you.'

She groaned. 'Dad, I hear what you're saying but I'll do as I see fit. Why did you wait until yesterday to tell me about Rachel? If you'd told me earlier, you'd have saved us both this upset.'

'I never dreamed you'd come home, so I didn't think you needed to meet her, but now everything's changed. We haven't decided what we want in the future. She stays over sometimes, but she went through hell when her husband died, and she wants to tread carefully this time. We get on well – but it's early days yet. But I want you to share in our happiness.'

'And I will, but not by living here. I'm sorry, Dad. My mind's made up.'

'And what will you do about John and baby AJ? I bet they both miss you.'

'I doubt that very much. John is sick of me and my tantrums while AJ is too young to understand.'

'You'd be surprised. I remember when you were a baby, whenever your mum came into the room, you used to stop crying. That was after only a few weeks.'

'I can't talk about that any more, Dad. I'll stay here until I find a place of my own, though.'

'OK, but I intend making the most of you while you are here. Let's have some quality time together – what do you say?'

'Yes, why not, but remember I'll be out looking for another job and a place to live too.'

'But not all day.'

'No, I hope not.'

A delighted smile spread across his face 'Good. Anyway, I'd better get on. I'll have a spot of breakfast and then I'm off to my workshop until lunchtime. I'm restoring a George IV walnut coffee table. It was in a right old state but now it looks like new. Come and have a peek when you've got a spare few minutes.'

'I will,' she said. 'Oh, and Dad? Do you have a computer? I left mine at John's.'

'I do, but it's old. Under the telly. I'll give you the user name and the password.'

'Thanks, Dad, you're a star.'

Once he'd gone, she searched for estate agents within a thirty-mile radius of Dexford; there were around twenty hits. She made a list of names, addresses and email addresses, then drafted a letter. She had her CV saved online, thankfully. If employers read this, she'd be sure to have a chance of a job.

<><><>

On the way home from work, John made a detour to Alan's house. As soon as he turned into the street, he saw her car – just as he'd expected, she wasn't with friends after all. And then, as he drove by, she came out and got into her car. He put his foot down hard on the accelerator. If she'd looked up at the sound of screeching tyres, she would have seen him – but she didn't.

What should he do now he knew the truth? If he wanted her back, he'd need to tread carefully.

He arrived at his parents' house only five minutes later than he intended. He could always say he'd been held up in traffic.

Although he had a key, he rang the bell to save any embarrassment.

His dad opened the door. 'Welcome to the madhouse.'

'Has he been all right?'

'Yes, as good as gold. Eating, sleeping and pooing to his heart's content.'

That raised a smile on John's face and as he followed George inside, he saw baby AJ in his mother's arms.

'Glad you're enjoying yourselves,' he said.

'We'd forgotten what it's like to have a baby in the family again,' she said.

'That's lovely. But much as I love you having him, I wish his mum was with him instead.'

'You've heard nothing, then?'

'Just a text message saying she needed some space and for me to leave her alone. I know she's at her dad's. Maybe I should phone him, see if he's willing to help.'

'Good idea,' Susan said.

'But I can't see him wanting to cooperate. Remember, Angie's his little girl.'

'Want to stay for tea?'

'No, no, you've done enough today.'

Susan shook her head in protest. 'John, he hasn't been any trouble, and we've got plenty of food. You're welcome to share it with us.'

John thought about returning to an empty house and having to cook his tea.

'OK, you've convinced me, but only as a one-off, seeing as you're having him every day until Friday.'

After eating, John didn't fancy going home yet, so he stayed a while longer until AJ's bedtime approached.

'Thank you for everything, Mum, Dad.'

They both hugged him and kissed AJ. At home, he kept wondering what Angie was up to. Did she regret leaving them? Would she realise her mistake?

<><><>

He'd just got up on Saturday morning when his mobile rang. He jumped, thinking it might be Angie. But no – to his amazement, Sarah was on the line. Strange for her to phone now.

'Hi John, how you doing?'

'Good, thanks, and you?'

'I'm OK. Listen, Jack's at football this afternoon, so I'm at a loose end. If you're free, can I come and have a look at the baby?'

John shuddered. Although they'd talked of him visiting her, he never expected her to take him up on it. He began to wonder what was behind this; perhaps she wanted to lecture him about his life again, but she meant well. 'I'm shopping this morning, but I'll be free this afternoon. So, by all means drop in. Have you told Jack?'

'When I mentioned it, he just shrugged his shoulders. He's in another world with his football. I'm sure he loves that stupid game more than me. But never mind that. How does two o'clock sound?'

'Sounds fine. But AJ might be having a nap.'

'That doesn't matter, at least I'll get to see him. Until later, then.'

'Yes, can't wait.'

'Me neither.'

John's heart beat hard against his chest. This sounded a little sinister to him. But since she'd been his confidante, he couldn't exactly say no. Now he'd worry until she arrived; and what if Angie turned up? She'd think he was having an affair when nothing could be further from the truth.

All morning, Sarah remained on his mind and he was sure he'd forgotten half of what he needed at the supermarket. Still, he'd deal with that problem later.

After lunch, he put AJ in his pram and got him to sleep in ten minutes. The baby never ceased to amaze him by how good he was for his age. If only Angie could see how easy it could be.

John kept the TV on low and waited for Sarah's imminent arrival. He didn't have to wait long – one forty-five had her ringing the bell.

She beamed at him when he opened the door, and followed him into the living room.

'Is he asleep?'

'Yes, unfortunately for you. He's only had half an hour so far – usually he has an hour or two. Let me get you a drink.'

'Just a coffee, please. White, one sugar.'

'OK, coming up. Make yourself comfy. I won't be long.'

'Thanks, John.'

He sat on the sofa, and they sipped their drinks.

'Nice house, John. I'm impressed. You deserve this, though, because you've worked hard over the years. Couldn't happen to a nicer guy.'

'I wouldn't say that. I've done my best but sometimes I wonder what the point of it was, now Angie's gone.'

'That's not your fault, nor Angie's. She can't help being ill. Such a shame, she's missing out on so much.'

'Yeah, exactly.'

'All right if I have a look?'

'Be my guest.'

She walked across to the pram, where AJ was still fast asleep. 'Ah, he's lovely – looks just like his dad. So calm and at peace.'

'I'm glad he doesn't know what's going on behind the scenes. He'd be upset.'

'Yes, true. Maybe you should be thankful it's happened now instead of when he's older.'

'I could do without it happening at any time, but I get your meaning.'

'I can't wait to see him awake. He's making me broody, John.'

She came back and sat closer to him.

'I'm surprised you still don't have any kids of your own.'

She smiled ruefully. 'Well, Jack's not keen, even though he knows I want a baby. All he cares about is his stupid football.'

'You must keep badgering him. One of these days he might surprise you and give way.'

'You're wrong. He won't. I thought I felt the same when we got married, but it's true what they say about biological clocks. I've realised I really would love to have kids. But he still says no.'

'Well, you can still afford to wait.'

'Yes, but it would be so much better to do it now. If we hang on much longer, I'll be in my mid-thirties. His football is the sticking point – he lives and breathes it. Trains twice a week, plays on a Sunday, goes to matches most Saturdays and in midweek, home and away. We hardly see one another and he refuses to see that it's a problem.'

'Why not go with him sometimes? You might enjoy the odd match together.'

'Ugh. I hate football – twenty-two grown men kicking a ball around a football pitch is so boring. I'd prefer to watch paint dry. Then he watches it on the TV. My God, I see those stupid players in my sleep.'

'I must admit I love football, but not to that extent. Some men are fanatical.'

'It gets to me. No wonder it's putting a strain on our marriage.'

'Does he know that?'

'He does, but he doesn't care. Football will always come first with him.'

'There are worse things in life. At least he's still with you.'

'True, but if I'm not happy, he may as well not be there. It's hardly a fulfilling relationship. And he won't let me have a baby.'

John raised his eyebrows. He was about to speak again when AJ woke.

'I'd better get him out,' he said, standing up. He picked AJ up and held him close, feeling the tears pricking his eyes as love for the boy welled inside him. AJ calmed down and wriggled his arms and legs happily.

'He's boisterous, isn't he? Careful you don't drop him.'

'I won't, he's in safe hands.'

'I can see that.'

'Do me a favour and hold him while I make his feed up?'

'Oh, I'd be so honoured,' she said, taking him off John's hands.

At once AJ started to cry.

'Oh dear, what have I done now?'

'Nothing, he's just used to me, I suppose. He'll be the same with you, if you give him time.'

'Ah, he's so small and vulnerable. I could eat him.'

He laughed. 'I wouldn't advise it.'

When he came back, AJ was quiet and calm in Sarah's arms.

'Well, it seems you do have the knack, after all.'

'All I've done is to hold him and hum to him.'

'Ah that's it. You sing well, I could do with you when I'm trying to rock him to sleep. Fancy feeding him?' he said, holding out the bottle.

'Do you mind?'

'No, of course not. I need a rest.'

Sarah set about the task with vigour; he noticed how entranced she was with his son.

'Wish Angie was more like you; I'd be so much happier.'

'Wow, he has a strong suck. He's hungry,' she said, without looking at him. Within fifteen minutes he'd drunk the lot and was gurgling contentedly.

'Excellent work, Mrs Benson. You're hired.'

'Thank you, I'd be very pleased to take up your kind offer if I wasn't employed as an accountant.'

'That is a shame. Never mind, I suppose I'll have to get someone else. Unless … say if I offered you a wage well over the going rate?'

'Stop messing around, John, you're making me sad.' She waved a hand in front of her face, about to cry.

'God, we're a right pair, aren't we? I never realised you were as miserable as me.'

'I'm sorry, I shouldn't have come. I was afraid this might happen.'

'No, I'm glad you did come. I wanted to show you what a proud dad I am, even if his mum doesn't love him.'

'Oh, I'm sure she does – and when she's better, you'll find that out.'

'I'll believe that when I see it. Get him to sleep if you want. And then I can hear you sing again.'

'I'd love to.'

He sat and watched while she sang. She had a good voice, and got the baby to sleep again within ten minutes.

'Success!' he exclaimed.

'Ssh now, you'll wake him,' she said as she laid AJ in the pram. She stood waiting for a reaction, but none came.

As she turned, he saw her weeping and when she reached him, he held her close. She shuddered and he wept too.

Then moving away, they stared at each other for a moment. Without a conscious decision, they moved together and their lips touched.

John pulled his face away. 'This mustn't happen. It's not right or fair.'

Sarah looked aghast. 'My fault. I'm so sorry, I needed someone to comfort me. Jack isn't interested.'

'No, it's both of us. I felt the same too, after all the terrible days I've had with Angie. You're the only person who listens to me, who I'd trust with my life. And now I've blown it.'

'No. We all need someone, John, and if that someone's love isn't returned then we look elsewhere. Let's forget it happened, shall we?'

'I'll be honest, Sarah – I wanted you. And I still do. But I won't destroy two families. We'd both end up with nothing.'

She nodded, tucking her hair behind her ear. 'We have to stop.'

'Yes.'

'I'd better go before I do something I'll regret.'

He took hold of her hand, amazed at how much he wanted her. She pulled herself free. 'Bye, John. See you Monday.'

<><><>

Later that Saturday night, in bed, John started shaking. He'd never dreamed something like this would happen. As if he didn't have enough problems! He should have been stronger, stopped it before it had begun. Now it was too late, and he doubted their friendship could even survive. He shouldn't have taken her into his confidence. Maybe he should just ignore what had happened; carry on as before and hope for the best.

He felt so guilty, even though Angie had left him. Didn't this make him as bad as her, if not worse? As he gazed across at AJ sleeping in his cot, he wondered what he'd jeopardised with the kiss. His job? His life with AJ? If Angie found out, she'd go crazy and might try to get AJ off him in spite. Or maybe he was being ridiculous; Sarah wasn't a girl to tell tales or act maliciously, and she'd be risking her own relationship, too.

The next morning, he received a message from Sarah.

'Thanks for letting me come over and see your gorgeous son. I loved every minute I spent with him. I now realise what I'm missing. It makes me broody but still hope we can do it again soon. Love Sarah.'

At least she remained friendly. But he wanted more – and if she did too, could he resist? If he refused, he'd upset her. Dear God, what a nightmare. He had to answer her text or she'd suspect something was wrong. He chose his words carefully.

'My pleasure. Love to do it again but I fear that might be difficult with our present commitments. Love John.'

Chapter 33

Having spent half of Monday morning looking for jobs, Angie began scouring the internet for flats to rent. A few looked nice but most of them were plain and ordinary – and even those were expensive. She saved the details of some she liked for later as she wasn't sure where she'd be working yet. This depressed her, but she had no alternative.

At two o'clock, her dad came into the house, covered in dust and dirt. He smiled at her and sat on the armchair.

'How's it going, Dad?'

'Yeah, not too bad. I've sanded it down, now it needs varnishing.'

'Good. Love to see it when it's finished.'

'OK, I'll give you a shout. So, what have you been doing while I've been slaving away?'

'Nothing much. On the computer, searching for jobs and places to live.'

'Any luck?'

'I've applied for five at various estate agents. And looked for rented property in similar areas. But until I'm offered a post, there's no point in viewing any flats.'

'I still say you're making a big mistake moving further away. What's wrong with this area? I appreciate you're not staying here, but there must be accommodation closer to home that would allow you to keep your job.'

'Dad, I've told you. I'm leaving in case I bump into John and the baby – it'll make me ill again. And they won't let me back for five months anyway. I'm surplus to requirements now Bethany's got my job. It's about their fear of me having more babies, perish the thought.'

'Won't you consider going back to John?'

'No, not a cat in hell's chance. That part of my life has gone.'

'But what about AJ?'

'Dad, I'm not interested. You were the one trying to get me to abort him, I seem to remember.'

'Yes, well you know why.'

'Yes, but even if he gets it, he won't develop symptoms until he's much older. And I still might get it, too. How will I handle that after what happened to Mum?'

'Rachel's upset you're leaving on account of her.'

'I'm not. It's your future happiness that concerns me – I won't jeopardise that.'

'You're very obstinate.'

'You don't say. Now I'd be grateful if you'd shut up. I'm not changing my mind and the more you carry on, the more liable I am to leave before my time.'

'OK, I'll just get my sandwiches. Help yourself to anything from the fridge when you're hungry.'

During the afternoon, she delved further into flats that were vacant, making a list of those she liked and where they were situated. But as the time dragged on, she was at a loose end and in need of something to do. Her urge to go out was strong, but where to? Having been around Dexford so many times recently, she was loath to do that again.

She browsed the contacts on her phone, remembering friends she'd hung out with before John. She'd message a few, to find out what they were doing now. As she scanned down her list, she came across Emma Jenkins and her sister Nicki. They'd gone to Dexford College together and had loads of laughs. Lots of boys were after them and they used to love playing one off against another. She could text them ... Yes. Why not?

Angie was stunned when Emma phoned half an hour later.

'Angie, I didn't know you were around. I thought you were all settled down and married?'

'I am, but we're separated. I wondered if you fancied meeting up – unless you have other plans. Be like old times.'

'Well, as it happens, both me and Nicki are in between boyfriends. We still go to *Jeeves* nightclub at weekends … and we're both free tonight. Come out with us! There's lots to catch up on. You'd be surprised at the eventful lives we've led. You'll laugh, I promise you!'

'Yeah, I certainly feel like a bit of a laugh after what's happened. I need a good night out with my friends, you're all I've got left now.'

'Ah, that's nice. We'll make sure you have a good time, Angie. I'll hire a taxi and ask the driver to pick you up at ten o'clock, shall I?'

'You've made my day.'

'Until later on, then.'

<><><>

When she got off the phone, she yelped with joy. This was what she'd been lacking, and she intended making the most of it.

She washed her hair, put on her best turquoise dress, and did her make-up. Not until she came downstairs did her father suspect.

He looked up from the TV, narrowing his eyes at her. 'Why are you so dressed up at this time of night? Shouldn't you be getting ready for bed?'

'Oh, I forgot to tell you. I'm out clubbing tonight.'

'You? I thought you were a bit past that stage?'

'Dad, I'm only twenty-five.'

'And a married woman, too, with a baby.'

'For God's sake. You sound like John. We're not a couple anymore and I'm no longer a mother, either. So why shouldn't I go out for one night? I'm not after another man. All I want is a good time with my mates.'

'Angie, I can't stop you, and I wouldn't even try. You're your own woman, have been for a while. I could voice an opinion, but at the end of the day, the choice is yours.'

'Yes, Dad. I'll do what's best for me.'

Ten minutes later, a car horn beeped outside.

'That must be my taxi. Don't wait up, I'll be fine. I can take care of myself.'

'I'm sure you can.'

'I'll be with Emma and Nicki Jenkins. Remember them from my college days?'

'Oh, the sisters? Didn't you get into lots of scrapes with them?'

'One or two. But they're a laugh, and that's just what I need. Speak in the morning.'

He smiled.

It was raining outside, so she pulled up the collar of her coat. The door of the taxi opened, allowing her to get in without getting too wet. Emma and Nicki sat there, looking much the same as ever, and giggled as Angie flopped down beside them.

'Angie, great to see you,' Emma said, a smile on her face.

'Angie!' Nicki cried, hugging her old friend. 'How are you?'

'Oh, not too bad. All the better for seeing you two.'

'We've got loads to tell you – it'll make your toes curl.'

'I've a few tales myself,' Angie grinned.

Once inside *Jeeves*, they found themselves a table at the side of the room. Music boomed out; the dance floor was filled with revellers dancing to the beat.

Angie's hands were shaking; she hoped her friends hadn't noticed. She'd had two cocktails which did nothing to stem her panic. 'Why don't we go out on the dancefloor? Let's find out if we still have that magic touch.'

The three of them danced by each other, laughing and giggling, having fun, but Angie still felt light-headed and nervous. She needed another drink. At the bar by herself, she picked up her drink and caught sight of a man looking at her.

He leered at her as he took a sip of his pint. 'Hallo, pretty lady.'

Angie ignored him and made to walk to her friends. He grabbed hold of her arm. Alarm flooded through her veins.

'Hey, I'm talking to you! Don't ignore me, you ignorant bitch.'

'Please leave me alone.'

'Only trying to be civil. Think you're too good for the likes of me – well, you're not. Sure, you're a looker, but that doesn't give you the right to treat me like shit.'

'Let go of me!' Angie wrenched her arm away then, in desperation, she threw the contents of her drink over him. His eyes widened. 'You fucking cow,' he growled but before he could react further, she pulled back her hand and slapped him hard across the face. The man moaned, touching his now red cheek. Angie rushed off, losing herself among the throngs of people, shaking with anger and fear as the adrenaline kicked in.

She gasped in shock, certain someone must have seen what had happened. But it served the guy right.

But she hadn't got the drink she needed. She spotted two on an empty table; after gulping down what was left in the glasses, she giggled to herself at her own audacity.

Returning to where her friends were dancing, she smiled at them. Emma shouted in her ear. 'What's going on at the bar? Sounded like a fight?'

'Yeah, that's why I'm back so quickly. This girl slapped this guy's face right in front of everybody. I never got my drink.'

'What say we get out of here, if there's trouble. The *Groundhog* across the road, maybe?'

'Great idea, the night is young.'

By the time they'd got into the new club, she was a little drunk but despite this and her friends' constant chatter and high-pitched giggling, she felt miserable. The alcohol, the dancing, the looks from men; none of it made any difference to her state of mind.

'You all right?' Emma asked. 'You seem quiet. Is it that kerfuffle back at *Jeeves*?'

'No. It's just that you two are having a great time, while here's me so miserable. With nothing or no one. I'm a failure, pure and simple. What did I do to deserve this?'

'Angie, what's wrong? I thought you were happily married, with a big house, a good job and a wonderful husband,' Nicki said.

'It hasn't lasted. Oh, sure, I had all that and more, but it's gone. And I'm in a mess.'

'How do you mean?' Emma looked bewildered.

'He ran off with another woman and took our son with him.'

'He did *what*? But why?'

'That's what I keep asking myself. The bastard. The thing is, he became a househusband, because I earned more money than him. Well, while I was at work, slaving my guts out, he meets this slut at a mother and baby group, would you believe?'

'Wow, Angie, that's devastating,' Emma said. 'Have you tried to persuade him to come back?'

'I would if I could find him. He's vanished off the face of the earth and took our life savings with him. He could be anywhere.'

'How about the police? It's kidnapping, surely? They'll trace them.'

Angie shook her head. 'I had to move in with my dad, because I hate it in that great big house on my own.'

'Oh, Angie. If only we could help.'

'It's helped, being with you guys again. You've no idea how much I've missed you. I wish I'd never met the guy. What makes a man do that? I trusted him and look what I got in return. I'd love to throttle the bastard.' Angie finished her drink. 'Anyone want another one?'

'Hey, Angie, haven't you had enough? It won't change anything,' Nicki said.

'No, nowhere near. So, what's your poison?'

'I'm fine, thanks.'

Emma shook her head.

'Neither of you. OK, suit yourselves.'

Angie stood up but once she was on her feet, her head was spinning. As though on a boat in the roughest of seas, she collapsed to the ground.

<><><>

They were in the taxi. Angie knew of her friends' presence but her images of them were blurred. She had a vague memory of throwing up and she knew her stomach ached. They were talking to her, but she couldn't take it in. Each had an arm around her as she sobbed.

The taxi jolted to a halt. 'Come on, Angie, time to get out,' Nicki said.

'Mm,' she muttered as they dragged her from the car and up the drive to the front door. Emma rang the bell. A light flickered on upstairs, then the window opened.

'What's going on?' Angie's dad asked.

'Got Angie here. Sorry, but she's had too much to drink. Mind taking her off our hands?'

'No, not at all. Give me a minute.'

He came out and picked Angie up. 'Thanks for bringing her home. I'll get her to bed.'

He carried her upstairs, pushing the bedroom door open with his foot, and laid her on her side.

'You ought to be ashamed of yourself, getting in this state at your age. Best sleep it off, you'll get no sympathy from me.'

He slammed the door shut and left her to her incoherent mumbling and her tears.

Soon she slipped into a troubled sleep, a nightmare of when her mum had died. She saw the terrified look on her mum's face as she fell off the cliff. In the early hours, she woke, trembling, her head pounding as if a hammer kept on hitting it.

Her watch said five o'clock. She needed something to calm her. But not a drink as it would make her sick. And then she thought of the antidepressants the doctor had prescribed; they were in her toilet bag, in the bathroom. She fetched them and took two, to be on the safe side; one extra couldn't do any harm.

She went back to bed and went out like a light. When she woke again, she saw the sun shining through her bedroom window, and checked the clock on her bedside table. Eleven o'clock. She felt groggy and fought to keep her eyes open. Time to get up, she thought, still finding it hard to stay awake. In the bathroom, she splashed herself with cold water, which almost brought tears to her eyes.

Down in the kitchen, her dad sat sipping coffee. The smell made her gag.

'So, you're awake at last,' he said. 'Got a sore head, have you, after last night?'

'Something like that.'

'What possessed you to do such a stupid thing?'

'I don't know. I was depressed, and I thought going out with the girls might buck me up. When it didn't, I had a few more drinks – but they didn't help either.'

'You should know better.'

'Dad, stop getting onto me, will you? I feel bad enough.'

'OK, sorry. I should have been more tactful, I suppose.'

He went over to the kettle and switched it on. 'Like a drink? Something to eat?'

'No, I'm fine, thanks,' she said, soothing her brow with her hand. She didn't feel like talking to him right now. Wasn't it enough that she'd made a fool of herself in front of everybody?

<><><>

On Tuesday morning, John woke early with a jolt. He'd been dreaming of Sarah and Angie fighting over him; he had been unable to pull them apart. He couldn't stop thinking of Angie, wondering what she was doing. He'd still take her back, despite her tantrums; he still believed the old Angie he'd loved so much was in there somewhere. What if he'd let her go too easily? And now he'd done nothing about contacting her apart from texting, since she'd threatened him. If he rang her dad, would he let him speak to her? Surely he'd want them to stay together. But would he cooperate or side with his daughter?

During his morning break at work, he went outside, took out his mobile and pressed it to ring Alan's phone.

John waited with bated breath but after only six rings, he answered. 'Hallo?'

'Alan, this is John. Wondered if Angie's with you … and if so, could I speak to her?'

'Sorry John, she isn't.'

'Is she staying with you?'

'That's none of your business.'

'I presume you're aware of what's happened between us?'

'Yes, she told me.'

'Well, if she's not there, do you have a contact number?'

'I'm sorry, John. I can't give you any information without Angie's permission.'

'Oh, come on, Alan. This isn't good for anyone. A husband without his wife, a baby without his mother. I just want to bring her back to us. Please, Alan.'

'Look, whatever's going on between you has nothing to do with me. I'm not taking sides, nor will I interfere. I'll pass on a message for you, but nothing more. Then it's up to her.'

'Ask her to contact me so we can discuss a few things. She is living with you, isn't she? I saw her car parked outside your house.'

There was a silence that spoke volumes.

'What if I came knocking on your door, demanding to see her?'

'You do and I'll get the law onto you – and that's a promise.'

'Don't worry, I'd never do that. I realise she's unwell but if she just came home I'm sure it would aid her recovery.'

Alan was silent for another moment, and it raised John's hopes.

'All right John, I'll tell her what you said. If it's any consolation, I'd certainly be happy if you were together again. Bye.'

So, there was a glimmer of hope. But if she refused, what then? He didn't like to think about that.

<><><>

After some time, Angie finally looked up to see her dad staring at her, scratching the back of his head. 'Had a phone call earlier on while you were out of it. From John.'

She felt the colour drain from her face. 'Oh no.'

'Don't fret – he was fine, just worried about you. I didn't give anything away, but he asked if you'd contact him. He wants to talk about where you two go from here.'

'I'm not speaking to him. He'll only cry like a baby when I tell him I won't go back, so it's out of the question.'

'Send him a text or write him a letter, then – explain how things are and what you want.'

'How can I, when I have no idea myself?'

'Don't keep him hanging on. The poor man needs to know where he stands.'

'Hey, whose side are you on?

'No one's. I'm on the fence, the adjudicator trying to find an answer to this problem.'

'I had the solution, Dad, but he didn't listen. Adoption would have solved everything. But no, he wouldn't consider my feelings.'

'Darling, what father would give up his own son? He's grown to love him, as well you might expect.'

She tutted. 'The subject is closed. And if he rings again, or comes around here, or writes to me, there'll be trouble. I'll slam the door in his face. When I get a place of my own, you're not to tell him where I am.'

'So you're still going through with this? Because of Rachel?'

'Dad, haven't you got a workshop to go to? I'm sick of being in the same room as you. Yes, I'm going through with it, and I'll be glad to leave, with you nagging me all day long!'

Alan drank his coffee and ignored her outburst. Eventually he said, 'Don't fret, love – give me a few minutes and I'll be out of your hair for the rest of the day.'

But when he'd gone, tears flowed onto her cheeks. She regretted being so horrid – if only he'd stop slagging her off.

She decided to check her emails; there were three replies to job applications. One had no vacancies, the other two asked her to fill in their own specific online application forms. What a perfect way to pass the time.

She took over an hour to fill them in then, looking at her phone, she noticed a text from Emma and Nicki, asking if she was OK. How nice of them to be concerned. She sent a message saying how sorry she was for her behaviour and hoping they might forgive her, but didn't hold out any hope of a reply.

Up in her room, she tried to sleep.

A little later, she was woken by a gentle knock; her dad popped his head around the door with a smile.

'Are you all right?' he asked in a quiet, soothing voice.

'I've been better.'

'Had a phone call from Rachel, she's invited us for dinner tomorrow night at the *Gypsy's Tent* in Broadcastle. She specifically asked that you come. Please, Angie – will you, as a favour to me?'

'A favour to you, eh? Well, that's an offer I dare not refuse.'

'So, you'll come?'

'I have to consult my diary. I imagine I'm booked up, so I'll have to put someone off.'

'Oh, in that case ...'

'Only joking.'

'You got me going then.'

'What time?'

'Seven? We're to meet her in the car park.'

'Promise I'll be teetotal.'

'Good, I'm glad of that.'

'It'll be nice to dress up, anyway.'

When he'd gone, she shook her head in wonder. How the hell had she talked herself into that? It appeared he still had a hold over her with certain things, because the idea of dining with them certainly didn't fill her with enthusiasm.

Chapter 34

Wednesday morning, John got up early with a groan, pondering over work and driving baby AJ over to his parents. It was the same mad rush every day of the week, and then the guilt over leaving his son with them. He dreaded twelve months' time when the lad was crawling and possibly walking. Still, that was a long way off yet.

'How goes it, son?' George asked once he had AJ and his things in the house.

'Oh, not bad. It's hard but I'm carrying on, I suppose. The worst part is taking him with me when I go out. Especially when I want to buy clothes or visit the supermarket.'

'We've said we'll have him on the weekends if you need us to.'

'Can't let you do that, Dad – you're already doing too much as it is. What if it's more than you can handle? What will I do then?'

'It won't be. You're on your own with it, whereas there's two of us. Heard from Angie yet?'

'Funny you should say that. I phoned her dad yesterday, but he wasn't very helpful. Said he'd tell her I want to discuss the future with her. But whether she will agree is a different matter. This mess needs to be sorted once and for all.'

'Well, you should see a solicitor.'

'Let's hope it doesn't come to that.'

'Your mum and I are worried over you. It's not fair.'

'Mum …?'

'She's tired. That's why I let her lie in today.'

'I'd better go, or I'll be late. Any problems, give me a bell.'

'Will do, son. But I'm sure that won't be necessary. You take care of yourself now.'

John smiled and set off to the office.

The weather was sunny and warm, so during his lunchbreak he went out for a walk, buying himself a drink and a bite to eat, then sitting on the bench opposite the office building. It always caught the sun at lunchtime.

There he was, with the sun beating down, eating his sandwiches when he looked up and saw Sarah walking towards him. She smiled and sat beside him with her own lunch.

'Don't mind, do you, John?'

'It's a free country.'

'Nice day, isn't it?'

'Yeah. Shame to be at work.'

'You know, I get the feeling you're avoiding me.'

'No, not at all – it's just that I've been very busy. This is the first chance I've had to get out of the place. Look, I don't want people getting the wrong idea about us. You know how people talk.'

'I suppose you're right. But I haven't had chance to talk to you properly. How have you been? Can't be much fun on your own with AJ.'

'I've had worse – when Angie was shouting and screaming at me – but nowadays I'm happy to settle for looking after myself and my son. I enjoy every minute with him, but I miss Angie, or the girl she used to be before she got ill.'

'Nice, though wasn't it, me and you and baby AJ? I loved it. I'd be a natural as a mother, if I ever got a baby of my own.'

'Have you spoken to Jack? I know you said you weren't keen on football, but why not offer to go to a few matches with him in exchange for letting you have a baby?'

'You're joking. He doesn't want me anywhere a football match with him. He wants to be with his boozy mates so he can get up to stuff.'

'Then you've a problem, babe. Why not trick him into it? He'd never know.' He grinned.

'Not sure I want a baby with him anyway. What sort of father would he be?'

'You never can tell. Angie was like you, before she got pregnant, and look how that turned out. What's his excuse?'

'He doesn't have one. He's a thug who only cares about booze and football. I must have been mad to marry him ... but I thought he'd mellow. But that won't happen so long as he's with his mates – they're a bad influence. And the number of times he's come home drunk after a match, I'm amazed he's kept his job. There have been loads of times when he's gone to work in a right old state. And he's been violent towards me more than once.'

'And I thought I had problems.'

'At least he hasn't left me – or should I say, I haven't left him.'

'Is it on the cards, then?'

'I can't decide. When I was with you the other night, it crossed my mind. I ... I think we both deserve better than we've got.'

She put her hand on top of his. Somehow, he didn't pull his hand away.

'I never planned for that to happen, Sarah. We've both got problems, and we let them run away with us. But one step further would put our friendship at risk.'

'So, you're not that keen then.' There was a touch of bitterness in her voice.

'It's not that. You're like the older sister I never had. And right now, you're the only person I can talk to. That says a lot – I mean, I didn't tell my mum and dad or any of my friends; I chose you.'

'Good. You've made me feel wanted for once.'

'I'm glad – but if we're not careful, our friendship could develop into something more, and ... well, to be honest, I'm frightened of being hurt again.'

'We gel together well, John, you know we do. We're on the same wavelength – don't you feel that too?'

'Yes, but an affair could change everything. We couldn't work together, for a start. One of us would end up in another department. People talk, Sarah. How do we know they're not talking already? We can't risk it.'

'I don't care.' Her eyes glistened with tears.

'You would when the time comes, believe me. Right now, my future is with AJ, and it will be for years to come. I hope we can stay friends but if that's not possible, I'm sorry.'

'You're not making it easy for me. We get on really well, you know we do.'

'Yes, but if Angie finds out she'll use it against me. I'd lose my son. And I can't live with that after what I've been through these past few weeks.'

'She'll never find out if we're discreet.'

'No. I won't do it, Sarah.'

'Well, then there's nothing further to say,' she said, getting up from her seat. 'You'll regret it, John, and then it'll be too late. You're throwing away a chance of real happiness.'

'I'm sorry, but my son must come first.'

She walked away, leaving John's emotions in disarray. But he wasn't willing to sacrifice his son for anyone.

<><><>

That Wednesday night, Angie purposely dressed in ripped jeans, a turquoise top and a khaki jacket, and left her hair unbrushed. She lay on the bed, waiting for the appointed hour. When her dad cleared his throat outside the door, she jumped.

'Coming, Dad.'

He breathed out with relief, put an arm around her shoulder and kissed her on the cheek. 'Thanks, Angie, I appreciate it. It's good to be in a family again.'

'Yes,' she muttered. 'Listen, let's go in my car, then you can have a drink. And it'll make sure I don't.'

'I won't have more than the one myself – at my age I need to be a bit more responsible or my health will suffer.'

'Pleased to hear you're trying to look after yourself.'

'Perhaps I haven't helped putting stuff in your tea and coffee. But I thought it might relax you.'

'It did at first ... but not anymore.'

Angie put the radio on when they drove off, so he didn't lecture her or try to tell her what to do. They made small talk, and that satisfied her for now.

Rachel got out of her car when she saw them driving into the car park. She wore a dark blue trouser suit with a white blouse, her hair curly and washed.

'Hallo there,' she smiled. 'So pleased you're here, Angie.'

'My pleasure. Dad had to drag me by the scruff of the neck, but I'll run off the first chance I get.'

'Sense of humour too, I like that.'

'Shall we go?' Alan urged.

'Yes, why not?' Rachel took his arm; Angie frowned behind their backs. She hoped they wouldn't be all lovey-dovey at the pub, because she'd cringe.

Rachel pointed across the room. 'Right, Angie, I've booked a table for three – there, right by the window. Why don't you sit in the middle?'

'Sure, whatever.'

Alan ordered the drinks, with Angie deciding on a lemonade. The menu sounded appetising, if you liked pub meals. Angie had a steak while her dad and Rachel decided on a lamb shank.

'Well, I'm so pleased you're here, Angie, your dad talks about you non-stop. From what he's said, I gather you're very close, especially since ... well, what happened with your mum.'

'Yes, you could say that. It was difficult because Mum was ill long before she died. It's not a subject I enjoy talking about, if you want the truth.'

'That's understandable. I'm not asking you to talk unless you want to. But your present situation concerns us. Both me and your dad, I mean.'

'Don't start lecturing me, or I'll—'

'No, not at all. This isn't about judging anyone. I'm just trying to figure out why it's happened.'

Oh, what the hell. May as well. 'It was John, tricking me into getting pregnant, when he knew I had no maternal instincts. He only has himself to blame. I tried my best but I can't cope with it, so now I've decided to make a fresh start. It couldn't be clearer than that.'

'That's very sad,' Rachel said.

Just then the food came. Angie suddenly found she was hungry and tucked in. They were quiet throughout; she sensed an atmosphere which she guessed was her fault.

'So how did you meet?' Angie asked.

'Through your mum, actually. I was her psychiatrist, and I used to see them both together. Once a week for over a year.'

'You didn't stop her from killing herself, though, did you?'

Rachel put her knife and fork down with a clatter. 'No, but that's – suicide, I mean – it's very hard to predict. I did my best for her and helped prolong her life, hopefully.'

Angie snorted. 'Oh, really?'

'And I helped your dad get through that traumatic period. He might have had a total mental breakdown and you'd have been taken into care.'

'I know,' Angie admitted.

'Anyway, we met again six months ago, bumped into each other in Dexford High Street. Went for a drink and talked about the past, and kind of took it from there. We hit it off straightaway and we've been together ever since. Your dad has told me of the problems you're encountered bonding with your baby, your mood swings and so on. Postnatal depression comes in many guises and it can take a long time to shake off. That's where my expertise can help: I'm prepared to offer you sessions with me for free. I normally charge from £100 a session, so I'll save you money. And if I can cure you, you could soon begin to lead a normal life again. What do you say?'

'I never saw this coming. I always imagined you weren't supposed to treat members of a family you're connected to.'

'That's true, but I'm not part of your family. Your dad and I are only good friends. But who knows what may happen in the future? That's why we should start our sessions at once.'

'What do you mean?'

'She means, darling,' her dad butted in, 'that all being well, we may get engaged in the new year.'

Angie's jaw dropped. She wanted to throw up.

Chapter 35

On the way home, Angie couldn't speak. Never in a million years did she expect this. Getting married again – well, that woman would never take her mum's place.

'You're quiet, love. Still taking it in, are you?'

'I never thought you'd want to marry again after what you had with Mum. But to each his own. You kept your secret well. Would you have told me if I hadn't been ill? Or waited until after the wedding?'

'We're not even engaged yet. And as I've said, it won't be until the new year. The wedding could be at least another year after that, if not more. There's no rush – we just want to enjoy what we have now. But at least we will make a commitment to each other. As for any future wedding, of course I'd want you there – that's only natural. This way I get to keep you both in my life. Been on my own for too long. I have my work, but there's always something missing, like happiness and contentment. What your mother and I had before the bad things happened. I want that again before I'm too old to enjoy it.'

'Oh, Dad. I don't blame you. You deserve that, I know you do, but I can't be part of this new family.'

'Oh, for God's sake, why ever not?'

'Because …'

'What have you got against her?'

'Nothing. You look well matched, I'm happy for you but it's just too much for me to take in.'

'You're being ridiculous, Angie. We could be a family again, like before.'

'That was then, and this is now. I'm a grown woman and I don't belong to you two.'

'But she's offered to help you for free and she's one of the best psychiatrists in her field – can't you understand that?'

'I understand it perfectly well. You're trying to manipulate me like John used to. I won't stand for it.'

'I'm not. You came to me because you were ill, and you're still not well. You wanted my help and that's what I'm giving you if you let me.'

'Yes – just you. Not the wicked stepmother.'

'Right, so that's it. Tell me what you don't like about her, because I'm at a loss to understand. Rachel is a wonderful person who got me through many bad days after your mum died. If she hadn't stood by me, what might have become of you? Adopted, fostered – who knows?'

'If she's such a fantastic psychiatrist, why didn't she save Mum?'

'She's not to blame for that. She did her best for your mum, but people with bipolar are unpredictable. They're irrational and when they're in that state, literally anything can happen.'

'I don't believe it. I've nothing against Rachel but I won't live with you and I'm not coming to the wedding. Take it or leave it.'

He gritted his teeth as he drove, not trusting himself to speak further on the subject.

Angie didn't care if it upset him; he never told her about Rachel until he had to, obviously fearing she might not accept the woman. He only cared about her, and himself.

They spoke no further until they were back in the house. It was too early for bed, so she switched on the TV. But if he started on her again, she'd walk out.

'Drink?' he asked.

'A Coke will be fine.'

He fetched one and took a sip of his beer. 'So, what are you going to do?'

'No idea. What about you?'

He laughed. 'I don't know.'

'I'm looking forward to seeing who comes first, your daughter or your girlfriend.'

'You can't ask me to make that choice, Angie.'

'I'm not asking you to. I've explained how it is – the rest is up to you.'

He finished his beer.

Angie put her can down. 'I'm off to bed.'

'Sleep well, my darling. Speak in the morning.'

She nodded, traipsing off with a symbolic wave. Just what had her father become? Rachel had made him into someone she didn't recognise. They were out to get her, like everyone else, John included. She intended being one step ahead of them. She had to find a job and a place of her own soon.

<><><>

Her dad was already up and eating his breakfast when she came into the kitchen the next morning. He looked up at her with a smile, but it wasn't returned.

'Good sleep?'

'No. I had another strange dream about Mum dying. I'm shouting at her, and then I push her off the cliff. Was it me that killed her, Dad?'

'Of course not. Don't fret. She did it herself and I couldn't get there in time to save her.'

'Why do I think I did it, then?'

'It's anyone's guess. That's why I want you to talk to Rachel, because she's the expert. Your mind is in a mess and someone has to untangle it. It may take time but I promise you she'll do it.'

'How could I think I'd killed her, Dad, when I was in the car?'

'Guilt, perhaps. Whenever a child experiences a tragic event, they blame themselves. It was no one's fault. Your mother got ill, and had a lot of disturbing symptoms which I found hard to understand. When the doctors diagnosed her with bipolar, I'd never heard of it. But when I read up on it, I realised all the descriptions were her to a T. There were periods when she was normal for a time, but gradually over time these got less and less.'

'Is that me too?'

'I don't think so. I think it's more likely postnatal depression and all this stuff about having no feelings for your own child is part of it. With the right therapist, you'll be able to manage your condition, maybe in a matter of months; from what Rachel has said, you're showing the classic symptoms. She says medication can help too. Please, at least give her a go, you've nothing to lose and a lot to gain. Surely you want to lead a normal life again?'

She nodded meekly. 'Yes.'

'Then will you let Rachel see you, say starting from next week? Go as often or as little as you like. No strings attached. Please, Angie.'

'I can't promise. But I'll tell you as soon as I've decided.'

'Well, don't wait too long – she's not available forever. She's a busy lady with lots of important clients.'

'All right, Dad, don't go on. Ask her about these dreams with me killing Mum.'

'I will, darling.'

She made breakfast – toast and marmalade was all she could face – and ate opposite him.

'Got much planned for today?' he asked.

'No. Might go job-hunting.'

'Oh, by the way, Rachel left you a few books to read. About your condition.' He pointed to a bag on the floor.

'OK, thanks. When I get time, I'll skip through them.'

'You do that.'

Soon after he'd gone, she made straight for the computer, clicked on her emails and scanned through them. Nothing. How disappointing. After an hour of surfing the net, she was bored out of her mind, and even contemplated looking through the books from Rachel. But she wasn't that desperate yet.

Around mid-morning, an email popped up from Davidson & Co in Burnfield; the subject line was 'Your Enquiry', which gave nothing away. Her heart fluttered as she opened it … an interview on Thursday the 4th! She tried not to get too excited, and decided she wouldn't say a word to anyone yet, not least because Burnfield was twenty miles from Dexford, and her dad was bound to be against it.

To emphasise her determination, she browsed the Davidson website for the prices of flats. Since Dad was letting her stay for free, she could easily afford the deposit for a rental…

On the Thursday, she slipped out and drove over to Burnfield, and had a bite to eat before going over to the estate agent's offices. She'd taken an extra tablet that morning but was still nervy and hoped to bluff her way through this without incident. This was her passport to a new life and if she messed it up, she'd cry a river of tears.

When she came out an hour later, she needed a drink. The barman in the nearest pub served her a double whisky that warmed her insides and calmed her down. Looking back, she had no idea how it had gone; they had seemed impressed with her qualifications and her achievements but wondered why she wanted to work so far away from home. A messy divorce and a new start were the answers she gave. Now all she could do was wait.

In the meantime, although she hadn't even got the job yet, she viewed a few rental properties. A couple caught her eye and when she expressed an interest, they gave her first option. But it would all depend on her getting that job.

When she got home, it was late; Alan was in the kitchen cooking the evening meal. He turned around when he heard her come, relief came over his face.

'Dear God, Angie, where on earth have you been?'

'Out.'

'I know that. Out where?'

'To a job interview.'

'Oh, any joy? Whereabouts is it?'

'Not that far.'

His eyes narrowed. 'How far?'

'I'm not saying yet. If I get it, I might tell you.'

'For God's sake, Angie, what's all this cloak and dagger stuff about?'

'That's my business.'

'Come on, love – we've never had secrets before.'

'Oh, haven't we? So what's Rachel then, if she's not a secret? How long had it been going on before I found out?'

'All right, a while, but this is different. Why you can't say where the job is? I can't stop you wherever it is?'

'No, you can't. We'll never be as close as we were before, Dad. From now on, you'll always be closer to her. There'll be lots of things you don't tell me, won't there?'

'Only stuff that concerns Rachel and me. It's only the same as you when you were with John.'

'I'm not arguing. Call me when dinner's ready.'

<><><>

A week later, a letter came in the post from Davidson & Co. The interviewer had said they'd only write to the person chosen.

She slit it open with shaking hands and stared at the job offer. To start in a week's time; she had told them she needn't work any notice because she was on maternity leave. Fantastic – she couldn't wait. And the money was better too. Now she must find a flat and be on her way.

She took a furnished ground-floor flat which was easily affordable, and paid the first month's rent so she could go in when she wanted. She wouldn't tell her dad as he'd do everything in his power to stop her. And she hated the hassle. Best to slip out at the first opportunity and leave him a note. The thought of Rachel picking over her private thoughts and those horrible dreams was too much to take. She needed to be out – now.

Chapter 36

'So, are you coming bowling or not?' David asked John on Wednesday, as they sat in the staff room with Joe and Sarah and a few other colleagues.

John flushed. Normally he loved these nights out – but of late he hadn't socialised much, because of Angie and the baby.

'I'd love to, but I have to take care of AJ.'

'How about a babysitter? You must know someone who'll help. Come on mate, you're our star player. If we haven't got you on the team, we'll struggle,' David said.

John groaned. 'There's only my parents, but they already have him five days a week. It's a lot to ask.'

'John, it's only one night – it should be over by nine or ten. When did you last have a night out?' Joe asked.

'Can't remember, must be before Angie got pregnant … early December, maybe.'

'That's a long time,' David said.

'Tell me about it. I'd love to go out, but I'd still have to pick up AJ afterwards.'

'Up to you, mate, so long as you don't leave before we finish the game,' Joe said.

'Oh, I'd never do that. OK, I'll speak to Mum.'

That evening, after work, he was on edge. He needed a boost since Angie continued to refuse his attempts to make contact. This bowling night would put his worries to one side for a few hours, but it wouldn't solve his problems.

He hated asking his parents. They sensed his subdued nature when he came to pick up his son and have dinner; even his mum's Lancashire hotpot didn't raise a smile.

George looked him square in the eye. 'You all right, son?'

John shook his head and took a deep breath. 'I ... I need your help again. Sorry, but I've got nowhere else to go.'

His dad put his hand on John's shoulder. 'John, ask away. To see AJ is a pleasure for us.'

'I'm being selfish, I know, but I need a rest. My work has a bowling night tomorrow night. Could you have Alan for the evening? It's a one-off, I promise you.'

Both his parents were beaming at him. 'Oh, love, it's no bother. We love having him. He's a little angel. Tell you what – say we have him overnight? So you can get a good night's sleep?' his mum said.

John was gobsmacked. 'You don't have to. I'll be home by ten o'clock at the latest.'

'By which time he'll be fast asleep. If we move him, he might wake. No let us have him for the night,' George said.

'Are you sure? It grieves me, it really does.'

'We're positive. You're our son and AJ's our grandson and we love you both to bits.'

'How will I ever repay you?'

Susan laughed. 'No need.'

John hugged and kissed them both; they were the best parents in the world, always supportive in whatever he did.

<><><>

Come Thursday morning, after dropping AJ off, John felt tearful; after all, he wouldn't see his son again until Friday morning.

He'd ring later to find out how they were getting on.

His day was busy, with enough work to keep him going beyond six.

Joe caught him wiping his brow with the back of his hand. He laughed. 'You look exhausted, John. Hard day?'

'You try looking after a baby on your own – and working full-time. It saps your energy, I can tell you.'

'I bet. You still coming, then?'

'Yeah, just shutting down my computer. Whose car are we going in?'

'Sarah's.'

John's heart missed a beat; this would be uncomfortable. Although the two of them were on speaking terms, they only discussed work-related items and no longer had lunch together. In fact, he was surprised she was in the team.

'Sarah, David, ready for the off?'

'Yes, just getting our coats,' Sarah said. 'We'll be outside in the car park.'

John and Joe sat in the back, David in the front by Sarah. They were chatty, the atmosphere good; even John joined in, although he was careful not to speak directly to Sarah.

'So, who are our opponents?' John asked.

'Brightwell Ellis,' David replied. He had organised the match.

'We played them two years ago, do you remember? They beat us four-nil,' Sarah said. 'Hope you're on form, John, we'll need you.'

'It's all of us. I can't do it on my own.'

Joe laughed. 'No pressure, eh?'

John smiled. He wanted to do well and not allow his troubles to defeat him.

They sat waiting for their opponents to arrive, and decided to have a few practice runs first. John was rusty but got a strike with his last ball. They cheered him, hoping he'd come good later on.

Sarah was clapping enthusiastically. 'Nice one, John.'

'Don't expect too much, or you might be disappointed.'

'I'm sure you'll be great.'

'Thanks for the encouragement – let's hope it does some good.'

'We'll see.'

The Brightwell Ellis guys arrived soon afterwards and exchanged familiarities. Then the match began.

Sarah delivered her first two balls down the gutter. They all laughed, but she picked herself up and gave her opponent a run for her money in the end, even though she still got beaten. Next came John. He was psyched up and started with a strike; he won his match easily, with five strikes. It was up to Joe and David.

David squeezed through his match in a nail-biter.

'OK, Joe,' John said, grinning, 'it's up to you now. No pressure, eh?'

'I'll do my best,' he said.

Joe played a blinder and beat Brightwell Ellis's best player. They whooped with joy once it was over.

'What a victory!' David exclaimed. 'This calls for a celebration! How about a drink and a bite to eat?'

The four of them were in raptures, and even John joined in with the celebrations as they all praised his play, saying he'd inspired them with his bowling.

'I reckon we could go further,' David said. 'So long as we keep our team together, eh, John?'

He blushed. 'I can't promise anything, David. I still have my family commitments.'

David tutted. 'The next game won't be until a month's time – surely you can manage one night?'

'I'll do my best.'

Sarah gave a knowing look and smiled but he looked away.

Around an hour later, they left. Sarah drove them to the company car park where they went to their respective cars. Just as John was about to get into his, she shouted after him. 'John, you've forgotten something.'

'What?' He turned and walked back towards her car.

'Fancy coming over to my place for a drink? Jack's out at a European match until lunchtime tomorrow.'

'Are you joking?'

'No, I'm not. And I'm fed up of this small talk and avoiding the obvious. Let's be honest with each other for once, shall we? For instance, Angie still hasn't come back, has she?'

'No, I haven't heard from her since the day she left and she won't return my calls. She isn't interested.'

'There you are, then. She could be having an affair – who knows, maybe that's the real reason why she ditched you. I know for a fact Jack's been seeing other women. I've seen messages on his phone. That's why he never wants me in bed and why he won't let us have a baby. John, we're doing nothing wrong. It's not as if we're really married to our partners anymore.'

'Yes, but having a kid makes it more complicated.'

'I disagree. She deserted you and AJ first. She'd never get custody of the child since you've always looked after him.'

John was tempted. What she said was true. A tiny voice inside egged him on.

He hesitated for two minutes. He missed the company of a woman and Sarah was very attractive…

She was still staring at him, a slow smile spreading on her face. 'I knew it. I was sure I could persuade you. She doesn't want you, John. I told you that before, didn't I?'

'All right, I realise that. I held on, hoping she'd recover from her illness and see sense. But as you say, the door's been shut in my face, so …'

'You're well rid of her. You'll never be happy with her and she'd have dragged you down with her. AJ needs a stable family life and maybe I can help provide that.'

'I hope so.'

'I know so.'

Within ten minutes, they had parked on the drive outside her newly built semi-detached house, and slipped inside. It was modestly furnished and decorated, and John couldn't help thinking that Sarah was the only one spending money on it; her husband spent his on a football team.

In the hall, she put her arms around his neck. Their lips met and John melted into her. He hadn't been so aroused since before Angie's pregnancy.

'Shall we have a drink?' she asked when they broke off.

'Only a coffee for me.'

'Not something stronger?'

'Absolutely not. I want to remember this in the morning.'

'So do I.'

They snuggled together on the sofa, Sarah leaning her head against his.

'When you told me what Angie was doing – the violence, I mean – I could relate to it straight away. Because he's been violent to me frequently, but to my body and not my face. He has a terrible temper. He flies off the handle over the slightest thing.'

'I hate men who hit women – it's such a cowardly act. And I don't go a bundle on women who hit men, either. I never wanted to retaliate, could never hit her and she knew it. I may be stronger than her, but I loved her.'

'Me neither although for different reasons. If I had, he'd have beaten me black and blue. If I'm not careful, one day he'll go too far and kill me.'

'Not while I'm around, he won't.'

'He's a tough cookie, John, been in a few fights in his time …'

'I can't think about him now, or Angie. Let's concentrate on the moment.'

She stood up and held out her hand, guiding him up the stairs.

'There's a bed in the second bedroom. I don't want to sleep in his bed. This bed will be ours, John.'

'Of course,' he said, his eyes never leaving hers.

Afterwards she lay in his arms and wept.

'That was so beautiful, the way it should be. I'll never forget tonight – whatever happens, this moment will be ours forever,' he said.

'Yes, but we must be careful. If someone sees us together, he might get wind of what's going on.'

'If it wasn't for AJ, I'd run away with you to where no one will find us. Make a fresh start and forget what I've left behind.'

'But AJ must come too, and then our little family will be complete. I love him as if he were my own.'

He hugged her close, but feared the dreams they had for each other would never come true. For now, he'd take what was going and be satisfied with that.

Chapter 37

John woke early; he hadn't got much sleep in the single bed he'd shared with Sarah. She was fast asleep, and he wondered if he should wake her. He slipped on his clothes and looked at his watch. Six-thirty. He had a wash, then returned to the bedroom.

'Hey, you,' he said, giving her a gentle shake. 'Got to go now.' He kissed on the lips.

'Stay a little longer,' she yawned rubbing her eyes.

'I'd love to, but what if Jack catches us here together? We can't risk that. And we should go into work separately. The fewer people know, the better. The bosses hate seeing colleagues having relationships, it can complicate matters – do you agree?'

'Maybe, but we'll have to come clean eventually.'

'Yes, but not right now.'

She seemed hurt. 'OK, John. As you wish.'

'I'll get my car early before anyone else arrives, then drive to Mum and Dad's to see AJ and be in at the normal time.'

'Sure thing.'

'Are you … are you sure you want to go through with this, Sarah? We'll be under a lot of pressure. What with your husband and my wife and baby AJ.'

'I never said it would be easy. But if we stick together, we'll get through this.'

'Yes, I hope so. See you later.'

'Thanks for a fantastic night.'

They kissed again.

'It's not light yet, so I should be safe.'

'There's a bus stop further on down the road, the number five stops there and takes you into Dexford town centre.'

'OK, wonderful.'

Daylight was breaking through as he slipped out and hurried to the bus shelter, where a timetable told him the next bus should arrive in ten minutes.

The bus was empty save for two early morning workers. He got off at the Town Hall and from there took just five minutes to get to Sachs Gordon's car park. Then he drove over to his parents'.

His dad let him in, looking pleased he'd come.

'Thought I'd look in at AJ. Is he all right? Did he sleep well?'

'He's fine – took a while getting him to sleep but since midnight, he hasn't woken once.'

'Good.'

John popped through to see his mum sitting on the sofa, her eyes glued on AJ who was still fast asleep in his pram.

'Glad he didn't give you too much trouble, Mum. I worry he'll wear you out.'

'Not at all. As I've said before, he's no problem. Any time you need us, let me know.'

'Well, I hate asking you, but ... would you be willing to have him one night a week?'

'No problem. The weekends are better because we don't have him during the day. And if you bring him over at seven or eight, he'll be asleep, anyway. He won't need looking after except if he wakes during the night.'

John beamed. He couldn't thank them enough.

'You pleased with that?' George said.

'I am. I'll be honest, Dad, it's bucked me up no end.'

'Well, you deserve a life of your own as well as bringing up AJ.'

'So how did it go last night?' Susan asked.

'I enjoyed myself. We even won our match, can you believe?'

'Good to see you happy again, love. After all you've had little to smile over lately.'

'I can't say I'm happy, Mum. Not yet. I miss Angie terribly, despite her tantrums, but I'm just taking one day at a time. I keep telling myself once she's learnt to control her emotions and got well again, we'll get back together.'

'Let's hope you're right.'

'I'd better go. I'll fetch AJ as soon as I can tonight.'

'All right – ring me when you're leaving, so I know when to do your dinner.'

'I will.'

For once he wasn't the first in work; David, Stuart and Sarah were in before him. When he entered the office, David came over to slap him on the back.

'Here he is, the hero of the hour! You played a blinder last night, John. You stuffed their guy good and proper.'

Stuart grinned. 'I've been hearing about your antics, mate. Sounded like a great performance.'

'Yeah, well. I was just lucky.'

'More than luck – skill and determination,' David said.

'Well, maybe a bit.' He grinned. 'Maybe we'll do the same when the next match comes.'

'We will.' Stuart smiled. 'If you help us win the Regional Trophy, a slap-up meal and drinks are on me.'

'That's a great incentive,' Sarah said. 'Hope you're up to the pressure, eh John?'

John smiled. He desperately wanted to speak to her – and more, if he was honest – but it was difficult to chat with everyone else about. Lunchtime, perhaps?

Lunchtime came. Joe and David went out for a drink but Sarah declined, saying she'd brought sandwiches. John asked them to bring him two cheese cobs from the pub. Once they'd gone, Sarah moved across next to him and ate her lunch.

'Good news. My parents offered to have AJ one night every week, on the weekend nights. That means we're free to go out so long as Jack's out of the way, I suppose.'

'Oh, that's brilliant! But you can't stay overnight that often – it'll just depend on where Jack's gone. For home matches he's back around six, and for away games it depends on where it is. Our best chance is when his team are in Europe – then he stays overnight.'

'You're saying I've been too optimistic.'

She put her hand on top of his. 'No, not at all. We'll be together, I promise. And when we are, let's make the most of it. And I want to see AJ as well, to bond with him, just the same as you.'

'That would be fantastic. Someday we'll be a real family.'

'But I do need to do something about Jack. And that's the sticking point. He won't take this lying down. He'll be as mad as hell and that's going to be hard to deal with. It'll be very challenging for me but I'll do it to be with you.'

'Yes, and the same goes for Angie. I keep trying to contact her, but she doesn't answer my calls. I rang her dad to get her to call me, but she hasn't. If and when she rings, I'll ask for a divorce. There's lots to sort out, but right now it's a question of wait and see. But that's for the future. Best enjoy being together while we can.'

'I agree. We'll have some difficult times ahead; it frightens me, but if we're brave, we'll get our reward.'

She moved to kiss him, but he pulled away.

'Better move, or people will talk.'

Sarah rolled her eyes. 'You're so sensible, John. OK – I think I'll go out for a walk, since the weather's so good.'

'Until later, then.'

By four twenty-five, he'd finished, said his goodbyes and was on his way. As he drove through the High Street, he caught sight of someone who looked a lot like Angie coming out of Elliott's estate agents. At the traffic lights he saw her again, walking in the opposite direction.

His heart beat faster. It certainly looked like her. Dear God, did he want to speak with her? He was tempted to shout after her, but feared she might do a bunk if he did.

Once the lights changed, he put his foot down and turned around at the first opportunity. Parking his car at the nearest spot, he ran in the direction he'd seen her walking. But she'd gone. He looked up every side road he passed, but nothing. How had he missed her? Perhaps she'd got in her car and driven straight past him.

However, as he walked back, a thought came into his head.

He opened the plate glass door and immediately saw Bethany on reception. She looked up but didn't acknowledge him; not a good sign. Still he walked straight up to the desk.

'Hallo, Bethany,' he said with a smile.

'Hi John. How can I help you?'

'Wondered if you'd seen Angie?'

'No – but she's on maternity leave, so I wouldn't expect to. Although she did come in a few weeks ago to say hallo.'

'I just saw her come out of your office a few minutes ago.'

'You must be mistaken.'

'Bethany, you're lying. Did you know she's left me and I can't trace where she is? I'm worried sick. She left our baby with me, too. Did you know that? If you've any information on her whereabouts, I'd be grateful.'

He noticed the tense expression on her face. She was holding something back.

'Err, I'm not sure if I can help. I'll speak with my boss, see what he says. Excuse me for a minute.'

'Be my guest.'

John took in a deep breath, praying they knew where she was.

The boss came out behind Bethany; John had never seen him before. He was tall and thin, with ruddy cheeks, thinning hair and bright blue eyes.

'Hi, I'm Taylor Winslow, acting office manager. I'm filling in for Duncan – he's off sick. You're enquiring about Angie?'

'I reckon you know where she is.'

'I'm afraid I can't tell you anything without her permission. She no longer works here. She resigned from the company and has a job with another estate agent.'

'Where?'

'As I said, I can't divulge that.'

'Look here, Winslow, it's in your own interest to give me the address or I might take the matter into my own hands ...'

'I don't respond to threats. I want you to leave the premises now – or do I have to phone the police to remove you?'

John laughed. Pompous arse. 'All right, I'm going. Angie is ill, her family and friends are concerned for her welfare. You owe it to us to tell me. If something happens to her, be it on your heads.'

'Goodbye, sir,' Winslow said.

John walked out, slamming the door shut. He hoped the glass shattered.

Back at his parents' house he knew he was in a subdued mood, but hopefully they wouldn't notice.

As soon as he came in the living room, his mum collared him.

'Hey, you told me you were coming home earlier,' she said.

'Yeah, well, I got held up.'

'I've left your dinner in the oven.'

'Thanks, Mum. Sorry I'm later than I said. Had to make a detour.'

'Oh, that doesn't matter, these things happen.'

'How's AJ?'

'Come and look.'

There in the dining room, John found his son in a baby bouncer, happily moving his arms and legs; John swore he saw a smile.

'Hey, what a mover,' he laughed.

'He's been sitting there for ages. Seems to be enjoying himself,' George said.

'He'll be a lovely little lad when he's older, and no trouble either,' Susan said. 'Sit yourself down, I'll just see if your meal is hot enough yet.'

'Thanks, Mum.'

John sat on the sofa, closed his eyes and yawned.

'Had a bad day?' George asked.

'Not that bad. Came out early – but then I saw Angie while I was driving. I got out and ran after her, but I lost her in a side street. So frustrating. She'd come out of the estate agent's and I thought she'd gone back to work there, but she hasn't. She's changed jobs, but they won't say where. I thought I was getting her out of my system, but now I'm back to square one.'

'It takes time, son. You were together for a long time, and she's the mother of your son, so it's not going to be easy to forget her. And I'd say AJ is looking like her too.'

'Thing is, Dad … I'm seeing someone else.'

'You what? Well, that'll complicate matters.'

'Yes, it will. And it's worse than that. She's married.'

George shook his head at his son.

'I guessed you wouldn't approve. She's nice, and so easy to talk to.'

Susan brought in his dinner on a tray. She put it on his lap and while he ate, George told her what had happened.

She looked horrified. 'That's a bit soon, isn't it?'

'I thought you'd say that.'

'I mean, there's still a possibility she might come home when she's well enough. Why didn't you wait instead of gallivanting with another woman? You risk losing everything, John. And what if she won't leave her husband?'

'She will. He's a violent thug who thinks it's OK to use his own wife as a punchbag. And he spends most of his time with his mates watching football matches.'

'So why hasn't she left him already?'

'I don't know. Either she's frightened, or she's waiting for the right moment.'

'A likely story. She's bored because her hubby is always out with the lads.'

'Anyway, I just wanted you both to be aware of the current situation. I have no idea what will happen, but we get on well and I intend seeing her when I can. She loves kids, too – she's met AJ and he took to her really well.'

'So, what's her name and how did you meet her?'

'Sarah. I work with her.'

Susan's mouth dropped open. 'You're playing with fire, love. And I promise you, it'll end in tears. But it's your life – it's up to you how you live it. I couldn't stop you even if I wanted to. Hope it works out for you, whatever you do.'

'Nothing's certain in life but I'll give this my best shot because Angie isn't coming back. And AJ needs a mother and a father; I can't be both.'

'That's true. But remember we're always at hand to help you.'

'Thanks for that but you've got your own lives to lead now you're retired. You need to be together.'

'They'll be plenty of time for that afterwards. Whenever you need us, we're here to support you.'

'Thanks, Mum. I'd better go, we've been here long enough.'

They helped him get AJ in the car and brought out his things to be put in the boot along with the pram.

As they waved, he knew he'd always be in good hands.

Chapter 38

The weekend was the best time to leave, Angie thought, a week later – and with her dad out shopping with Rachel that Saturday morning, she had the perfect opportunity. The night before, she'd packed her belongings in a large suitcase and stored it in the wardrobe.

She had breakfast as normal, but began to shake when she saw Alan come into the kitchen, all smiles, ready to pick Rachel up.

'Right, I'm off,' he said, putting on his coat. 'Anything you want while we're out?'

'Yes, a packet of hot cross buns and some chocolate biscuits if you don't mind.'

'OK. See you later.' He bent over and kissed her cheek.

She stopped trembling once he'd gone; giddy with excitement, she rushed upstairs, pulled out her suitcase from the wardrobe and dragged it to her car. Without looking back, she drove off. The journey of over twenty-three miles was uneventful, and by ten o'clock she was unlocking the door of her new apartment.

On the first floor, it had two bedrooms, a living room, kitchen and bathroom, all decorated to a high standard. The rent was higher than she'd expected but she felt comfortable away from Dexford. Surely nothing could go wrong here.

Around twelve o'clock her mobile rang; her father. She didn't answer it. He rang six more times and then resorted to texts. She deleted all of them. Even Rachel got in on the act, which made Angie angry enough that she decided to change her phone and get a new number. Now none of her family or friends could bother her unless she wished to contact them. Sheer bliss.

The next week dragged, with nothing to do and no one to talk to. Without the incentive of going back to work, she might have gone crazy.

Come Monday morning, she was eager to go and arrived at Davidson and Co half an hour early.

She waited outside the office and spotted two young girls walking towards her. The brown-haired one smiled at her and the blonde girl spoke. 'Hi, you must be Angie.'

'Yes, I'm due to start today.'

'I'm Susie, this is Deb.'

'Pleased to meet you. Sorry I'm a bit early.'

'Better early than late,' Susie said as she unlocked the door.

Angie smiled. 'Yes, I suppose so.'

'OK, Angie, you'll be with me for the first week. It's your job to look after prospective sellers and buyers. You find a good mix here, but it's mostly wealthy and middle-class clients, searching for properties at the higher end of the market. As you're aware, as a small rural town, we have lots of farmers, country squires, that kind of thing. Most of them still living in another era!'

'Sounds really interesting.'

'Yeah, can be, although some of them are very stubborn, not willing to budge on their asking price, and then they blame you when they can't get what they want.'

Angie smiled; despite taking an extra tablet that morning, she felt nervous. If she messed up again and lost this job she'd be devastated.

Luckily, she bluffed her way through with Susie's help. At home, she was glad it was over – but now faced an evening on her own. She opened a bottle of wine to ease her anxiety; slowly, the alcohol took effect, and she felt better. She finished the whole bottle and fell asleep.

The next morning, she woke on the living room floor with a pounding headache, the empty bottle beside her. When she sat up, she threw up all over the carpet.

How the hell had she let herself get in this position again?

As she wiped the sick off her clothes and the carpet with a wad of tissues, she glanced at her watch. It was eight-twenty.

'Shit!' She should be at work in thirty minutes' time. She'd never make it. So she found her mobile and phoned Susie.

'Sorry to phone you, but I just realised I have a dentist's appointment at nine. I should have told you yesterday, but what with everything going on, it slipped my mind.'

'All right, Angie, that's no problem. When will you be in?'

'About nine-thirty, with luck.'

'OK. I'll see you later, then.'

Once Susie had rung off, Angie breathed easier. She had to stop drinking. She felt better for a time but soon came down with a bump.

She skipped breakfast, had a quick shower and dressed, had a cup of black coffee and got into her car. Still light-headed, she knew she shouldn't be driving and was relieved to get to the car park in one piece.

From there, she ran to the office building; it was nine-forty. Susie was with a client.

'Hi, Deb, sorry I'm late. What I can do while I'm waiting for Susie?'

'Er ... tell you what. You could hold the fort on reception while I carry on with some paperwork, please.'

'Sure, no problem.'

Deb disappeared into an office, leaving Angie to fend for herself until Susie was free. Her hands trembled as she waited for someone to come in. Her heart beat hard against her chest when a young couple came in and showed a keen interest in the display of new properties for sale, but they didn't enquire about any of them.

Then suddenly she had the urge for the toilet and ran off, leaving the desk unattended. Upon her return, Susie was manning it.

'Who's supposed to be on reception here, Angie? I saw Deb at her computer and she told me you were covering. Yet when I came out of my office, two people were waiting but no one was there to see to them. On no account are you to leave that desk unmanned again.'

'Sorry, Susie, but there was no one in when I left, and I was back in five min—'

'That's no excuse. If you need the toilet, ask someone to take over. This could have left us in an embarrassing position. Not only that, it's very unprofessional. Customers come in expecting help and advice, and if we're not there to serve them they leave. If I hadn't noticed when I did, Lord alone knows what might have happened.'

Tears streamed down Angie's cheeks. 'I'm sorry – I promise you it won't happen again.'

'You're right, because if it does, you'll be on a warning. I have to say, I'm surprised, after the glowing praise your previous employers gave you. Anyway, I've said my piece, so dry your eyes – we have work to do.'

This mortified Angie. No one had told her off in this way before. She felt humiliated; she wasn't sure if she could carry on.

Susie left her to attend to the customers on her own, which was another bombshell. To do this after one day, when she was already fragile, seemed unfair – almost as if they wanted rid of her. Well, she'd show them.

She got through the rest of the morning unscathed. Her confidence grew and by the afternoon she was dealing with everything herself without assistance.

But in her apartment, the gloom descended once more. Everyone was conspiring against her; even her beloved father had gone off with another woman. Only drink helped – wine, in particular, but not the whole bottle this time. Just enough to send her to sleep.

The week passed; she settled in and gave Susie no further cause for complaint. But the approaching weekend filled her with dread. Isolated, she worried over how to get through the days. On the Thursday night she thought of John, and wondered how he was coping with baby AJ. Maybe she'd drive past, see what he was doing. She was reluctant to admit it, but she missed him. Perhaps she should contact him about a divorce – or a reconciliation. She didn't know which.

Chapter 39

John had just put AJ down and was watching TV when the phone rang that Thursday night. When he saw it was Alan, his heart flipped.

'Hallo, John, it's Alan here. Sorry to disturb you, but I wanted to speak to you about Angie. Have you got a minute?'

'Oh God, now what? Is she OK?'

'Good question, John – one I haven't an answer for. But she's been living with me for the last few weeks. She made me promise not to say anything. The thing is, though, a fortnight ago she flitted away from me too. She'd threatened to walk out because she found out I had a girlfriend – but I never thought she'd go through with it. She left while we were out and didn't say where she was going. I rang her but she refused to return my calls. Her employers said she'd left but wouldn't tell me where she'd gone.'

John nodded. He knew the feeling. 'Yes. I drove past the estate agent's a few days ago and saw her leaving, but when I went after her I lost her in the crowds. I went in and spoke to them, but I got much the same answer as you. And how was she when she was with you?'

'Oh, she was all right until I mentioned that Rachel, my girlfriend, is a psychiatrist. That's when she got nervous. And now I haven't a clue where she is, or what she's doing. Rachel wanted to try and help her, but Angie refused. I'm sure that's why she left. I kept thinking she'd come back, but now it's been so long without hearing from her, I'm beginning to worry.'

'Hope she hasn't done anything stupid.'

'That's why I've contacted you.'

'Maybe I should make a few enquires with the police, hospitals, that kind of thing – see what they turn up. And I'll keep you in the loop, all right?'

'Thanks, bud. I'm so worried. One minute she was full of beans, the next she was so low.'

'Leave it with me.'

'Thanks. Let's just pray nothing's happened to her.'

John switched his phone off, butterflies flying around in his stomach. He felt guilty and wished he'd done more after she'd left him. Might he live to regret this?

He made the calls at once, hoping he might get some answers soon.

<><><>

He got in to work early the next morning and filled Sarah in on the developments. After he'd told her, she said, 'Do whatever you think's best. I hope she's OK, John, but if you're thinking of getting back together, you'd better tell me now.'

'No – not a chance, but I am concerned about her welfare. And she's the mother of my child. Forgive me, Sarah. I have to do the right thing.'

'I know. Don't be long finding her, eh? We have little time together as it is.'

'I realise that. Once I'm sure she's all right, I'll be back, I promise.'

'But John, just remember: she walked out on you and your son. How can any woman do that? I'd say she's a cold callous bitch and the more you fall for her drama, the worse she'll be.'

'Maybe.'

'Remember, I'm working hard to pluck up the courage to leave Jack – I'll do it very soon but not if I'm not sure of you.'

'I realise that. I promise I'll never jeopardise our happiness.'

'You'd better mean that.'

When the police and the hospital returned his calls, neither had any record of Angie; he couldn't decide if that was good news or bad. When he mentioned she'd left her job and her former employers wouldn't say where she'd gone, the police promised to make some enquires. But since he was no longer the next of kin, as they'd split up, it would be down to her father to chase up.

John rang Alan that night.

'They know where she is, but they won't give me any information because we've split up. You'll have to ring them since you're the next of kin now.'

'That's understandable, John. Glad you've made progress; I feared the worst.'

'They didn't sound unduly worried, but you're to inform them if there's any news. Can you let me know what you've found out tomorrow night?'

'Yes, of course – that's the least I can do.'

Next, he rang Sarah on her mobile, hoping Jack wasn't on the scene.

'Can you talk?'

'Yes, he's out football training.'

He then told her what he'd learnt.

'Brilliant. Now, forget about it. And, listen – Jack's out on Saturday, from first thing in the morning until midnight. An away match in Southampton. If the weather's decent, I could come over, spend the day with you? We could take the baby out. What do you reckon?'

'Great idea. I'll look forward to it.'

He felt able to smile again.

<><><>

Saturday afternoon; Angie had the TV on low, a glass of wine in her hand. Her eyes were heavy, and she was dozing when a beep came from the intercom at the front door. She jumped, wondering who it could be. Someone must have pressed the button by mistake.

'Hallo, Angie, it's Dad.'

She had to catch her breath before answering. 'Oh my God. How did you find me?'

'It wasn't difficult. Can I come up?'

'You must be joking! Not if you're trying to get me to see that psychiatrist girlfriend of yours.'

'No, I'm not here for that. I just want to talk, make sure you're OK.'

'All right – but don't badger me or I'll ask you to leave.'

'Fair enough. Thanks, love.'

She pressed the button to open the main door, and let him into the flat without smiling. He sighed with relief when he saw her.

'Very impressive,' he said. 'It's a nice apartment – you've done well. Nice job, too, by the look of it. On more money than before?'

'Yes. I've been lucky.'

'And how are you?'

'Not too bad.'

He raised his eyebrows at her. 'Oh, Angie. Why did you leave without telling me? I've been worried sick and searching all over for you. I had to inform the police you were missing – John suggested we ask them for help. They got Elliott's to tell them your new employer's address, and that's how we found you.'

'You haven't said anything to John, have you?'

'Not yet.'

'Don't. I'd rather he didn't know.'

'Angie, you're being silly. The man won't wait around forever. He's on his own with your baby son – how long before he finds someone else? And then what will you do?'

She winced. 'He wouldn't dare do that.'

Anger spread through her body. Her legs shook.

'You have to go back to him while you still can. Or you'll lose him and little AJ, and neither of us will ever see him again. Surely that's not what you want? And it's certainly not what I want. Come on, Angie, swallow your pride and go back to him.'

'He'd never dare go with someone else, not while he hopes I'll come back to him.'

'Well, if this goes on much longer, he'll lose all hope. You couldn't blame him for looking at other women. I mean, it might be too late already – have you thought of that? You can't afford to waste any more time.'

'No. John wouldn't.'

'Wouldn't he? Dare you take that chance?'

'Shut up, shut up, will you?' She covered her ears with her hands.

He pulled them away. 'Stop trying to avoid your responsibilities, Angela. Now's the time to face them. Sort this out with John once and for all. The man knew you were sick when you left, so I'm sure he'll make allowances for you – God knows, he's made enough already. But he won't wait around forever.'

She shook her head. 'My John will wait forever if that's how long it takes.'

'You can't take that for granted.'

She burst into tears. 'Dad, what shall I do? What if I get what Mum had and AJ has it too? It'll be a nightmare. I keep having these horrible dreams about Mum on that cliff top. I dream I was the one who pushed her off because she didn't love me. It's as if my head's going to burst.'

He took her in her arms and comforted her, his hand smoothing her hair. 'Don't, my darling. Once you've sorted this out with John, the pain will disappear. You've made a great start by getting a new job and a new home. With John and the baby back, you'll live in peace. It will change your life forever. That's what I felt when for your mum before she died and now with Rachel, I've been born again too.'

'I can't take this, Dad. I need you to go. I'll sort out my own mess, in my own good time.'

'You can't afford to waste time, love. But don't forget – even if the worst did happen, Rachel and I are here to help. I've been through it with your mum, so I know what to expect. And Rachel has studied this condition for years; she's an expert.'

'Please, Dad, just go.'

'If we can help, ring us.'

She gave him a forced smile.

When he'd gone, she took out another bottle of wine from the fridge and drank a third of it from a mug. As she sat there, many images went through her brain: of her mum screaming as she fell off the cliff, of her dad shouting and then of herself, riddled with guilt for not grabbing hold of her in time. Why couldn't she shake the impression that she'd been outside, when her dad had told her she stayed in the car? Those pictures wouldn't go away.

The next morning was a Sunday. When she woke, she was lying on the settee, groggy, sick and tired. And her first thoughts were of her dad, angry at her for running away and for leaving John in the lurch. She was annoyed at him for insinuating he might find another woman; had he said it to make her go back with John, or was there something else?

It nagged at her over the next few hours as her hangover slowly receded. Lunchtime came and went, with only a sandwich and a black coffee to help her think straight. She took her antidepressants, too, and they helped for a while.

By two o'clock, she'd decided to return to Dexford herself to see if anything untoward was going on.

She parked away from the house and lay in wait.

The afternoon was dragging, with no sign of activity, even though his car was outside. It was cold out here; she shivered and buttoned her coat, but despite her discomfort she was determined to stay until she learned the truth.

She was brought out of her reverie when the door to her former home opened.

Out came John, followed by a pram ... and a woman who looked vaguely familiar, young and pretty. They lifted the pram over the threshold like a well-practised team.

Angie's heart beat like an express train. She banged her hands on the steering wheel, her whole body shaking with rage.

They were walking away from where her car was parked. She started up the engine and rolled behind them, windows open. The sound of them laughing and joking and the sight of them holding hands made her feel sick.

She watched them walk into the nearby park without a care in the world. As they turned into the gateway, she finally recognised the woman: Sarah from his work. To find out he was going with someone she knew made her worse.

'You bastards. You dirty stinking fucking toe-rag. You'll regret you ever walked on this earth.'

Chapter 40

The sun was bright, but it was cold; they wore thick jumpers, and baby AJ had two blankets covering his padded pram suit. The hood of the pram was up to keep out the cold wind.

'What a beautiful afternoon,' Sarah said.

'Yeah, it is, even though it's freezing. They say nice weather improves your state of mind. Glad your Jack's playing football this afternoon.'

'Me too. Nice of him to give us an extra afternoon!' She smiled. 'I'm so glad Angie's OK. Now you can forget her troubles and concentrate on your own life.'

'Yes – her dad says she's on the road to recovery and seems to be making a new start there. He told me where she lives and works, but not her phone number; she still won't speak to me. Well, if that's how she wants it, very soon she'll be receiving a letter from my solicitor. I wanted to tell her face to face, but why should I waste any more energy on her? She doesn't want me or the baby – I should have realised that a long time ago.'

'Seems that way, yes.'

'I worry more about what Jack will do to you when you tell him you've met someone else.'

'I'm saying nothing. He'd kill me. I'll have to sneak out and leave him a note. Hopefully, he'll never find me.'

'What if he comes to work?'

'I don't think he will. Anyway, without a pass he won't get past the front entrance – and if he makes a nuisance of himself, security will call the police.'

'I suppose so.'

'So Tuesday's still on. I've made an appointment with the solicitor, to file for divorce. I want to set this in motion as soon as possible. You'll have your own little family again, John – and we might even add to it! What do you say?'

'That would be fantastic.'

AJ woke with a yawn and a sigh. John smiled at his son, sad at how his life with Angie had panned out – but to meet Sarah was a godsend; maybe in later years, AJ would even think of her as his mother. The truth would come out one day, but that was for the future.

Sarah took the baby out of his pram and held him close. John noticed how drawn she was to him, and he, her.

'He's gorgeous, isn't he? Looking more like his dad every day.'

'It's hard for me to make comparisons this early. I leave that to other people,' John said as AJ grabbed hold of his father's little finger. 'Hey, he has a hell of a grip, even at his age.'

'Hasn't he just!' Sarah squeezed his hand and moved to kiss John on the lips.

<><><>

Seven o'clock Tuesday morning. Sarah was up as usual, wanting Jack to think she was off to work. So she forced herself to eat breakfast while he occupied the bathroom, readying himself for his trip to Russia for a Champions League game. He stomped down the stairs, wearing his blue replica shirt, and an excited smile on his face. He dropped his overnight bag – in the club colours, of course – on the floor.

'Hi,' she said, glancing up from the kitchen table.

'How are you, my sweet?' He gave her a kiss on the cheek.

'You're in a good mood.'

'Yeah, well I'm looking forward to my trip. Never been to Russia before, heard so much about it, can't wait to see it for myself.'

'Maybe we should book a holiday there.'

'Sounds cool. I'll check it out while I'm over there.'

'What time are you starting out?'

'Soon. I've checked I've got everything – match tickets, plane tickets, passport, money. Got to pick up Roy, Ewan and Barry and we need to be at the airport by eight-thirty, so I'll get breakfast there. And maybe a cheeky pint, eh?'

He picked up his bag.

'Best be off, my sweet,' he said, kissing her again.

She tried not to flinch.

'So when will you be back?'

'Stopping overnight, the plane leaves at about ten tomorrow morning, so it'll be sometime in the afternoon. You'll still be at work. How about I get the dinner on, eh?'

'That'll be the day!'

He laughed. 'No, I will, and that's a promise.'

She smiled. She'd be long gone by then.

He slammed the front door shut and drove off. She pulled back the curtain and waved, waiting until he'd disappeared before getting herself ready to start her new life.

It took two hours to get her things packed. Amazing what you accumulate over the years, and so difficult to decide what to take. She had three large suitcases ready and was about to put them in the car when she heard a noise at the back of the house. Her heart raced and, turning, she rushed to the kitchen. The back door was open, much to her surprise. Fuck – it couldn't be Jack, could it? What if something had gone wrong with the trip? She moved towards the door, her breathing irregular, her hands shaking. A hand enveloped her mouth and nose, stifling her scream. He was so strong; she had no chance of escape. And then he stuck something sharp into her back, again and again and again. Blood was everywhere. Death overcame her before she hit the ground.

<><><>

John took the day off, excited by the prospect of Sarah moving in. Her text had told him to expect her by twelve o'clock, so he imagined they'd spend the best part of the afternoon putting her belongings away, in the spare room for the time being as some of Angie's stuff still remained. He'd speak to Alan and tell him to ask Angie to remove her things, pronto. Or maybe he'd just put them in bin bags in the garage.

When she hadn't come by twelve-thirty, he started to worry.

He texted her, asking if she was OK. No reply. By two o'clock he was frantic. What was going on? He wondered if perhaps Jack hadn't gone to the football match after all. But why hadn't she let him know?

Another thought struck him. What if Jack had found out? He'd go berserk. What if he'd hurt her?

His hands were sweating, but he told himself there had to be a logical explanation. Best keep calm, not get worked up ... but by five o'clock he decided to ring her. He tried her number, and it rang out for minutes before going to voicemail. Why didn't she answer her phone? Was someone stopping her?

What if she'd changed her mind because she was frightened of what Jack might do? The speculation was driving him mad; he needed to take action. But first he had to phone his parents.

His father answered.

'Hi, John, you OK? You sound anxious.'

'Yeah, I am. Sarah's supposed to be moving in with me and AJ today but she hasn't turned up. I'm worried her husband has found out about us. He has a history of violence. Can I bring AJ over while I go and sort this out?'

'You need to be careful. I warned you over taking up with her, John, but you wouldn't listen. You should give her up, or you'll end up in more trouble than you can handle. If he's violent, who's to say he won't hurt you, too? And you might even lose your son over this if Angie finds out.'

'Dad, this subject isn't open for discussion. Now, will you help me or not?'

'Yes.'

'OK, thank you. I'll see you in twenty minutes.'

He got AJ ready, making sure he packed extra clothes and nappies. When he arrived, his parents were washing up after their dinner.

'I'm sorry for putting on you again,' he said.

'Don't worry, love, we'll look after him. You get off and find out what's happened to your girlfriend,' Susan said.

'I'll be as quick as I can.'

'Take as long as you need. AJ's safe with us.'

'And keep us informed, won't you, John?' George added.

'I will, and thanks again.'

John rushed out and drove over to Sarah's house. What he'd do when he got there, he had no idea; he would just have to play it by ear.

The closer he got, the faster his breathing. He didn't fancy confronting Jack – but if it came to it, so be it. He turned the corner into the road where Sarah lived. Straight away, he saw a blue and white police cordon around the front of the house. His stomach lurched. There were three police cars and an ambulance. Officers were everywhere and a large crowd had gathered; some of them looked like TV reporters.

He parked his car a distance away, got out and walked on shaking legs towards the fracas, deciding his best bet was to mingle with the chattering crowd.

'What's going on here?' he asked a middle-aged man who was staring at the house.

'There's been a murder, mate. Pathologist fella's just gone in.'

'My God. Who?'

'Woman who lives there, is what people are saying.'

'Jesus …' he whispered. How he kept himself together was impossible to say, but he did.

The man continued. 'You never imagine this happening in your own backyard, do you? Unbelievable – they were a lovely couple, kept themselves to themselves. Friendly, though. Always said hallo with a smile.'

'Is he in there too?'

'Not as far as I know. Someone said he's gone off to a football match, abroad somewhere. I saw him drive off early this morning, anyway. But I heard a whisper the police will be waiting for him at the airport when he comes back. Could be he's a suspect.'

'Wow! That's terrible.'

'The cops are asking for witnesses.'

'Well, let's hope they find the killer.'

'I imagine it'll be on the news tonight. And in the newspapers tomorrow. Not much of a claim to fame, is it, living in a street where a murder's been committed. The value of the houses here will drop like a stone … Here, you all right, pal? You look terrible.'

John forced a smile. 'Yes. Just a bit of indigestion. Anyway, I'd better be off before the law have a go at me for sightseeing!'

The man laughed and John made a hasty retreat back into his car, where he threw up. Just what he didn't need. He had nothing except a handkerchief and a few tissues to mop it up. Time to get out of there.

What if the police came looking for him? After all, he'd sent her a text message, and tried to phone her. What if they suspected he was the murderer? What if they found his fingerprints around the house? And if she'd packed her bags before it happened, they'd realise she planned to walk out on her husband. This was getting far too incriminating. What should he do? Come clean or lie his way out of trouble? The thought of spending years in jail for a crime he didn't commit was horrific. Then he'd never see his son again.

Somehow, he avoided an accident as he drove back to his parents' house, blinded by his tears. He took a few minutes to pull himself together.

He rang the bell, waiting for the door to open. His mum's eyes widened upon seeing his grief-stricken face.

'Oh my God, what's happened?' she asked, ushering him inside.

He collapsed into her arms. 'It … it's Sarah. She's dead,' he whispered.

'What? How?'

He shook his head.

'Come on, let's go into the living room to talk.'

His parents sat him down, one either side of him on the sofa. He told them everything, leaving nothing out.

There was a silence.

George cleared his throat, then spoke. 'What a mess. Why did you get involved with that woman? It makes no sense.'

Susan frowned at him. 'George, now isn't the time. Go to the police, John. And tell them the truth.'

'But what if they charge me with murder?'

'They've no evidence and you've got an alibi. You were with your baby the whole time until you brought him to us. And by that time Sarah was long dead.'

'Your mum's right, son. Best go, before they come for you – because they will, eventually. It'll look better if you go of your own accord. They'll see you've nothing to hide and it could help prove your innocence.'

'I don't know what to do. But like you say, the police will want to interview me anyway. I haven't got a choice.'

'Why don't I come with you? Your dad can look after AJ while we're away.'

<><><>

Together, John and his mother spoke to the duty sergeant in the local police station, only a few hundred yards from where he worked. They were taken to an interview room and within minutes a middle-aged man, tall and thin with a pock-marked face, faced them.

'Detective Sergeant Howe,' he said. 'And you are?'

'John Greaves and my mum, Susan Greaves.'

'I understand you may have some information for us.'

'It's about Sarah Benson, she's the girl you found dead today.'

'OK, so what can you tell me?'

John went through everything he had told his parents earlier on. The detective took the details.

'Very interesting. So, Sarah was leaving her husband for you. That certainly ties in with what we already suspected – there were three bags in the hall. Just as she was about to go, someone disturbed her. We assume this was the person who killed her.'

'Any ideas who it could be?'

'We can't say yet, sir. We're still at a very early stage of the investigation. But you can rest assured the perpetrator will be brought to justice.'

John was unsettled by the detective's hard stare. 'I only wish I'd gone to her house earlier; I might have saved her life.'

'We shall never know. Now, if you don't mind, sir, I'll get down what you've told me in writing. Then I'll need you to read it and sign it.'

John grimaced. It would take ages to get this written. But it had to be done.

When it was done, John read it through. Seeing the details there in black and white suddenly made the nightmare seem real, and his hand shook violently as he signed. He hoped the officer hadn't noticed.

'OK, thank you, Mr Greaves. We may need to contact you again, so if you could just fill in your address and phone number there at the top, please – and I'd advise you to remain in the country until we can eliminate you from our enquires.'

John did as he was told.

'That wasn't so painful, was it?' his mum said when they got outside.

'No. It wasn't much fun, but I suppose it could have been worse. I don't think they've finished with me yet, though.'

'We'll see. Let's hope they put an end to the matter soon. It's got to be her husband – it can't be anyone else.'

'Yes, I think so too.' He stopped walking and leaned against a wall. 'But now I've lost both of them, Mum. That's hard to take. How do I recover from that?'

She squeezed his arm. 'You will, love. You're still young – young enough to meet someone else.'

He couldn't begin to think about that. And besides, who on earth would want him in this state?

Chapter 41

After the trauma he'd suffered, John was given two days' compassionate leave. He grieved for Sarah as he had for Angie when she left him. Thank God for little AJ, who always brightened his day.

Early Thursday afternoon, after he'd had a quiet first morning back at work, his mobile beeped. He picked it up casually – then nearly dropped it.

'Angie?'

'Yes, John, it's me.'

'My God – after all this time …'

'I know … But …'

'So why are you suddenly phoning me now?'

'Because I want to see you, and … and AJ, too.'

'What the … But why?'

For a few seconds she didn't speak. Then he could hear her sobbing.

'Angie? Are you OK?'

'No. I hate being alone in my flat, and I miss you. I miss you so much.'

'Is that where you are now?'

'No. I'm visiting Dad.'

'How come?'

'I phoned in sick, then I felt lonely and miserable and I had no one to talk to.'

'Well, at least you're not far away.'

'No.'

'Do you have you any idea what you've put me through these last few weeks?'

'Yes, of course. I've been awful to you. And AJ.'

'You have. But you were ill, Angie – you still are, by the sound of things.'

'I'm better than I was, but life is difficult. My new job is fine, but I miss Dexford. My fresh start hasn't come off. That's why I need you and AJ, John. I must find out if I can take to him now, and if I can, I need you both back in my life – if you'll have me. I can't promise you much, but I'll give it my best shot.'

'I don't know. It's not a good time right now. My ... a friend of mine was murdered on Tuesday.'

'My God, how awful for you. Who?'

'A work colleague. You know her, actually – Sarah.'

'How terrible. Yes, of course I remember, we were talking to her at the Christmas do, weren't we? Isn't she the one with the football fanatic husband?'

'That's right. I think the police suspect him, but he seems to have disappeared as well.'

'Incredible what goes on behind closed doors. I can only imagine what you're going through, but perhaps it would do you good to talk about it. When would be a good time to meet up?'

'I don't know, Angie. You hurt me before and I've struggled so hard to get over it. I can't face another upset ...'

'You won't have to, I promise. I want us to be together as a family, if you'll be patient with me.'

The agony of losing Sarah gnawed at his mind. But Angie was still his wife, albeit estranged. Should he do this or not?

'All right, I'll drive over, but if you've got me over there on a fool's errand it's the last time you'll ever see me or AJ. Understand?'

'Yes, of course. I promise I won't let you down this time.'

'All right. You say you're at your dad's? But where do you work and live now?' He didn't want to betray Alan's confidence.

'In Burnfield – I'm working for Davidson & Co. If you've got a pen and paper handy, I'll give you my address.'

'OK, hang on … go ahead.'

'Flat 5, Borewood House, Penny Street, Burnfield.'

'Thanks, that's just in case I need to get in touch.'

'Dad said I can use his kitchen to cook you a meal if you can manage it tonight. Say at six o'clock.'

'I'm not sure … I won't be very good company right now.'

'Well, she was only a work colleague. It's not like she was family …'

Christ, if only she knew. 'I know, but I worked with her for years. It came as such a shock. Surreal to think you knew someone who's been murdered.'

'I bet. So, will you come or not? It won't bring her back if you don't come.'

'You're right – perhaps I am overreacting. I'll see you at six, then.'

'And don't forget to bring the baby. I bet he's grown.'

'You'll be surprised.'

'I have to admit I'm nervous about meeting with you, but I must face this, or I'll live to regret it.'

'I understand. But remember I'm not at my best after what happened to Sarah. So don't expect miracles.'

She cried again. 'I'm not. I am so sorry, John. Can you ever forgive me?'

'We'll have to wait and see.'

Once she'd gone, he found his hands were shaking and though he tried hard to stop them, he couldn't. If Sarah had still been alive, he wouldn't have considered this for a second, but right now he couldn't face any more upset.

After he picked AJ up from his parents' house – having not breathed a word about his plans for the evening – John dashed home to put everything he needed for a baby in a big bag.

At five-thirty he started out again. He was glad he hadn't told his parents. The idea of him getting back together with Angie may not appeal to them, but it wasn't their life – it was his. And he'd do what was best for him and his son, no matter what anyone else said.

Because of the rush hour, he got stuck in two traffic jams but finally reached the house just before six. He knew that Alan's presence would mean they couldn't talk freely, but perhaps having him there as a buffer would be a good thing.

He carried the car seat in one hand, the bag with AJ's things in the other. The rain poured down, making him curse. He pressed the doorbell and saw the outline of Angie coming towards them.

<><><>

'Hallo,' she said.

'Hi.'

'Oh, John, thank God you're here. And AJ too?'

'Of course.'

She leaned over and kissed him on the cheek. And the baby too, but he was asleep.

'Come through. I've been so looking forward to seeing you both.'

He hung his wet coat over the banister, and she led him through to the living room.

'Drink?'

'Tea, please.'

'Dinner should be ready within half an hour.'

'Smells lovely. What are you cooking?'

'Beef casserole. You always used to say it was one of your favourites.'

'It still is.'

She went to the kitchen, her heart racing, and made the tea. And one for her dad too; he was currently in his workshop, repairing a Victorian Welsh dresser.

'Dad!' she shouted, opening the door above the din of a drill. She showed him the mug, and he nodded, smiling.

'John and AJ are here,' she said.

'Give me five minutes and I'll be with you.'

Angie returned to John, who was feeding the baby.

'Oh, how lovely, he's awake,' she said.

'Yeah – must be that racket in the garden.'

'Sorry, you know Dad and his antiques. He'd be in there all day if I let him.'

John smiled.

'I'll just see if the dinner's ready.'

She opened the oven; the casserole was bubbling away, the roast potatoes were browning nicely. Twenty minutes at the most, she guessed.

Back in the living room, John had AJ in his arms, the empty bottle on the table.

'Sorry to hear about Sarah,' Angie said.

'Thanks. It was a big shock. The police interviewed me – as one of her friends, I mean – which was an ordeal, I can tell you. Reading between the lines, I think they suspect Jack. He has a history of violence, and I heard she was going to leave him because of it.'

'How horrible.'

'Yes, it is.'

Fifteen minutes later, Alan came in, looking dirty, but grinning. He went over to his grandson.

He bent towards him. 'Hallo, son,' he said. He tickled his grandson's chin. 'My, he's grown, hasn't he? I'll just get changed – won't be long.'

'He has, I hardly recognised him,' Angie chuckled. 'I'll dish up.'

John put AJ in the bouncer, then sat at the table.

Angie divided the casserole into three and brought the plates in.

'Looks delicious,' John said.

'Well, they say the way to a man's heart is through his stomach …'

'I couldn't say, but it certainly helps.'

'Hope you don't mind Dad being here.'

'No, not at all. We'll talk later.'

She smiled. 'Let's wait for him – it's bad manners to start without him.'

'Sure, no problem.'

Alan returned, washed, in jeans and red jumper; he'd even combed his hair back. He sat next to Angie at the end of the table.

'How's the dresser progressing, Dad?'

'Good – should be finished by tomorrow, if I'm not interrupted.'

'John's had a big upset. A friend of his was murdered yesterday. They think it was her husband, who's since disappeared.'

'Wow, that's terrible. You have my heartfelt sympathy.'

John mentioned the theory that Sarah had been having an affair and that she was about to leave her husband.

Alan slammed his fork down. 'Well, if that's the case, she's got what she deserves. Can't abide infidelity. When you get married, you don't go off with other men.'

'Dad!'

'No, I'm sorry, but it makes my blood boil.'

'Anyway, let's talk about something else,' Angie said, determined to change the subject before things got out of hand.

'Like what?'

'Baby AJ, for a start,' she said.

'Right. I'm sorry, John. Yes, AJ's a belter, and it's lovely to see him. Even better is seeing you two in the same room, and talking.'

John nodded and Angie smiled.

'I'm so glad I persuaded you to get in touch, love. I want you two to try again because before this upset you were the perfect couple. And you can be again. What do you think, John?'

'I think ... I'd love you both to play a part in AJ's life. A child should always have a mother and a father, don't you think?'

'You should ask Angie that question. All I'll say is that I did my best under difficult circumstances.'

'You did well, Dad, but no one can ever take Mum's place, you know that. How is Rachel, anyway? I expected her to be here with you.'

'She's in London at a conference. Should be back in a few days. I miss her. Pity she's not here, she did so want to meet the baby. Never mind – there'll be other times.'

Once the meal was over, Alan got up. 'OK, time I made myself scarce. You two have got plenty to sort out, without me being in the way. I'll go up and watch TV in my bedroom. Give me a bell before you leave, though. I'd like to say goodbye to my grandson.'

'Of course. Shouldn't be too long,' John said.

'And don't worry about the washing-up. We'll do it in the morning.'

'Well, I'll just take the dirty dishes out and put them in the sink,' said Angie.

<><><>

John sat in front of the TV, keeping the sound low because of the baby. His breathing quickened as he waited for Angie to return from the kitchen. It had suddenly hit him that he had no idea what to expect, or what he wanted after having lost Sarah in such a catastrophic way. He didn't look forward to a meaningful discussion.

She sat down opposite him, but looking straight ahead instead of at him.

He couldn't think of a single thing to say.

'I know you were seeing her, John,' she said suddenly.

'What? Seeing who?'

'Sarah.'

'And what makes you think that?'

'Because I saw you together outside the house, acting all lovey-dovey.'

'Oh, did you now? And where were you?'

'In my car up the road. Dad had dropped a few hints about you, so I decided to find out the truth for myself. You bastard – I've only been gone a few weeks and already you're seeing someone else.'

'Did you expect me to live like a monk for the rest of my life? You never contacted me, or answered any of my calls. I was under no illusion where I stood with you. Why shouldn't I find a girl who wanted me when you didn't?'

'I was fucking ill, you moron.'

'Keep your voice down, you'll wake the baby – and your dad will wonder what's going on.'

'Couldn't care less!' she yelled. 'How could you do that to me?'

'Well, it hasn't done me any good, has it? I haven't got her anymore, have I? That demented husband of hers must have found out and killed her.'

'Serves you right.'

'Thanks for being so sympathetic – sounds to me like you're glad she's dead. So why did you ask me round in the first place? Looks like I was right about coming here on a fool's errand. Think I'd better leave.' He got up from his seat.

'Please yourself,' she said indignantly.

He put on his coat and took AJ, still sleeping, to the car. He slammed the door shut and turned the ignition key. The car coughed … but wouldn't start. He tried again, with the same reaction. And once more. What was the matter with the damn thing? He tried a dozen times, but still no joy. He was desperate to get away from this place once and for all, but for now that was impossible.

He got out and opened the bonnet, but he knew nothing about cars except how to drive them. Glancing up, he saw Angie coming down the drive towards him. He'd need to phone someone to come out to it – only as he searched his coat pocket, he couldn't find his mobile. Unbelievable.

'Something wrong with the car, John?'

'It won't start – and now I've lost my phone, too.'

'You'd best bring AJ back inside – he'll catch cold.'

John stared at her as if she was to blame, but he had no choice.

So he carried the baby back into the house, wondering what on earth to do next. He'd have to borrow Alan's phone, or Angie's.

'Can I use your mobile to phone the AA?'

'No, it's all right, I'll phone for you,' Angie said, producing her phone.

'They'll want to speak to me,' he said.

'I seem to remember we're both on the policy. Don't worry, I'll sort it.' She walked towards the window, and he heard her talking. When she'd finished, she returned to sit by him.

'One to two hours, they said.'

'This is ridiculous. What shall I do about the baby?'

'If it comes to it, you'll both have to stay here – nothing more you can do.'

'I suppose not.'

John heard a cry from inside the pram. He laughed.

'It never rains but it pours,' she said. 'Did you bring enough bottles with you?'

'Yes, I always do.'

'So, it's not a problem, then.'

'No. I'll get him out if you'll warm the bottle for me. Think I left one in the fridge.'

'OK.'

Five minutes later, AJ was sucking away on his teat. In no time, he'd drunk it and had his nappy changed. Angie hadn't volunteered any help, and although she watched, she still didn't want to get involved.

'Like old times, isn't it?'

'Yes – with me doing everything.'

'Well, you always liked to take control.'

'I'm surprised your dad hasn't come in, wondering what's going on.'

'Probably immersed in a film.'

'I'll try to get him to sleep. If the AA arrive in the meantime, can you take over?'

'Be my pleasure, John.'

It took half an hour before the baby was asleep. John was worn out and irritable. 'What the hell's happened to them? It's been ages.'

'They'll be here soon enough. Want a drink while you're waiting? I'll do you a whisky special if you want, like Dad gives me.'

'No thanks, I'm driving. A coffee would be nice, though.'

'OK – coming up.'

John was thirsty and drank the coffee almost in one go. It was strong and bitter, but he didn't care.

'Nice?' she asked him.

'Yeah, fine.'

'Good. If that AA man doesn't come until late, sleep over here until the morning. Dad has another spare room besides mine.'

'I'd hate to impose on you,' he said, yawning and rubbing his eyes.

'You all right?'

'God, don't know what's come over me. I feel a bit strange – giddy and sick. Probably just everything finally catching up with me. Think I need some fresh air.' He got up and almost fell over, grabbing on to the sofa for balance.

John moved towards the kitchen and felt the room going around; he had to get outside quickly. Reaching the back door, he opened it and staggered out into the garden, taking in deep breaths. His sight was fuzzy. He reached Alan's workshop and, making for the door, caught sight of a mound of grass cuttings. And at the bottom, he thought he saw a pair of feet. Christ, what was the matter with him?

His legs went from under him and he collapsed onto the grass mound.

When he tried to get up, he was confronted by a woman's face.

Her eyes were wide open and she was definitely dead.

'Oh my God,' he cried out. 'Shit, shit, shit!' His legs felt rubbery and he was unable to get up. He gasped, frantically trying to get away from the body.

<><><>

Angie rushed out and found John on the grass, wondering what was wrong with him. Then she caught sight of the body too and stopped in her tracks.

She recognised her at once: Rachel.

Before she had time to scream, a hand grabbed her arm. She froze and turned to face her father, his eyes wide and full of anger. There was a demented scowl on his face, as if he meant her harm.

'Get inside and stay there,' he growled, pulling her into the kitchen and slamming the door so hard it bounced open again.

Angie looked up, and now the scream came. In his right hand, he held a carving knife, pointing it straight at her.

'What the hell were you doing outside? I told you to keep him in the house!'

She shook her head, weeping, unable to look at him.

'Dad, what have you done? That's Rachel out there, dead! And what about John? Did you do something to him too?'

'Just a little something in his coffee, to calm him down. I heard you rowing, so I disabled his car and took his mobile. He needed taking care of.'

'Dad, I ... I ... what's going on? Why would you kill Rachel? It makes no sense! You love her!'

'I had to. I told her what I did to Sarah, and she threatened to go to the police, the silly cow.'

'W ... what did you do to her?'

'I went to her house and killed her – with this knife, as it happens. She was going to move in with lover boy John – I saw the suitcases in the hall. You would have lost him forever.'

Angie shook her head and tried to pull her hand away but his grip was like iron.

'I got rid of that Sarah so you could get back together with John. But I when I heard you fighting, I realised the bastard didn't deserve you, and I couldn't let him hurt you. You've been through enough.'

'I never asked you to do that. You're frightening me, Dad. I'm not sure I know you anymore.'

'Doesn't really matter. You're going to die as well – you know too much now. And soon you'll get bipolar anyway. I can't look after you and AJ.'

'Please don't hurt me, Dad. I'd never tell anyone, I promise. And I might not get bipolar, you said so yourself.'

'It's too much of a risk – I can't trust you. You'd go to the police, your conscience would make you,' he said, pulling her closer, the tip of the knife pressing into her stomach.

'But I love you, Dad.'

'Really? You don't know what it's like to love when you have something wrong with you. But now you'll never find out.'

'What are you talking about?'

'I'm talking about bipolar. Your mother was ill, but she had depression and not bipolar. I'm the one with bipolar. I've kept it hidden for years; only my psychiatrist – Rachel – was aware of it.'

Angie gasped.

'Your mum didn't kill herself, and you didn't do it – I did. When she was on the hill and slipped, I could have saved her but I chose to let her go. She was out of control. Wouldn't do as she was told. And wanted to shop me to the police. So she had to die.'

Angie stood still, then tried to make a run for it, but he was too quick. He tightened his grip on her arm. 'You'd betray me as well, so sadly although it pains me you have die too...'

Out of the corner of her eye, she glimpsed John, unsteady on his feet but with a large stone in his hands. Alan had his back to him.

Oh please God, don't let him see. Don't let anyone else die needlessly.

Alan pulled back his arm.

She closed her eyes.

John brought the stone down hard onto the back of Alan's head.

Alan grunted, turned around and tried to grab John, but blood was streaming down his neck, and he fell backwards onto the kitchen floor.

Then John collapsed, the effects of whatever he'd taken sapping his strength.

Angie screamed and screamed and didn't stop until the police arrived.

<><><>

John woke, his eyes fuzzy, hardly able to move due to exhaustion. He was in a bed and felt as sick as a pig. He could just make out Angie, the baby in her arms, and tried to smile, holding a shaky arm out towards her. He felt her hand clasp his own and saw tears in her eyes.

'Where am I?'

'In hospital. They had to pump your stomach or you would have died.'

'What happened to me?'

'I'm sorry. Dad told me to make you a drink. He must have put something in it – I had no idea. Then when he got me inside the house he told me he was going to kill me too. But you ... you saved my life.'

'I thought I was dreaming that. Did I hit him with a boulder?'

'Yes. He's dead, John. You killed him to stop him from killing me. It was self-defence, the police assured me of that, so you're not in any trouble.'

'But why? I don't understand what it was all about,' John said, his tired eyes fluttering.

'I've got a confession to make,' Angie said, looking downcast. 'I've kept a secret from you because I feared I'd lose you.'

She squeezed his hand, and his stomach flipped as he tried to imagine what she'd tell him.

'I told you Mum died in a car crash – but I lied. Mum was very ill; everyone, including the doctors, thought she had bipolar. She and Dad used to have terrible rows, and this last time, she threatened to kill herself and drove off. Dad and me followed in his car, but we couldn't catch her up or stop her. She drove for ages and we ended up on top of this great big hill, where she got out and ran off. I wanted to go with him, after her, but he ordered me to stay put and locked me in the car. I can remember shouting and screaming but it was no good.

'He went after her; I saw her turn around and they started arguing again. She ran off and raised her arms as if she was about to fly, but instead she jumped. Dad managed to grab hold of her, and I thought he'd got her. And then he hesitated and let her go.'

'Oh my God.'

'I went berserk, banging on the windows and the doors but I couldn't get out. And when Dad came back, I started hitting him and he had to slap my face to calm me down.

'Later, Dad told me she'd killed herself and there was nothing he could have done to save her. But he did let her die – I know, because I saw it with my own eyes. After that, I sort of blanked it out, although later I did start having these horrible dreams where I was the one who failed to save her. I blamed myself and Dad let me believe it.'

'So, you've had that on your conscience ever since? That's awful.'

'I couldn't tell you about the bipolar because it can be passed down to the next generation. There's a chance AJ could get it – and me too – and I thought you'd leave me if you knew, or you wouldn't want any more children with me.'

John shook his head. 'Of course, I wouldn't have left you, and I would have still wanted children, despite the risk. No wonder you were so het up, with all that fear on your shoulders. You should have trusted me, had faith in me. I love you and always will.'

'And then I found out Mum didn't have bipolar at all, but depression – he'd lied all along, to put the blame on her. He was the one with bipolar, diagnosed before I was born, and I never guessed. He always seemed so normal to me, looked after me so well after Mum died. He'd concealed it from everyone. except Rachel, but it cost her, her life. He killed Sarah to make you come back to me, but then when you discovered Rachel's body, he knew he had to kill both of us too.'

'This is incredible,' John said.

Her lip trembled. 'The police have searched the house.'

'Fucking hell. We're all lucky to be alive.'

'When you were behind him, I kept praying you'd be able to stop him but when you collapsed, I thought I'd lost you too.'

'How could I die, when I have such a beautiful wife and a gorgeous son waiting for me? Angie – after this, we can face anything together.'

She went to him, and held him as close as she dared along with baby AJ, aware of how lucky they were to have each other. From now on, he knew, they would be together for as long as they lived; even if the worst happened, they were ready to meet the challenge.

THE END

Dear reader,

We hope you enjoyed reading *The Art of Deception.* Please take a moment to leave a review in Amazon, even if it's a short one. Your opinion is important to us.

Discover more books by Peter Martin at
https://www.nextchapter.pub/authors/peter-martin

Want to know when one of our books is free or discounted for Kindle? Join the newsletter at http://eepurl.com/bqqB3H

Best regards,

Peter Martin and the Next Chapter Team

You might also like:
The Last Tiger by Tony Black

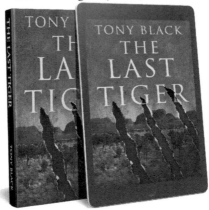

To read the first chapter for free, please head to:
https://www.nextchapter.pub/books/the-last-tiger

Printed in Great Britain
by Amazon